# TO CATCH A RABBIT

*by*

Helen Cadbury

**Magna Large Print Books**
Long Preston, North Yorkshire,
BD23 4ND, England.

British Library Cataloguing in Publication Data.

Cadbury, Helen
   To catch a rabbit.

   A catalogue record of this book is
   available from the British Library

   ISBN   978-0-7505-4251-7

7/16

First published in Great Britain in 2013 by Allison & Busby Ltd.

Copyright © 2013 by Helen Cadbury

Cover illustration © Tim Daniels by arrangement with
Arcangel Images

Published in Large Print 2016 by arrangement with
Allison & Busby Ltd.

Magna Large Print is an imprint of Library Magna Books Ltd.

Printed and bound in Great Britain by
T.J. (International) Ltd., Cornwall, PL28 8RW

# TO CATCH A RABBIT

A dead woman sits slumped against the door of a grubby trailer. She's on Sean Denton's patch, but who is she, how did she get there and why doesn't CID want to investigate? As Doncaster's youngest PCSO, Denton takes the case into his own hands, but he's way out of his depth. When people are reported missing, Denton must work backwards – facing corruption from outside and inside the force – before anyone else falls victim to South Yorkshire's deadly underworld of migrants and the sex trade.

*for Josh, Isaac and Reuben*

# NOVEMBER 2007

# CHAPTER ONE

There were two of them. As they came closer, Sean could see that the larger boy had been crying. He was wiping something from his mouth with the back of his hand. The smaller boy was pale, with a hard face. Behind him, a Staffordshire bull terrier pulled on a rope. It wanted to get back up the hill, but the boys were heading straight for Sean.

There had been a frost and Sean's breath hung ahead of him in the still air. He rolled his shoulders back and let his arms fall by his sides. He'd been on a course on dealing with young people. It was important to get the body language right. An open gesture, the trainer said. You had to get the facial expression right too. He adjusted his smile to *inquisitive but friendly.*

'You a copper?'

'Police Community Support Officer Denton. Call me Sean.'

'That a copper?'

'More or less.'

They edged closer, the skinny one shifting his weight from side to side like a toddler needing to pee. Sean thought about crouching down. Height can be an intimidating factor, the trainer had said, but he didn't like the look of the dog.

'She found summat.'

'Who?'

11

'Ruby did.' The dog squatted on the cracked pavement and a trickle of piss snaked towards Sean's foot. 'Over the ring road. Brandon said you have to go on the fields if you want to catch a rabbit.'

The sickly one gave a numb nod and rubbed his face on his sleeve.

'What did she find?'

'I'll have to show you.'

He turned and let the dog pull him back up the slope towards the bypass. 'Come on,' he called back over his shoulder. 'You better have a look.'

There was a whimper but it wasn't from the dog. Brandon wasn't moving.

'You stay here then, you big pussy, me and the copper'll sort this.'

Sean wasn't sure whether he should go on his own. He was meant to be on patrol with his partner, Carly Jayson, but she had phoned in poorly so there was no one free to cover. It couldn't do any harm to see what the boy had found. He decided to follow; the dog setting the pace. It was an ugly animal, with back legs too thin for its barrel body, a bit of whippet thrown in with the bull terrier.

They passed the recreation ground, where a stack of old pallets, broken chairs and cardboard boxes waited for Bonfire Night. After scrambling up the embankment, Sean looked back. Brandon was sitting on the wall of the rec, bent over. It looked like he was throwing up. The dog sniffed at the dual carriageway and Sean looked at his watch: 08.12 hours. The boy was talking again, as fast as he walked. A gap opened up between the cars and they crossed over.

12

'We was throwing sticks and she's no good at that, so she went off to sniff around that old snack bar van up there and she wouldn't come back when we shouted for her.'

Sean realised that he should be writing this down. Sounded like evidence, but he wasn't sure of what. They climbed over the battered metal barrier in the centre of the dual carriageway and reached the lay-by on the other side, crunching over loose stones and broken glass. A hedge had swallowed up the broken remains of a wooden fence. The boy stepped through a gap in it and onto a well-trodden path along the field edge. There, hidden from the road, was a grubby, box-like trailer with faded red lettering. Sean spelt it out in his head: REFRESHMENTS. The boy stopped and yanked hard on the dog's rope.

'Ruby! Stay!'

Sean looked over at whatever it was the dog was straining towards. A pair of feet, naked, an odd colour. Wrong colour. Blue-black like ulcers. He got closer. The girl was sitting on a step at the back of the trailer, leaning on the edge of an open door. She seemed to have folded forwards, as if she was resting her head on her knees. He went closer still, the boy's nervous chatter behind him.

'Brandon thought it were some lass, fallen asleep, said she's going to be cold. He poked a stick at her. She's dead, isn't she?'

The girl was wearing a T-shirt and knickers. Her straight black hair was spread over her face and her cheek rested against her knee. As Sean got nearer, he noticed her blue lips were parted, and he could see her teeth. It was the smell that made

13

the vomit rise in his throat. He turned away fast, drawing quick breaths to keep his breakfast down.

He called it in, as calmly as he could. Gave directions as the boy watched.

'What happens now?' the boy said.

'Some police officers will come.'

'And take her away?'

'Yes. They might want to speak to you.'

'What for?' He pulled the dog closer, coiling the rope in his bony hands.

'Just to ask you some questions.'

'I've told you. Dog found her. There's nowt else.'

'I know, but–'

The boy yanked the dog, 'Hup, Ruby! Hup!'

They ran along the path, her tail wagging with this new game.

'I don't even know your name!' Sean called.

'It's Declan,' he called back. 'But I ain't talking to no other coppers.'

He and Ruby scrambled through the broken fence. Sean looked back at the dead girl. She could wait. He went after Declan but, as he reached the end of the path, his foot slipped on an ice-coated puddle and his leg twisted under him. His knee went down on the jutting edge of a stone. He checked his radio was still in the pocket of his vest and pulled himself up, rubbed his knee and limped towards the lay-by, just in time to see Declan dodging the traffic to the other side. He didn't even know where he lived.

He'd been in the job less than two months. He hoped they'd take that into account back at the station. He got out his notebook, made a wild guess at how to spell the boys' names. What else should he write down? No idea. He tried not to look at the body again, but he needed to see if there was a registration plate. She was there, still and dead, just the wind lifting two strands of hair and blowing it back over her shoulder.

The plate was missing. The only detail he could record was the brand name of the vehicle itself: *Motorhead?* No. He looked again and the word reformed: *Motorchef.* That made more sense. He could feel a hysterical laugh bubbling up inside him. It was just shock. He forced himself to look past the body and saw that the van's interior fittings had been stripped out, the catering equipment replaced by a mattress.

By the time he heard vehicles pulling into the lay-by he was shaking. He hadn't noticed the cold at first, but the longer he stood, the less feeling he had in his feet. Two men got out of their unmarked cars and seemed to be sharing a joke as they shook hands. He recognised Detective Chief Inspector Barry 'Burger' King, limping from a barely recovered stress fracture in his right leg. There was a rumour at Doncaster Central that he'd broken it standing still, his own weight cracking the bone. The other man was thin. He was wearing a green waxed jacket and a tweed flat cap, a black medical bag in his hand. A little rhyme danced across Sean's memory, *Miss Polly had a dolly who was sick sick sick, she called to the doctor to come quick quick quick, the doctor came with his bag and his hat...*

'You've checked for vital signs, I take it?' Burger asked when he reached him. Sean hesitated. It hadn't seemed necessary to check the pulse of someone who was already in a state of rigor mortis. 'And given her mouth-to-mouth? You know you're supposed to do everything possible to preserve life?'

Sean tasted sick rising again as Burger wheezed a laugh through his teeth.

'Huggins can take a look at him. Pathologist,' he added, in answer to a question Sean hadn't voiced.

Huggins approached the body, while Burger held back, casting his eyes over the trailer and taking out a cigarette. The pathologist had a go at lifting her head away from her knees. Sean wanted him to be careful with her, almost called out. But what was the point? She was dead, wasn't she? Her neck was stiff, but Huggins got it far enough up to move her right arm away. The skin inside her elbow was peppered with puncture wounds.

'A tenner says it's a straightforward smack OD. This estate's awash with it,' said DCI King.

'I'm not arguing, Barry. I'll give you an estimated time of death and certify it. Then I need to be off. Crying shame, a young girl like this.' Huggins's fingers reached out and touched her hair.

Another car pulled in and a young woman got out. She had a roll of incident tape, which she started wrapping over the gap in the fence between the field edge and the lay-by.

'Not now, Lizzie. How the hell d'you think we'll get the body through?' Huggins shook his head and mumbled to no one in particular. 'Graduate training scheme, fast-track, I ask you.' He took another look at the body, then at Sean. 'You'll have to check in your shoe size and brand with the lovely Lizzie Morrison. She's our new crime scene

16

manager; very keen on tread patterns.'

'Anyone else been up here?' Burger stared out across the road towards the Chasebridge estate.

Sean assumed the question was directed at him. 'Two young lads and a dog, sir, they found the body.'

'How old?' Burger eyed the estate with an impassive stare.

'About ten, sir.'

'And the dog?'

'Sir?'

Sean felt himself blush as he realised he was having the mick taken again. Burger let out a belly laugh and Huggins smirked. Only Lizzie looked suitably serious, as if she disapproved of the whole lot of them. He almost felt sorry for her, having to work with this team. The laughter was definitely a bloke's joke, and Lizzie didn't look like she was one of the lads.

'Have a look for footprints will you, love? See if there's a couple of kiddy's sizes in there.'

'The ground's pretty hard, so I don't think there'll be anything in the mud. Maybe something in the frost itself,' Lizzie said. She had the kind of voice that Sean's nan would have called 'proper'. 'Where are the SOCOs? They should be here by now.'

'I don't think we'll need them.' DCI King headed back to the car with the doctor. 'This one's low priority. You and Plastic Percy can manage.'

Bastard, Sean thought. Not proper police, plastic police. Pig. Percy. He couldn't meet her eye, didn't want her to see how much it bothered him. Burger walked Huggins back to his car and Sean watched

Lizzie pull on a white, cover-all suit and tuck her dark hair neatly under the hood. He was glad someone was taking this poor girl's death seriously.

'Make yourself useful and lend us a hand, will you?' She tossed a packet of latex gloves to Sean. 'As soon as this is signed off, we can get the morgue van up here.'

He struggled into a second white suit. It was hot over his uniform and his movements felt as subtle as a Teletubby's. Lizzie issued instructions and Sean did as he was told. He tried to switch off mentally, shut down his feelings, as he held the dead girl's head in both his hands, while Lizzie looked in the mouth and ears. He turned away to catch his breath. Lizzie gestured to him to steady the body by the shoulders while she lifted the T-shirt away from the girl's skin and looked for any signs of injury. Even through the cloth and the gloves, he could feel hard, cold flesh. Burger lit up another cigarette.

'Nothing obvious, sir.' Lizzie didn't look up as she spoke. 'Except the needle marks. Discolouration of the skin could be septicaemia, post-mortem. Dirty needle could have done that as she was losing consciousness. Face is bloated, so hard to say, but features look East Asian.'

'Good, well, let's get her on the slab and see what's what.' Burger flicked the ash off the end of his cigarette.

A grey Mercedes van pulled up in the lay-by and two men got out. The stretcher they carried had a built-in body bag, like a suit carrier from a smart dry-cleaners. Once the body was on the

18

stretcher and zipped in, Lizzie fetched some evidence bags from the car and gave Sean some paper towels. Where the girl had been was now a sticky mess on the step. He was becoming an expert at not breathing through his nose.

'Sir, am I looking for anything in particular inside?' Lizzie asked.

'Whatever takes your fancy, love,' Burger shrugged. 'I'm going to sit in the car and keep warm, the lad'll give you a hand.'

'Right.' She stood in the open doorway and paused for a moment to survey the interior of the trailer. 'There's not much room, so you stay there. Open me up one of the larger bags.'

Sean fiddled to separate the plastic, fumbling in the latex gloves. Lizzie reappeared in the doorway with a bundled-up sheet, which she slid into the bag. 'Take this back to the car and get the sharps box, I think I've found the murder weapon.'

'But I thought it was a drug overdose.'

'Duh! I'm talking about the needle. If this were a murder, they'd have sent me an actual team instead of having to make do with a... Sorry, I didn't catch your name?'

'Sean Denton, I'm the–'

'PCSO, yes I know. Well, it must be nice to do a bit of proper policing for a change.'

She smiled a tight smile and he was reminded of the girls in the top set at his secondary school, who dated older boys and played in the orchestra; unattainable middle-class girls who ignored boys like Sean or, worse still, pitied them.

Burger was sitting in the passenger seat of the unmarked police car, holding a cigarette in one

19

hand and hanging out of the open door talking into a mobile phone. Lizzie's car was parked further along the lay-by. Sean looked for a way to get round Burger without disturbing him, but the detective had parked right in front of the gap to the field. Sean found another section of hedge low enough to climb over. A bramble caught his trousers and nearly had him down for a second time, but not before he heard a snatch of Burger's conversation.

'Looks a lot like her. That's all I'm saying. No. I'll keep you out of it. Just thought you might want to know.'

On the loose Tarmac of the lay-by, Sean's footsteps gave him away.

'Hang on,' Burger said to his caller.

Sean kept walking towards Lizzie's car and if there was any more to the conversation, he didn't hear it. He stowed the evidence bag in the boot and took out the yellow plastic sharps box. When he turned back, Burger was out of the car and watching him.

'If you pick up fag ends, you'll burn your fingers,' the detective growled.

'Sir?' Sean eyed the gap in the fence and the ragged section of hedge he'd just crossed. He opted for the gap, even though it meant squeezing past Burger, who showed no sign of moving.

'You weren't earwigging, were you?' the DCI said.

'No, sir.' He was close now, breathing in the cigarette smoke that hung around them both.

'Good.' Burger suddenly grabbed Sean's ear and twisted it tightly. 'Because you've got to learn to mind your own fucking business in this job.'

Then he let go, lowered himself back into the car and slammed the door. Sean heard the radio come on, a talent-show singer belting out a ballad. His ear was burning.

When Lizzie had retrieved everything she thought relevant, she told Sean to tape off the snack-bar trailer with blue-and-white incident tape. He stood back and looked at it. It was like a huge gift-wrapped present. Christ. He tried to shake the thought away. He wasn't a sicko. He silently promised himself that he would never be that disrespectful or cynical, how ever many bodies he saw, and he made another promise, that he would never forget this dark-haired dead girl; his first.

## BONFIRE NIGHT: 6 a.m.

'Now then, Phil, mate.' On the other end of the phone, Johnny Mackenzie sounded like he'd been wide awake for hours. 'I knew you'd be up.'

'I wasn't.'

'I've got a job on today,' Mackenzie said. 'Need a driver.'

Philip Holroyd took his phone out to the landing and sat at the top of the stairs. Stacey was working late last night and he wanted to let her sleep. The glass above the front door framed a perfect, shiny rectangle of night sky and the cold air made the hairs on his legs stand up like a tiny forest.

21

'Be up at the farm in fifteen minutes,' Johnny was saying. 'I'll see you right on this one. Stacey said you could do with a bob or two.'

'I'll be there.' He shivered and flipped the phone shut.

Stacey's eyes flickered under a crust of yesterday's mascara as Phil crossed the bedroom and scooped his clothes up from the floor. She half-smiled in her sleep and the little worry-line between her eyebrows almost disappeared. He went to get dressed in the bathroom. He was buttoning up his shirt when Holly appeared in the doorway, rubbing her eyes.

'What you doing?'

'Getting ready for work, sweetheart. Daddy's got a job today.'

'Can I come?'

'No, 'fraid not. I'll bring you something back.'

'A rabbit,' Holly said decisively and turned to go back to her bedroom.

Phil cleaned his teeth and hoped he'd be back home in time to take Holly to the fireworks at the pub. His daughter was five and fearless. She'd been talking about it for days. As he dragged Stacey's hairbrush back through his thick hair, he fancied he was receding a bit at the temples and around his widow's peak, but at thirty-two there was still no sign of any grey. Picking up a purple hair elastic, he pulled his ponytail up and through. He sat on the edge of the bath, rolled a cigarette, licked it, sealed it and tucked it behind his ear. Tiptoeing down the stairs so he didn't wake the dog, he stepped into his trainers and let himself out of the front door.

Up at the farm, puddles filled the cracked concrete of the farmyard, lit only by the neon light from the office window. He dropped the butt of his cigarette and heard it hiss in the silence. He leant his bike up against the prefab wall, opened the office door and stepped into Mackenzie's world.

# CHAPTER TWO

In the office of The Refugee and Migrants' Advice Centre in York (known as RAMA), Karen Friedman flicked the kettle on. It ticked and rumbled gently as the element fought with the build-up of limescale. Like most of the office fittings, it had seen better days. She went back to her desk while the water boiled and opened up a black box-file marked *Asylum Refusal 3rd Quarter*. The box was almost full. Her fingers thumbed through its contents until she pulled out a clear plastic wallet stuffed with documents. There was a sticker on the front in Jaz Kumar's spidery writing.

*Rudo and Florence Moyo/ Zimbabwe/ Claim refused 18/10/07*

She'd tried to show him how to do the labels on the computer, but Jaz, her boss, was a Luddite at heart. Karen pulled the papers out of their cover and spread them out in front of her. There was a letter from a St Jude's Church, with a cheerful rainbow-coloured logo, offering to sponsor Mr and Mrs Moyo and their daughter, Elizabeth. The Reverend Wheatley was big on warmth, but short on details. She opened a photocopy of the Moyos' asylum application form, meticulously filled out in black ink.

*...and then I was hit many times across my back until I was bleeding...*
*...all this time I didn't know where I was...*
*...that was when they took my daughter to be questioned. She was fourteen years old...*

The bubbling roar of the kettle reached its peak. Karen got up and crossed the uneven floor to where a box of peppermint tea and three mugs were lined up on the windowsill. She wondered if she would ever get used to the details of man's inhumanity to man. Nearly a year into the job, her caseload still gave her nightmares. Her face frowned back at her in the window. It was already dark outside. She'd give it another half hour and then she'd have to go home.

The night sky over York was peppered with coloured fireworks. Karen got off the bus and hurried up the path that cut through to the school playing field. As she emerged opposite an embankment full of spectators, a rocket whistled up and burst into a shower of stars, bathing the faces of the crowd in green fluorescence. She spotted her own children, Sophie and Ben, open-mouthed, staring upwards. Behind them, one hand on Ben's shoulder, was Max. Her husband's bald head reflected the light from the sky, turning from green to pink. Even in the chill of a November evening he didn't wear a hat and if he felt the cold, he certainly didn't admit it.

The first time she saw him, he was on the dance floor at a wedding, wearing a tight 1950s suit that was somehow beyond fashion. She'd liked his smile and the way he flung his legs out when he danced. Sometimes she wondered how long they would have stayed together if she hadn't found herself pregnant within just a few months, but it had worked out all right, for the most part. He'd done well, bought them a Victorian house on a good road, got the children into a good school. His word: good. She had to believe it was; it was costing them enough. Looking at him now, stiff, upright, under an immaculate black overcoat, she understood why people often misjudged his age. Still in his early thirties, and four years her junior, he looked ten years older. She couldn't pinpoint exactly when it had begun, but along the way he'd morphed from an idealistic young architect into a middle-aged company man. Karen wasn't stupid, she'd changed too, aged certainly, but after twelve years of marriage and three pregnancies, going back to work had made her feel younger.

A huge explosion was followed by a burst of silver. The crowd let out 'oohs' and 'ahs', as stars fell like a waterfall. Karen looked up too and when she looked back towards the embankment, she could no longer see Ben. Max and their daughter Sophie were still watching the sky, but beside them was a gap. A taller boy pushed forward to get a better view. Karen scanned the crowd, but she still couldn't see her son. She hurried round the side of the field, avoiding the launching area of used tubes and a taper-wielding teacher. She stumbled on unseen tussocks of long grass, glancing towards the embankment. There were parents and children she recognised: her next-door neighbour and his new wife, a group of mothers whom Karen knew by sight. There was still no sign of Ben. She had almost reached the crowd when everyone began clapping. The display was over. People began to move, the stillness of the watchers undone as they broke ranks. People surrounded her, saying good-night to one another, catching up on gossip. Dry-mouthed, she pushed on.

'Max!' she called.

Her husband turned. He nodded, gave her a wave.

'Have you got Ben? Where's Ben?' She was at Max's side.

'He's here somewhere.' Max shrugged, he went to kiss her on the cheek, but she was already turning away.

'Sophie? Where did Ben go?'

Her daughter was looking down at her phone, thumbs dancing over the screen. 'Oh, hi, Mum. Dunno. He was here a minute ago.'

Karen pushed between clusters of families, swallowing the urge to shout. The lights of the school building only reached the top of the embankment. Here, on the field, the dark deepened towards the river. She spotted a small boy in her son's class.

'Do you know where Ben is?'

'Yes,' the boy pointed behind her. At the same moment she felt a tug at her sleeve.

'Mummy, you came!' It was Ben, his eyes wide

26

in the darkness. 'You missed it.'

'There you are!' She pulled him close and stroked his hair.

'You missed the Roman candle, it was awesome.'

She tried to calm her breathing, hide her fear from him. 'How come there's no bonfire?'

'Don't know. Daddy said it was the healthy safety Nazis took it away.'

'Health and safety, and not Nazis, not real ones.'

Karen took his hand and they wove through the other families, back to their own.

The next morning, in the boardroom at RAMA, Florence Moyo sat with her elbows on the table and her head resting on her hands, as if it was too heavy to be held by her neck alone. She was a large woman, her eyes heavily lidded and circled by shadows. Karen stole glances at her in between taking notes. Mrs Moyo was five months' pregnant and Mr Moyo was explaining to Jaz that they had reached the end of their patience and their hope. The refusal of their claim meant he had lost his right to work and soon they would lose their accommodation too. They had a teenage daughter, settled in a local school. They couldn't go back to Zimbabwe, even if they wanted to. There were things that were hard to say out loud. A silence grew in the room.

'Shall I...?' Karen stood up.

Jaz finished her sentence. 'Get the leaflet, yes.'

They had a leaflet to help people through the appeal process, step by step. As Karen left the room to get a copy from the shelf, Rudo turned to Jaz Kumar and began to lift his sweater.

27

'You see what they did to me in my own country? How can I go back?'

She pulled a chair up in front of the tall bookshelf in the office. As she put one foot on it to test it wasn't going to wobble, a breath, no more than that, made her turn.

'Can I help you, perhaps?' Florence Moyo's voice was low, each consonant clearly enunciated. 'Maybe I should steady that chair. It doesn't look very safe.'

'No. No, it's fine, really.' It came out more snappily than she'd intended.

'You have children?'

Karen nodded.

'So you understand. It's a habit. You will do anything to make sure they are safe. You find yourself mothering everyone. I'm sorry.'

Yes, of course, Karen thought, of course you would do anything to keep your children safe. But you can't always. She pushed the thought away.

'My daughter is only fifteen,' Mrs Moyo continued, her hands resting on the chair back, 'but she has the look of someone twice her age. She has seen too much. Here she can be normal again.'

Karen stood on the chair and reached for a magazine box on the top shelf. 'Yes, of course.'

'She works hard in school. Goes to the Girl Guides. She helps out.'

'Nice. That's nice.' Karen took a copy of the leaflet. She hesitated about getting the whole box down and putting it somewhere more convenient, but the office was so tiny, there wasn't a spare inch. 'Thank you.' She stepped down. 'I wish my daughter would do something like that, but my husband, I mean, we don't go to church or anything and they seem, mainly to ... excuse me.'

Mrs Moyo's body filled the doorway, as if she wanted to hold Karen there, to forge some connection between them. Later Karen realised that it was to protect her from hearing what the men were talking about in the boardroom. Little did Mrs Moyo know that Karen would be writing it all up for Jaz as soon as they had left and she would soon know every painful detail.

## CHAPTER THREE

At nine in the morning, there was only one other occupant in the staff canteen and Sean Denton thought it would be rude to ignore her. But he wasn't at all sure whether she would acknowledge him. Crime Scene Manager Lizzie Morrison might just think it was beneath her to share a table with a PCSO.

'All right?'

He hovered, ready to go on to the next table, depending on the response. She was probably too well brought up to tell him to get lost, but she might still freeze him out. He wouldn't mind having a chat with her. In fact, if he was honest, he'd been looking for an opportunity for the last three days. If he could just talk to her about that dead girl, then maybe he wouldn't feel so bloody haunted. The girl's face was there in front of him when he closed his eyes at night. When he woke, there was a second or two when everything felt the same as it always had, until it dawned on him that everything had changed. He'd seen a body. He needed to know whether Lizzie still saw her too.

She was reading the paper and flashed him an automatic smile before returning to the page in front of her. He sat down.

'I've been thinking,' he said, 'about that girl.'

'Have you? There's a SOCO going down this afternoon to dust for prints. We'll see if he finds anything, but it's down as an overdose, nothing suspicious, so don't hold your breath.' She met his gaze. 'There was DNA from over fifteen different subjects on the bedsheet. Semen.'

He swore under his breath and saw her smile. She'd meant to shock him and she'd succeeded.

'The prints on the needle were hers.'

'So,' he blew on his coffee, squinting through the steam, 'we're looking at an accidental overdose by a woman who was, what, on the game?'

'Pretty good.'

'What are they dusting for?'

'Rule out foul play,' she said. 'Mind you, I had to push to get Burger to agree.'

'Why was she outside?'

'There's another question you need to ask first.'

'How long had she been dead?' he offered.

'Good question. Twelve to eighteen hours. It's not easy to be exact, especially at this time of year. One day can be sunny and the next freezing; decomposition can be slowed or accelerated, depending.'

He thought back to the weather on the day before they found her.

'It was sunny.' He'd helped his nan peg out the washing in the back garden; it was what she called a good drying day. 'Maybe the girl sat on the step to shoot up and enjoy the last of the afternoon sun.'

'You'd make a great detective.' Lizzie's smile seemed genuine.

Sean took a sip of coffee and occupied himself with the little plastic stirrer. He wasn't going to tell her that he didn't think he could pass all the tests. It wouldn't have crossed her university-educated mind.

'I never thought... I don't know, that I'd be doing that sort of work, as a support officer I mean.'

'Yeah, well. It looks like our friend Burger doesn't exactly follow procedure.' Lizzie folded her paper and stood up.

'Who was she?'

Lizzie shrugged. 'We don't know. She had no ID. Burger says she's not known to the police. She was in her mid-twenties, probably Chinese, and her clothes were all from British shops.'

'I wonder if anyone will come for her?'

'Don't hold your breath. Unless someone in Vice can ID her. A drug-addicted prostitute from the Chinese community isn't likely to have stayed close to her family.'

He shook his head. Chasebridge wasn't just his beat; it was where he grew up. He'd played all over the estate, crossed the potato field behind the lay-by with his mates, and gone off exploring in the woods. Who would have thought there'd be a brothel in a snack bar trailer, right under his nose?

That evening he was on duty at the Doncaster Rovers Community Fireworks Display. It was supposed to be a perk to be rostered for events like that, but as his feet turned numb he longed for the boredom of his first job, night-time shelf-stacking at Pets At Home. At least that had been warm.

He had a surprise at the Keepmoat Stadium. Up in the VIP box, a familiar face was looking down at him, although it took him a moment to recognise her, fully made-up and with the collar of an expensive camel coat pulled up to her ears. It was Lizzie Morrison and she actually waved. Later, as the spectators were leaving, milling around in front of the ground, she detached herself from a group and came over.

'Fancy meeting you here!' She smiled broadly and Sean was taken aback. Maybe she'd been on the champagne.

'I bet you were a sight warmer up there than we were down on the pitch,' he said, taking in how pretty her face looked with a spot of lipstick. 'How did you wangle a ticket?'

'My dad,' she nodded over her shoulder to a cluster of men with Doncaster Rovers scarves tucked into their dark coats. 'He's on the board.'

'Fancy that.' Sean thought he might have frostbite in his toes.

Back home in front of the gas fire, he rubbed his feet in his hands. He'd been planning to drop into the pub for a game of pool on the way home, but didn't think he'd stop shivering enough to hit the ball straight. His nan had waited up for him. Maureen was his mum's mum, and she'd had looked after him since he was twelve. She still hadn't got used to the fact he'd grown up. She had offered to run him a bath, but he'd settled for a can of lager and a packet of crisps.

He stared at the telly, a nice flatscreen he'd got on instalments when he started the job, trying to make out the flavour on his tongue. Worcester sauce, maybe. He washed it back with a mouthful of lager, cold and fizzing in his throat.

'Carole popped round with them. A whole box was only three pound. They're a bit too spicy for me, but I thought you might like them.'

'Carole?'

'From bingo. She gets them wholesale.'

He didn't know why she bothered with bingo: a bunch of old women staring at a set of numbers. She'd be seventy next year and she said it kept her young, said he ought to give it a go, but he wasn't tempted. The living room table was covered in home-decoration magazines and she'd marked several pages of wallpapers. That was going to be their next project together. She directed; he did the labouring. She entered competitions on TV makeover programmes, but she hadn't won yet.

'Any trouble at the fireworks?' she said and passed him another packet of crisps. The writing on the back looked foreign. Arabic or something.

'Not really. Had to ask a feller to put his sparklers out, but he wasn't too fussed.'

'It's been like World War I round here, some of these bangers they've got now, sound like they could take your head off.' The cat jumped up onto her lap, turned a few times before he settled. 'He's been right funny all night, but at least he's indoors.

33

Better when they do it properly, organised, much less bother for everyone.'

The feeling was coming back into his feet. A thousand pinpricks of returning blood made his eyes water and he wished he'd been less distracted when he spoke to Lizzie Morrison. He should have asked her how the SOCO got on taking prints at the trailer. On his bedroom wall, above the chest of drawers, was a sheet of flipchart paper that he'd taken from one of the conference rooms at the station. He'd helped himself to a set of marker pens too. It wasn't stealing; it was just bringing work home. The bosses did it all the time. In the centre of the sheet of paper was a photograph. It wasn't very good quality. Sean had taken it on his mobile, not at the scene, he hadn't thought of it then, but later, when the girl's picture was on the incident board. He'd given her a name, Su-Mai, which sounded sort of Chinese, and written it underneath in green. Then he'd used different colours to draw lines out from the picture in a clock pattern. At the end of each line he was going to write all the information gathered so far. Right now, all the lines were empty.

The following morning, Sean was glad of a late start. At the station he went straight to the canteen for a cup of coffee. Standing in the queue, he was aware of an argument going on at one of the tables. DCI Barry 'Burger' King was tucking into his lunch, or possibly his second breakfast, when a middle-aged man in a navy boiler suit, carrying a heavy, black case, approached him. The man's epaulettes said Scene of Crime Officer.

'Donald, mate!' Burger waved him over. 'Donald the Duck, how did you get on, any good prints?'

'Next time, give me the right bloody address. I've been up and down that stretch of road all morning and there's no snack bar van or catering trailer, or whatever you want to call it. Not there, not anywhere. No trailer means no prints.'

'I don't know what you're talking about,' a gobbet of something flew out of King's mouth across the table in front of him. He studied a map that was thrust under his nose and jabbed at it with a ketchup-covered fork. 'Right there, bit of a hedge, broken fence, just inside the field. You'd have to slow down to see it. What speed were you doing?'

'Very funny. I pulled up at every single lay-by along a three-mile stretch. There are six in case you're interested. Then I went back and checked them all again. There's nothing.'

King caught sight of Sean and beckoned to him.

'Here, take Percy with you. He knows it. He's a native.'

The SOCO looked less than impressed when Sean asked if he could go and transfer his coffee into a disposable cup.

As they pulled out of the car park, the SOCO broke the silence.

'Chaplin, Donald. No jokes about the name if you don't mind.'

Sean wasn't about to make one. 'Denton, Sean. Not Percy.'

Chaplin flicked on the radio. Classic FM. It was loud, but he turned it up louder.

'Helps the stress,' Chaplin shouted. 'Blood pressure, you know. Not helped by arseholes like our friend King.'

'How come you didn't go yesterday?'

'What?'

'Lizzie Morrison said you were going yesterday.'

'Violent burglary in a house at Bessacar!' Donald shouted back. 'And a nasty knife crime the day you found the body. Stretched resources, mate, it's a sign of the times. Smack ODs just don't cut it.'

Not a priority. Poor Su-Mai. They drove the rest of the way without speaking, listening to some tune like a film score blasting out of the speakers. Sean showed Chaplin where to stop and they pulled up onto the gravel of the lay-by. Sean twisted round in his seat and stared back through the gap in the fence. There was nothing there, just a space where only three days ago there'd been a mucky old snack bar trailer with the word RE-FRESHMENTS peeling off its side. He got out of the car.

'So it was definitely here?' Donald followed him.

'You can check my notes, if you can read my writing.'

The same break in the fence, the trodden grass, even a shred of incident tape caught in the hedge, told Sean he hadn't imagined it. There was a rectangle of yellow-brown grass and four matching dents where the stands had been. If the soft tyres had left a smudge, last night's hard frost had covered it over.

Back at the station Barry King shrugged it off.

'The farmer probably moved it. I'll get someone to ring him. He won't have been too pleased

36

about having a mobile brothel on his land.'

'We'll have to find it,' Sean realised he'd spoken out of turn as soon as King fixed him with a pointed stare.

'Oh, we will, will we? Well, sunshine, I think you'll find it's not in your job description to tell me how to allocate this department's meagre resources. We had a major burglary last night, violence to the person and kiddies in the house. No, I'm not putting any more manpower into a dead junkie. Let's get on with protecting the public from real criminals.'

After work, Sean walked up through the estate as it was going dark. He stood and looked across the ring road. The air was heavy with exhaust fumes and the scent of frying onions was coming from one of the blocks behind him. Eventually there was a long enough gap in the rush-hour traffic to risk crossing. There was still no trailer, just a flicker of blue-and-white tape from the hedgerow. It had been a crime scene, his crime scene, and now some idiot had moved the evidence and nothing more was going to be done about it. Su-Mai was dead and nobody except Sean gave a tinker's cuss.

## BONFIRE NIGHT: 6.45 a.m.

Phil rammed the van into gear and pulled away. The engine ground against itself then roared with the effort. When Mackenzie told him the van had seen better days, he hadn't been wrong. But it still

37

had a cassette player and Phil reckoned he had time to stop off and grab some sounds. The light was on in the bedroom and the dog greeted him with a thud of his tail against his legs. Upstairs, Stacey was sitting in bed with Holly curled around her.

'Sorry, did I wake you?'

'No. This one did. Said you'd gone a-hunting. Don't squash me, Holly,' Stacey shifted her daughter off her legs.

'Johnny Mac's got a job for me.'

'Good. He's going places, you know?'

'Yeah?' Phil rummaged in a box on the top shelf of the wardrobe.

'He might have something permanent soon. He'll need someone to run the office full-time.'

'Here it is. I knew I put these tapes somewhere.'

'Are you listening, Phil?'

'I can hear you.' He turned and looked at her. Stacey was prettier when she didn't frown, but it seemed to be her default expression these days. 'I can't see how answering the phone for Mackenzie is a fantastic career move.'

'The bills don't pay themselves,' she said. 'Maybe I should apply for it.'

'Maybe you should.' He bent down and kissed her on the forehead. 'I need to go. I should be back before you have to be at the pub. Bye, little chicken.' But Holly rolled away and stuck her thumb in her mouth.

As he left Moorsby-on-Humber, the sky was growing lighter. Phil reached over to the passenger seat and grabbed a tape from the carrier bag. The delicate percussive opening of Betty LaVette's 'Let

Me Down Easy' made him smile. Any second now the vocal would kick in with a swift boot to his guts. It was one of those tunes that landed him back at another time in his life, over a decade ago. A girl called Katie, kissing him goodbye at the airport in Ibiza, the salt still on her lips from her morning swim. She said she'd wait for him, wished she could come with him, but he was on his way home for a funeral. His mother was dead and he had to face it on his own.

He hit eject and failed to catch the tape. It skittered across the floor under the pedals. He grabbed another. The call and response of Chris Kenner's 'Land Of A Thousand Dances' shuddered through the speakers. Rewind to six months before his mum died. Chuck Everett's Soul Bar in Playa d'en Bossa. Chuck made him these tapes when they were getting a band together for the bar. For a blissful few months they'd played in paradise to packed houses; Phil on trombone, bigging up the brass sound. But when Phil got back from that wet, English funeral, he found that his so-called mate, Chuck, had moved in with Katie. No. Chris Kenner had to go too. Phil managed to get the action right this time and caught the tape. He dug a little deeper in the bag, finally settling on Beverley Knight. Good driving music, 'Moving On Up (On The Right Side)'. Phil laughed, the van wasn't moving up on anyone. A few bars in to the song, he was overtaken by a hearse. When the Humber Bridge came into view, his heart lifted. You really felt like you were going somewhere on that bridge, even if it was only Hull on the other side. People knocked Hull, but Phil liked it. A port was always full of possibilities; it was a way in and a way out.

He had the instructions in Mackenzie's wobbly handwriting: pick up the stock from a warehouse on the industrial estate and take it to an address in Doncaster. Easy money. He thought Stacey would be happy for once that he'd got some work. But somehow it was never enough. She didn't seem to understand that he needed to be flexible in case any bookings came in. And whatever else Johnny Mackenzie was, he was certainly flexible. He always had something on the go and was good for a bit of cash in hand.

Phil sang along, drumming the wheel with his index fingers. Driving jobs were all right. Even in this old heap of junk he could get into the music, be with his thoughts and get paid for it. He'd done his fair share of bar work but he hated it, it was all too rushed. That was how he met Stacey. He'd come back from playing a stint with an Abba cover band on the Hull–Rotterdam ferry. He'd been trying to hitch south; thought he might stay with the old man until he got straightened out. The ferry company had fired him for smoking spliffs in the staff restroom, but he was ready to leave anyway. The playlist was driving him nuts. He'd hitched a lift with a Dutchman in a refrigerated tulip truck. Just the other side of the Humber Bridge, the driver decided he needed a pie and a pint. The Volunteer Arms in Moorsby-on-Humber was warm and the jukebox played Otis Redding and Aretha Franklin. As the Dutchman was coming to the end of his third pint, Phil saw the sign above the bar: Staff

Wanted. The barmaid had a wide smile and a great laugh. Her name was Stacey. He decided to stay.

# CHAPTER FOUR

The RAMA office was one floor up above a doll shop in an uneven row of buildings just outside York's city wall. As Karen came round the corner, with a half-eaten sandwich in one hand and a carton of orange juice in the other, a man was looking at the dolls in the shop window. She let herself in at the office door and he turned round.

'Is your boss in?' he said.

Her mouth was full of dry chicken and granary bread.

'Well, is he in? Your boss? Jasvinder Kumar? My name's Moon. DCI Charlie Moon. Human Trafficking Service.'

He was very tall. Long arms hung from wide shoulders, the rest of his body hidden under a black puffa jacket. He held a police ID card out to her.

She swallowed the last of her mouthful. 'He's getting some lunch. Do you want to come up?' He nodded and followed her up the wooden stairs. 'He won't be long. Take a seat.'

DCI Moon crossed the room and sat down on the rattan garden chair that usually had Jaz's coat slung over it. One big hand ran through his hair, leaving it just as messy as when he'd come in.

'Nice place.' He looked around, taking in the beamed ceiling. 'Small, but perfectly formed.'

She wondered about sending him into the boardroom, to sit at the oval table where they'd interviewed the Moyos in the morning, but she felt like keeping an eye on him. Watching the detective. He looked like he was prepared to wait; took out his Blackberry and checked his messages. Even sitting down he gave the impression of height.

'Charlie!' Jaz bounded into the room, his coat half off, looked for a place to put it and decided the floor would do. The two men shook hands then pulled together in a backslapping man-hug. Jaz seemed to disappear into DCI Moon's arms. 'Has Karen given you a coffee?'

She hadn't. Somewhere between curiosity and a lingering irritation at having her lunch break interrupted she'd forgotten that part of her job description. She asked Moon how he liked it.

'Strong, and a tiny bit of milk.'

There was an upward inflection in his voice. Not local. Welsh maybe. Another 'blow-in'. The city was full of them, people like her and Max and Jaz. He looked like he'd want the good stuff, so she went into the boardroom where they kept the coffee machine. There was an old photograph above the fireplace captioned: 'Nineteenth-century Slum Housing for Irish Railway Workers, Just Inside the City Walls.' Two muddy-faced children were staring, hollow-eyed, at the photographer. Part of an earlier wave of immigration to York, it must have been even harder for them.

When she brought the coffee through, they

were reminiscing about a case they'd worked on. It sounded like Jaz had been defending someone Charlie had arrested.

'I still can't believe you thought he was legit,' Moon was saying.

'I thought he had a reasonable asylum claim. My job was to make sure the law was applied fairly.' Jaz interlaced his fingers and tried to hide a smile.

'He was a pimp for God's sake!' DCI Moon took the coffee and thanked her.

'Well at least you can be sure I'm on the side of the angels now,' Jaz replied. 'You were saying...?'

'We need to track down anyone connected to a haulage firm in Grimsby belonging to a guy called Xhoui Li, or anyone who could have come in on one of his trucks.'

'There's a girl at HMP Moreton Hall,' Jaz said. 'She was picked up in a Chinese restaurant by Immigration. Her solicitor approached me about her grounds for appeal. The dates fit and, if I remember rightly, she named Grimsby as her port of entry. Karen, could you...?'

She was already crossing the sloping wooden floor to get the file from the boardroom. The sound of her mobile stopped her. It hardly ever rang during the day. The two men watched as she fumbled to silence it. The name on the screen read Dad. In her haste, she hit the screen and realised she hadn't stopped the call, but answered it on speakerphone. The sound of her father's voice saying, *Hello, hello, Karen* filled the room. She looked helplessly at Jaz, mouthed, 'It's on the table, middle stack,' and slipped out through the other door to the landing at the top of the stairs.

'I'll call you back, Dad. I'm at work.'

'Wait, no, listen. Karen, please.'

It was a tone she didn't recognise. Later she would say that she knew something was wrong the moment she heard her father's voice. She stood against the wall, turning her back to the office door.

'What is it? What's up?'

'Is Philip with you?'

'Phil? Why would he be?'

'I'm sorry. Yes, it's a long shot. Stacey phoned. She thought he might be here. But he's not. I thought he might have come to you.'

'I don't understand.'

'He's gone missing. Didn't come back from a job yesterday. Stacey's had no message from him and his phone's just going to voicemail.'

'Do you think he might have turned up at our house? I can go home if you like.'

'Could you? I tried your home number but, obviously, you're not there.'

Why would her brother come to York? He made no secret of hating Max. She spoke to him on the phone every couple of months, but they hadn't seen each other since they went to her father's house in Hertfordshire, just before Christmas. Phil had brought little Holly down, but his wife had stayed at home. It was too near London and London – according to Stacey – was full of terrorists.

'I'll call you back when I get home,' she said.

Karen leant against the cool plaster of the wall, trying to make sense of what her father had told her. When she went back into the office, the detective was alone again. She could hear Jaz in the boardroom shuffling papers.

'I'm sorry about that. I don't normally leave it on.'

'These things happen,' the detective said. 'You OK? You look like you've seen a ghost.'

'I'll be all right.'

'Got it!' Jaz emerged, waving a manila folder.

'You know, we haven't been properly introduced.' Moon offered his hand and she took it. It was as if he was offering her some of his strength and, just for a moment, she held on.

'God, I'm so sorry! This is Karen, Charlie Moon. Charlie, Karen Friedman. Karen's my right-hand woman.' Jaz put the folder on her desk and began to shuffle through it.

'Karen's had a bit of bad news,' Charlie Moon said.

She wondered if he'd heard every word through the door.

'If no one minds, I think I need to go, I'll make up the hours.'

Jaz shrugged. He was reading the file of the restaurant girl.

'I've left all the papers for Mr and Mrs Moyo on your desk,' she said, as she put her coat on.

'Brilliant. Did you make another appointment for them?'

'It's in the diary.'

'Right, Charlie mate,' Jaz said. 'I can give you ten minutes, then you'll have to piss off.'

The two men turned their attention to the papers and she said goodbye. As she reached the door, Moon looked up briefly and she caught his eye.

45

In the doorway to the street, she hesitated. The air outside was cold and the light sudden. She could still smell last night's bonfires. Philip was missing. She wasn't sure what that meant or what she was expected to do about it. Missing people were posters in bus stops, appeals in the paper, they weren't your family. He could be anywhere. In every face, every body, every passing car, there was the possibility of Philip. Maybe she should have asked the detective's advice, but she wasn't sure what to ask. There was no point in causing a fuss if her brother turned up again in a day or two. People wandered off all the time, had rows or went to find themselves.

Around the corner from the office, waiting for the lights to change, Karen noticed several sleeping bags in the porch of the Methodist church. It was hard to see which of the filthy cocoons were occupied and which were empty. These people were missing too, even though they were right here in front of her. Somewhere a sister or a mother might be looking for them, but just didn't know to look on these particular church steps, in this particular city. They might, even now, be pasting up pictures at bus stops in another part of the country or another part of the world.

Her father's words, 'gone missing', rebounded in her head. One boy, sitting against a stone pillar with his knees drawn up, looked about fourteen. An old man was bent over, rearranging the contents of several plastic bags, his oversized suit jacket tied at the waist with a bungee. He reminded Karen of Philip at their mother's funeral. Phil only just made it back from Ibiza in time and she'd met him at the airport. He smelt of stale beer, cigarettes and several nights on the dance floor. He arrived at the crematorium in a suit borrowed from one of their dad's party comrades who was Phil's height, but three stone heavier. Her brother's tanned neck towered above the starched white shirt collar, which circled his throat like the ruff of a buzzard. The jacket hung from his bony shoulders and a tight belt gathered and bunched the extra fabric of the trousers round his waist. He looked like an elegant tramp, a Heathcliff, in that neat, suburban cemetery.

As she watched, the old man on the church steps looked up at her and she turned away towards the bus stop.

## BONFIRE NIGHT: 7.10 a.m.

Phil Holroyd hit the Clive Sullivan Way and Beverley Knight started to stutter and squeak. He ejected the cassette, but part of it stayed hooked inside the machinery and a slew of tape unravelled like spaghetti. A car hooted as he swerved into the outside lane. He dropped the cassette and it swung like a pendulum. He prayed it wouldn't snap. Steadying the wheel with his right hand, he scooped up the cassette with its trail of tape and laid it on the dashboard. The teeth of the machine held on, but the tape didn't break. Result. He would untangle it later, but in the meantime he'd have to make his own enter-

47

tainment. In the drone of the engine, Phil found several harmonies. Third gear launched him into a chesty rendition of 'Amazing Grace' and shifting into fourth switched him up a key to 'Swing Low, Sweet Chariot'. By the time he was turning into the industrial estate, his throat was dry. He pulled up at a row of low breeze-block sheds with metal shuttered doors. There was no one there.

Phil was ready for breakfast. He swung round and parked by a little café he'd spotted on his way in. A grey-faced girl pushed a stray lock of hair out of her face and served him without speaking. He thanked her, determined to get a smile out of her, but she wasn't interested. Balancing a bacon sandwich and a lidded paper cup on his lap, he drove back, one-handed, to the sheds. This time, at the last building before a high brick wall, there was a short, thickset man in a green parka and navy wool hat, standing with his arms folded, watching.

Phil wound down the window. 'I've come for Mackenzie's pick-up. The name's Phil, Phil Holroyd.'

The man nodded and waved him down the side of the last building. A red freight container filled the gap between the building and the wall. Its doors hung open like a toothless mouth.

Phil heard the man opening up the back of the van as he jumped down onto the rutted Tarmac.

'Mr Mackenzie would prefer you to keep the back doors locked,' the man said with a smile, revealing a flash of gold on one side. 'You never know who might jump in. My little joke, don't look so serious. Call me Len, Laughing Len.'

The smile vanished and Phil shivered. Inside

the container, he could see cardboard boxes and plastic-covered cases of soft drinks, each one made up of a stack of about eight trays.

'Take your time.' Len jerked a thumb at Phil's bacon sandwich, oozing fat and ketchup down his wrist.

'Cheers. Bit peckish, early start.'

'You southerners need a bit of feeding up. Cockney, are you?'

'Not exactly,' Phil's mouth was full and he wiped his greasy lips on the back of his hand. He didn't feel like chatting and he had a fair idea of how this kind of conversation would go. Jibes at soft southern bastards; questions about what he was doing up here and if he were to let on he was a musician, the inevitable: have you been on the radio?

'Been on Mackenzie's payroll long?'

Phil shrugged. 'On and off.'

He finished the sandwich and screwed up the soggy paper napkin. He looked for somewhere to throw it but there was nowhere obvious so he chucked it on the floor of the cab. They loaded the van in silence until it was full. Phil reckoned there was still plenty of stock left in the container. Mackenzie had asked him to make several journeys until that consignment was shifted. Pallets of soft drinks, boxes of crisps and sweets, destined for export to somewhere with Arabic writing, diverted back to the pound shops and market stalls of South Yorkshire.

'I'll be seeing you later, sunshine, unless Mr Mac has other plans for you today.' The gold tooth twinkled from Len's cracked grin.

'Yeah, see you.' Phil slammed the door of the

49

van, catching his cup of tea just in time as it bounced off the dash. He wedged it between his knees as he pulled away. Back on the first stretch of straight road he steadied into fourth gear and took a sip through the tiny hole in the plastic lid. Cold.

## CHAPTER FIVE

Karen lay in bed watching Max reading an auto-biography of Thierry Henry. She rolled onto her back and stared up at a hairline crack running down the sloping ceiling, like a tear in fabric.

'What if he's in trouble with the law? Or had a breakdown?'

'He'll be OK. He's an adult. You worry too much.'

'What makes you so sure? What if it's not all right? What then?'

Max put his book down and turned to her. He propped himself up on one elbow.

'What do you want me to say?'

'I don't know. If I have to tell you what to say, then there's not much point in you saying it.' She turned her head away. 'But I don't worry too much. And who's to say what's too much anyway? There have been times when I haven't worried enough.'

Then she started to cry and he held her.

'Hey! Don't give yourself a hard time, but you can't solve everything, that's all.'

Finally she turned over and lay with her head on his chest, wrapped around him, skin-to-skin, alone with her fear. A light snore caught in the back of his throat and she envied him his ability to fall asleep in seconds.

In the middle of the night, she woke and listened to the ticking of the cooling radiators. This was originally Sophie's room, but she'd got scared of the monsters who clicked their teeth in the darkness. When Ben was born, he had the room next to his sister's on the middle floor because Sophie refused to swap with her parents. Karen fixed up an alarm and got used to listening to his breathing, watching the red lights flicker up and down in sequence. She didn't have an alarm for Sophie or for their second child, Cara. The one they lost. Their cot-death baby. She sometimes wondered if Sophie felt it too, the need to check on Ben, be nearer to him in case anything happened to him. Perhaps the monsters were just a ruse. Baby Cara was six weeks old when she died, but the space she left behind had been with them for eight slow years.

The next day, Karen was in the office trying to organise the notes that Jaz had left. He wanted a report on the Moyos' reasons for refusal. There was a page labelled *Passport Issues*. The writing was swimming like tadpoles. She'd spent the last two nights lying awake, thinking about Phil, hoping that tomorrow would be the day the phone would ring and her dad would say, it's all right, he's turned up, all a fuss about nothing.

Her eyes were dry and her shoulders ached …

51

*used cousin's South African passport ... reasonable?*
*Stress circumstances re. detention in home country...*
The urge to tip forward and rest her head on the desk was almost overwhelming, but she needed to get this done before she broke off for lunch to meet up with her dad. Reg Holroyd had been to Lincolnshire to see Stacey, and now he needed to see his daughter, they needed to talk, he said.

When the buzzer went her heart sank. She picked up the intercom phone.

'Hello, RAMA.'

'Hi there.' The voice surprised her. Big hands, coal mines and Tom Jones all competed in her head in a crazy game of free association. 'Jaz in?'

'No. Sorry.'

'Can I come up and leave him a message?'

She buzzed DCI Moon in and hoped he wouldn't stay long. She didn't want to be late to meet her dad.

'How's things?' He smiled a twitch of a smile that sent sunbeams of fine lines shooting up around his eyes. She wasn't in the habit of noticing men's eyes, but she thought it was an interesting effect.

'Me? Oh, fine.' She looked at her watch. 'You wanted to leave Jaz a message?'

'Quite a result on the Grimsby case. Your man Jaz did us a favour.'

Karen started putting her coat on. Her father's train would be here in twenty minutes.

'The girl at Moreton Hall checked out.' He was talking fast, unable to hide his enthusiasm, like a big kid. 'Thanks to her we've pulled in the owner of a haulage firm and forensics have picked up skin, faeces and urine samples from the back of three of the trucks. Male and female. All human. Seven different ethnic markers.'

'Nice.'

'At least this lot are coming in alive. So far. Looks like we've nipped something in the bud. I was hoping Jaz might be around to celebrate.'

*Coming in alive.* She was glad Moon turned round to help himself to the cooling coffee jug, before she gave herself away. For a second she thought her eyes were about to fill with tears. She hated being so bloody sensitive. After Cara she thought she'd cried all she could, but it had left her vulnerable and now this business with Phil. She blew her nose and held her breath.

'I don't mean to be rude, but I'm going to have to lock up. I've got a lunch meeting.'

'Sure, no problem.' He swallowed the coffee and wandered into the boardroom to stick a Post-It on the whiteboard. Then he walked down the stairs humming. It sounded like 'Oh, What a Beautiful Morning'.

Karen watched the London train unload its passengers into the cold air of York Railway Station. Reg Holroyd was the last one off, his brown corduroy jacket and green scarf marking him out as a country mouse among the town mice. He gave her a little wave and looked down at his feet as he approached her, as if he was trying to work out what the protocol was. She kissed him on the cheek and met his eyes. He'd aged. Perhaps she had too. They walked towards Lendal Bridge in silence. She'd heard about a new place in one of

53

the bridge towers, with tables outside.

When she brought their drinks out, he remarked that the smoking ban had suddenly turned the British into Europeans, with pavement cafés all year round.

'Can't even smoke at party meetings any more and I'm too old to stand around the dustbins.'

She thought it was strange that they were once considered a threat, Reg's tiny Home Counties' branch of the Communist Party; a group of aging comrades, now driven from their subversive activities by health-and-safety rules. She watched him fill his pipe and press the tobacco down with his thumb. As he lit it, a plume of sweet smoke billowed up and over her face.

'Sorry, love, you're down-wind, should have sat on the other side of you.'

'I don't mind.'

It was the smell of her childhood, of following him round the garden with her own little trowel and bucket, squatting down to bury her fingers in wet earth and pulling out the weeds as he'd shown her. Reg was in no rush to start talking about Phil, but Karen was getting impatient, she only had an hour for lunch and the Moyos' case notes were waiting for her in the office. She put her cup down too hard and the flimsy aluminium table rocked drunkenly on the stone paving.

'How did Stacey seem?' she said.

'She seemed worried enough when she phoned last week.'

'Yes, I spoke to her.'

'I had to ask her if she thought he'd done anything stupid. I didn't want to say it, but you have to consider these things.'

He tapped his pipe out on the edge of the chair. It was chilly out here. She wished she'd worn a scarf.

'But that's so unlikely, don't you think, Dad? Phil's always been so ... optimistic.' The frothy milk sank into her coffee. She stirred it and the separate strands of colour merged to fawn. 'When I got there, she behaved as if I was over-reacting.'

'What? But you're his dad for God's sake!'

Two girls at the next table glanced at her briefly and then looked away.

Reg lowered his voice. 'When I asked her what the police had said, she told me she hadn't called them.'

'But ... I don't understand. Does she know where he's gone then?'

'She made out that he's done this sort of thing in the past. He gets cold feet. Those were her exact words.'

Karen bit into her sandwich. It tasted like card-board.

'She thinks he's just driven off with his employer's van. A fellow called Mackenzie, who's hopping mad and wants his van back.'

'He wouldn't walk out on Holly, I'm sure about that.'

'Poor little Holly,' Reg said. 'She looks like her mother, that one.'

'It makes no sense. He's seemed really settled since Holly was born. Did you ask her if his pass-port was missing?'

Reg looked at his daughter with a weary resignation. 'Maybe you should have gone. I didn't want to pry too much. I'm not a detective. I'm just an old man.'

They sat in silence while a pigeon landed next to the table and looked hopefully for crumbs. Karen swung her foot at it.

'Look, I'm sorry, Dad. I'm just worried. That's all.'

'Me too, love. Me too.' He reached across to squeeze her hand.

## CHAPTER SIX

Sean followed the herd into the morning briefing and stood near the back. All available staff had been called in for this one, so they were packed into one of the conference rooms. A DI from the drugs squad was speaking. Sean knew him by sight; Rick something, a pretty slick pool player.

'...similarities with the Chasebridge girl. But the other side of town...'

Sean spotted Lizzie, looking like she was in the front row of the maths class, waiting for her turn to deliver the scene-of-crime report. The light reflected off her smooth hair, like in that shampoo advert. She was most definitely worth it. He forced himself to tune back in to Rick.

'...not officially a cluster, but two deaths with a similar MO needs looking at. Early toxicology suggests poisoning from a high-grade batch of heroin, in combination with amphetamines in the first girl's case. We're just waiting for a second run of tests on the body from Balby. Meanwhile, the Chief Super's ordered an information campaign and my team will be making it a high priority. Any questions?'

The hand dryer in the gents hadn't been working properly for months. Sean gave it the obligatory thump on the side and it rattled into action. Two men came in. As the dryer cut out, Sean heard 'prostitute' and a question about suppliers on a different patch. He recognised Rick, the pool player. He didn't know the other man. He wanted to hear the answer, but they'd moved to the urinal. Sean decided it would look weird to hang around any longer.

When he got back to the conference room, it was empty. The whiteboard and the flipchart with the details of the victim were still there. Flora Brikenda Ishmaili, aged twenty-three, born in 1986, in Kosovo. The blown-up photograph showed a girl with messy brown hair, her head angled like something in her neck had just snapped. If you hadn't already guessed she was dead, her skin confirmed it. Neither white nor yellow, it was an ageless, ivory grey. He felt in his pocket for his phone and took a picture. He had to get in closer to the one they had of her alive, a photo-booth image of Flora pulling faces with her friend; the girl who found her. On the whiteboard there were details of the place, names, times. He snapped that too.

'What are you doing?' Lizzie Morrison said, from the doorway.

'Just trying to keep a record. So I can remember

stuff.' He shoved the phone deep into his pocket.

'Why don't you use a notebook like everyone else?'

'I better get off.' He edged towards the door. 'I'm supposed to be back on the estate in twenty minutes.'

'What do you think the connection is?' She sounded like it mattered what he thought, not taking the piss or anything. 'I mean with our girl?'

'Don't ask me, I'm just a PCSO.' Passing her in the doorway, he could smell her. It was a clean perfume and soap smell. Like fresh sheets.

Outside Chasebridge Health Centre, Sean was being ignored. Carly, his partner, was doing better, pressing leaflets into the hands of women surrounded by sticky kids. She acted like one of the lads back at the station but out here she switched on some secret woman-talk thing.

'Come on girls, give us a minute, cheers, duck.'

Bold black letters warned of a batch of high-strength heroin in circulation, with a helpline number and the usual details of local drugs agencies. Most of the leaflets ended up in the hoods of buggies or stuffed in pockets, while others were blown away down the parade of shops. Sean couldn't help thinking that this was not the target audience. This lot were more at risk of an overdose of trans-fats than heroin.

A woman pushed a double buggy across the pedestrian crossing, a baby in front, a toddler behind and a little girl of about four standing on the back axle. Her face was pale and the knuckles of her hands were hard and white. Alongside her, a youth kept pace, his hands in his pockets and his head down. Sean couldn't decide if he was the father of the children or an older son. The way she launched her family off the pavement and across the road, without looking, was beyond careless. It was beyond caring. Sean decided that this one needed his leaflet.

'Excuse me.' He stepped forward. She was level with him but her eyes were fixed on the glass door of the health centre. 'We're giving out information and a helpline number. A potential risk from high-grade heroin...'

'Come on, Neesha.' The youth was holding the door open for her. The hood of his sweatshirt framed his profile and Sean had a feeling they'd met before.

It was starting to rain. He stepped back under the overhanging roof, but the wind was gusting the rain in horizontal sheets. Carly had gone to put up a poster in the little branch library at the other end of the parade. She was taking her time, but it was warm in there and she'd probably been offered a cup of tea. Ten minutes later, and nobody else had taken a leaflet, the door opened and the over-loaded buggy was shoved back out onto the pavement. The youth was pushing this time and as he reached the crossing the woman turned back.

'Give us one of your leaflets then.'

'Right.' Sean fished a dry one out of the middle of the stack. 'And if you have anything you'd like to tell us, anything at all that could help, you can phone the number, here...'

She looked like she wouldn't take it, but a glance over at her family told her that nobody was watching. The leaflet disappeared inside the pocket of her thin jacket and she set off across the road.

'Oi, you lot! Wait for me, you bastards!'

Sean watched her go. Her thin legs were bare below her leggings and, despite the cold, she was wearing those plastic clogs that everyone bought last summer.

'Take care,' he said, knowing she couldn't hear him.

Sean handed in his radio at the end of his shift. He had no plans for the evening. A DVD and a take-away with his nan would suit him fine. He saw Lizzie Morrison rounding the corner of the corridor a split second before they would have crashed into one another. She was sending a text and looked up at him, startled and slightly embarrassed, as he jumped out of her way. He liked how it made her eyes extra large, like a cartoon rabbit. There was one in a chocolate advert when he was a kid with a really sexy voice; only later it turned out it was just some old actress. Lizzie was saying something but he couldn't get the advert out of his head.

'Did you hear a word I just said?' Lizzie was laughing. It was his turn to look embarrassed. 'I said, it's like there's been a nuclear holocaust and nobody's told me. I can't find a single person who's up for going out tonight. It's like I have literally no friends.'

'Where do you fancy going?' The words were out there before he realised he'd said them and there was no way to haul them back in.

'Well, I have to eat something or I'm going to

pass out. Don't mind what, but I could eat a horse.'

'Don't know any horse restaurants, but there's a nice Chinese near the swimming baths.' He made her smile. Almost made her laugh. She checked her phone again as if it could tell her what to do.

Twenty minutes later, they were sharing a basket of prawn crackers at The New Moon Restaurant and Take Away. They'd agreed not to talk shop. Which left them sitting in silence after a brief attempt at 'where did you grow up' and 'where do you live now'. Her one-word answers told Sean everything he already knew about how little he had in common with Lizzie Morrison. Half-way through the spring rolls, she broke first.

'Did you know that the second overdose girl, the one in Balby, had form?'

'What for?'

'She was known to Vice. Three arrests.'

He nodded. 'What about the girl who found her?'

'We've got nothing on her. She was from Kosovo too, but is technically married to an Englishman. The dead one, it's really sad, she came here as a refugee when she was only a kid. Her parents died in the war over there.'

'Shit.' The waiter put a dish of chow mein in front of him, but he felt his appetite going. 'What a waste of a life.'

She picked up a pair of chopsticks and hooked a bean sprout into her mouth. 'We can't stop people destroying themselves.'

She was right. He thought of his dad, his voice

61

cracked with whisky and his memory gone. He looked like an old man and he wasn't even fifty.

'The job of the police, and we humble civilians who've thrown in our lot with the Force,' Lizzie saluted with her chopsticks, 'is to lock up the people who are making money exploiting the vulnerable.'

'OK, Wonder Woman,' he raised his pint to her, 'I'm right behind you.'

He'd imagined them going on somewhere, a club or maybe the little Spanish bar near the Civic, but when she'd cleared her plate, she sat back and thanked him for saving her from boredom. She fancied getting off home now for an early night. They paid the bill and got their coats. Outside on the pavement, ready to go in opposite directions, she turned to him.

'There's something I wanted to ask your advice about.'

'Mine?' he said.

'I started at Donny Central the same time as you, so we're in the same boat.'

'I wouldn't say that.'

'Just between the two of us – I'm not sure how to put this – but if you thought something, or someone, wasn't quite right. Let's say, someone wasn't playing it straight, who would you go to?'

Sean walked up from the bus stop, round the curved crescent of Winston Grove and into Clement Grove. There were lights on in the front rooms and the silver-blue flicker of TV screens. Beyond the Groves, the first block of the Chasebridge flats loomed in the dark.

There was a woman in a navy tracksuit sitting at the kitchen table with his nan.

'You know Carole, don't you?' Maureen said, as she got up to put the kettle on.

'All right?' Sean greeted the woman. 'No tea, thanks, Nan, I'll get a beer.'

'Carole's got some nice T-shirts, only a fiver, all good labels.'

A few months ago, Sean would have shown more interest. It would never have crossed his mind to ask where things came from. A bargain was a bargain. As he bent down to get his beer from the fridge, he caught sight of Carole reaching for the zip of the holdall on the floor beside her. She closed it quickly.

'Mostly just kiddy sizes. I don't think I've got anything that would fit you.' She must know what he did for a living.

'I'm going up.'

Maureen wasn't thinking straight, letting Carole bring her knock-off gear round here. He'd have to find a time to tell her, but he had stuff to do just now. In his bedroom he hooked his phone up to the computer and uploaded the photos from the conference room. When they were printed, he added them to his flipchart. He sat on the end of the bed and took a long drink from the can. Bloody hell. He'd been out for dinner with Lizzie Morrison. And she'd asked his advice, although he wasn't sure whether he'd given her the answer she was looking for: keep your head down and your mouth shut. All the same, he couldn't help wondering who she was talking about.

# CHAPTER SEVEN

Max had taken the car to Scotland, so Karen decided to take the train to Doncaster and pick up a hire car when she got there. For half an hour, the flat landscape licked past the window of her carriage and she felt ashamed of how seldom she'd visited Phil and Stacey. It wasn't all that far. She and Max had driven down after Holly was born, got lost on the smaller roads and argued. It always seemed too much effort after that. This time she'd printed a map from the Internet. She ran her finger along the blue line, tracing her route and trying to memorise the names of the villages between Doncaster and Moorsby-on-Humber. The road zig-zagged into North Lincolnshire, suddenly straightening out for a few miles, along the side of a man-made waterway, then curving round again until it reached the side of the Humber estuary, whose mouth opened towards the sea like a huge fish.

She tested the pedals in the hire car and tried to adjust the seat, wishing she'd paid extra for an upgrade. She put her foot on the accelerator and the tiny vehicle lurched out of the station forecourt. The one-way system drew her through the town and out onto a main road that led east, through semi-industrial villages, past farms and warehouses, until finally she came to a signpost telling her that Moorsby-on-Humber was just two more miles. The road began to look familiar and soon she was on the outskirts of the village, passing the pub where Phil had been working last time she came. She had a feeling Stacey worked there now. She rounded a bend and pulled up in front of a row of terraced farm cottages. She cut the engine, pulled on the handbrake and sat still, waiting. Stacey hadn't told her *not* to come, but she hadn't sounded particularly welcoming either. Karen took a deep breath and got out of the car. The house was in the middle of the row. It was rented from a local farmer. She noticed that the windows and door had been recently replaced with PVC double-glazing. She'd come this far with the conviction that she should do something: support Stacey, help her and help Phil, if he could be helped. Now she wasn't so sure. She rang the bell. The chime triggered the frantic barking of a dog and a weight hurled itself against the door.

'Marvin! Get back, you stupid mutt!'

After a scuffle, Stacey opened it. She'd become thinner, but harder. Still pretty, but some of the effortlessness had gone.

'Karen. Hi. You'd better come in.'

'Marvin? I didn't know you'd got a dog.'

'She's Phil's.' Stacey said. 'Silly bugger didn't ask what sex it was. Got her from a feller whose house he was decorating. Called it after Marvin Gaye.'

Typical Phil, Karen thought.

Stacey disappeared into the kitchen to put the kettle on, while Karen sat down in the front room, taking in the tidy toy corner and the neat row of framed pictures on the mantelpiece. One was a photograph of Phil on a beach with Holly on his shoulders, her white-blonde hair against a sky full of rain.

'Cleethorpes.' Stacey handed her a mug of coffee. 'You wouldn't believe it was July. He had a summer season with an end-of-the-pier band.' Karen winced at the chemical smell of instant. 'Is that all right? You do take milk, don't you?'

'Yes, it's lovely. Thanks.' They sat in silence for a moment. Karen wasn't sure how to frame her questions. Max said she mustn't be too bossy, so she chose her words carefully. 'Have you thought any more about talking to the police?'

Stacey looked into her mug. 'I told your dad. There's no point.'

'What about a helpline? There's a missing persons' helpline.'

Stacey pressed her toes into the pile of the carpet. Her nails were painted the same shade of purple, like chameleons disappearing into their habitat. Karen could see Holly's features in her, the same wide brow and open face.

'Would you like me to do something?' Karen offered. Stacey shook her head. 'Are you in some kind of trouble? I don't really understand.'

'Look, Karen, I don't want to be nasty, I thought we were all right, me and Phil, apart from the fact he's never had a proper job, but it turns out it's worse than that, he's been a right bastard and I didn't know the half of it.' A rush of air and water gurgled through the radiator. Marvin pushed through the kitchen door and wagged her tail hopefully at Stacey's feet. 'Now he's buggered off and I haven't even had the chance to have it out with him, face-to-face.'

Getting no response, the dog turned to the visitor and pricked up one ear. Karen reached out a hand and Marvin sniffed it.

'I'm sorry...' She wanted to say something else, defend her brother, but she wasn't sure what the charges were.

'It's OK. I was proper worried an' all the first couple of days. But then a friend set me straight. Told me a few home truths. I think he's just legged it, if you must know.'

'Has he gone off before?'

Stacey shook her head.

'Dad said–'

'I'm sorry for your dad. He looked, right, I don't know, disappointed. I told him Phil gets cold feet about marriage, and being part of a family and that, because it didn't sound as bad.' She took a slurp of coffee. 'Look, this friend of ours, Johnny, came round and told me some stuff about Phil and, well, it weren't just one other lass, but a few. Johnny says he's been covering for him ever since we've been together.'

'And Phil's with one of these women?'

'There's a married one. Don't know her name. Her husband left her and she was doing up her house to sell. Phil worked out there for a few weeks, decorating. I never thought...' Stacey rubbed a mark on the arm of her chair with her thumb. It looked as if she was trying not to cry.

'And where is she now?'

'Johnny says, last he heard, she's got a place in Florida. He reckons they've gone there.'

Karen looked away from her and out of the window. She wanted to say, 'I don't believe it,'

67

but she knew she had no right. She stared out at the dove grey sky over the flat fields and watched a gull wheel in and out of view.

Karen gripped the dog's lead tighter, wrapping it round her wrist. Marvin was part Border collie and looked like she might have a tendency to round things up. When Stacey said she needed to collect Holly from a neighbour, Karen offered to take the dog for a walk. She wasn't sure if Stacey really wanted her there any more, but she wasn't ready to leave and her sister-in-law was probably too polite to ask her to go. Anyway, she wanted to see her niece now she'd come all this way. A public footpath sign led Karen across a field, pulled along by Marvin. They approached a hawthorn hedge and, as the heels of Karen's boots sank into the soft ground, Marvin pulled harder. At that moment, a small woman with a large German shepherd stepped through a gap from the next field. Karen tried to get past, but she'd forgotten the sociability of dogs. Marvin began to circle the other animal until their leads were completely entangled.

'Come on, Marvin.'

'Oh they love each other these two, old friends they are!' The woman peered up at her. 'You a friend of Stacey's?'

'Sister-in-law. I'm Phil's sister.'

'Oh.' She bent down to untangle the dogs' leads and Karen couldn't see her expression. 'He's back then, is he?'

'No. I came to see if I could help at all.'

'Such a shame, with a littl'un.'

'I've been worried,' Karen offered. 'It doesn't seem like him just to disappear.'

'I usually let Caesar off here, do you think Marvin would like a run?'

Karen's arm was aching from the constant pull of the dog. When she unclipped the lead, she and Marvin shared a moment of relief and the two dogs raced away after the scent of a rabbit.

'My name's Jackie, by the way. Me and my husband Stan, we run The Volunteer Arms.'

'Karen Friedman.'

It was an oddly formal moment in the damp, dead grass of the field, as she stuck out her hand and Jackie took it with a firm shake. They walked together for a while and Jackie told her about how she met Phil when he first arrived in the village, how she'd offered him a job and what a lovely guy he was, always singing or whistling a tune. Karen found herself sharing a memory of Phil getting into trouble at school for humming and driving the teacher mad. And then it crossed her mind that this was the sort of conversation you have at funerals.

'You older than him, are you?' Jackie asked.

'Yes, I looked after him when we were little. My mum had MS, she was ill for a long time.'

'You have a look of Phil. I can see the likeness.'

She'd always thought how different they were, in habits and behaviour at least, but maybe the code that was written across their features and in their bone structure was stronger than that.

'Did he... Stacey thinks ... he may have been seeing other women?'

'Really?' Jackie peered ahead, as if trying to visualise it. 'I wouldn't know. I don't listen to gossip.'

The two women walked together without speaking, while the dogs returned, circled them and chased each other away along the edge of the field. Karen found herself thinking about how her mother used to do jigsaw puzzles. She found them harder and harder as her condition worsened, until in the end they only frustrated her. Karen remembered her struggling to force in a piece, which wouldn't go, and then crying over the loss of that simple function. It was a picture of two retrievers chasing a rabbit in an autumn landscape. Now Karen felt like she had a piece of a puzzle in her hand, but she couldn't see where it fitted.

'Who's Johnny?' she asked Jackie.

'Johnny?'

'A friend of Stacey and Phil's?'

'Johnny Mackenzie?' Jackie stopped and looked at Karen. 'Local lad. He and Stacey used to go out together when they were younger.'

'What does he do? I think Phil was working for him.'

'Bit of an entrepreneur. Got an agency with all foreign types, Poles and that. They clean the posh houses out towards Barton. Some of them do the fruit-and-veg picking.'

Karen made a mental note to mention this to Jaz. 'Phil was driving a van. He was doing some sort of delivery job for Mackenzie, I think.'

'Oh yeah? Well, Johnny Mac's got a lot of little schemes.'

Karen listened to the squelch of wet ground under her boots. The leather was spattered with chocolate-brown mud, which had reached the

70

hem of her skirt. Her calves ached and her legs longed for Tarmac.

'Would you trust him? This Johnny Mackenzie?'

'Would I trust him?' Jackie's tone was as flat as the fields. 'Well, I don't know really, love. I don't know.'

When she got back to the house, the dog whined at the front door while they waited for Stacey to answer. She could hear the sound of the television, a nursery rhyme cranked up high. Behind it, a man's voice was raised in some kind of argument and then she could hear Stacey calling to Holly to turn the volume down. She rang the bell again. Stacey opened the door with Holly pressed between her legs.

'Stop it, Holly! You'll trip me up!'

'Marvin!' She was not much bigger than the dog, this little girl who wrapped her arms round its grubby neck. She smiled up at Karen.

'Remember your Aunty Karen, Holly?'

Karen let go of the dog's lead and closed the door behind her. She thought she felt a sudden draught, as if another door had been opened at the back of the house. Holly didn't show any sign of remembering her, but she took her hand anyway and led her into the front room to show off her toy box.

It was only later, when they were sitting down to a pizza in front of the TV, that Holly asked where Uncle Johnny had gone.

'Isn't he having pizza, Mummy? Can I give his bit to Marvin?'

'He had to pop out, love.' She turned to Karen

and said quickly, 'He's just a neighbour. Every-one's Uncle or Aunty to her.'

'He's the guy Phil was working for.'

'So what?'

'For God's sake, Stacey!' Karen stood up. The jigsaw piece had just clicked into place. She had a dizzy sensation of filling the room as her plate slipped off the sofa and the pizza landed face down on the purple carpet. Holly started to cry and Marvin rushed in, seizing her chance.

'Can't you see?' Karen could hear her voice pitching out of control. 'He was probably the last person to see Phil. He could be telling a pack of lies! And you just believe everything he's said.'

'Nobody asked you to come here!' Stacey was on her feet too. She scooped Holly up into her arms.

'That's right.' It was a man's voice behind her. 'So I think you'd better leave.'

He was standing in the doorway to the kitchen, a small and squarely built man of about thirty, with wind-burnt cheeks and reddish hair.

'I know who you are and I want to know where my brother is!'

'You know nothing, lady, not a bloody thing. This your bag?'

He crossed the room in three strides, picked up her handbag and opened the door to the hall in one seamless action.

Karen looked at Stacey, but she couldn't see her face, buried in Holly's hair. She felt hopeless and huge, like Alice in Wonderland, grown too large for the tiny room. She went to the door and took the bag from Mackenzie's outstretched hand. When she was level with him, he whispered in her face:

'Ten thousand pounds, that's what you owe me for that van. Your old feller didn't look like he had that sort of money, but you do, lady. I take cash or a cheque.'

On the way out of the village, Karen slowed down outside The Volunteer Arms, leaking warmth and yellow light into the darkness. She was tempted to go in and find Jackie, but she was scared; not just of Mackenzie and any friends he might have, but of herself. She'd never been one for picking fights, but now she'd started she was afraid she might not be able to stop. She tipped the lights to full beam, put her foot down hard on the accelerator and headed for the main road to Doncaster.

She parked in the allotted space and posted the keys through the door of the car-hire office. Her heels rang out in the station forecourt. It was Saturday night, but the place was almost deserted. In the ticket hall a couple leant drunkenly against a shuttered counter, lost in each other's faces. The girl pressed against the boy, and he gripped her to stop himself from falling. Karen checked the departure board. The last train to York had left half an hour ago. She walked outside to a scratched metal bench where she sat down, breathed in cold, damp air and let the tears come. When she'd exhausted the only tissue in her pocket, she got up and walked away from the station. A man passed her, weaving slightly, he paused to look at her for just too long. She wasn't sure where she was going, but on the next corner she came to a large Victorian pub with a vacancies sign trapped behind a grey net curtain. She pushed open the door and there was a brief murmur, which she just caught the end of, '...lady present. Thanks, Sid.'

There were four men in the warm room and a television set high up on the wall. The picture was frozen. She caught sight of a leg and a head of long blonde hair. She looked away, feeling the men watching her as she walked to the bar.

'Do you have any rooms?'

'We do, love.' The barman was large and smiling, a diamond-patterned jumper stretched over his belly. 'How many would you like? Eat in or takeaway?'

She smiled weakly at his joke. 'Just one, just for tonight.'

'Follow me, madam, or would you like a drink first?'

'I'll take one up, if that's OK. A glass of red wine please.'

While she waited for him to pour her drink, she found herself looking at the pictures on either side of the bar; two Turner prints, their cloudy colours smudged under dirty glass. She knew them like old friends, *The Fighting Temeraire* and *Rain, Steam and Speed*, two of a set of place mats her mother used to get out for Sunday lunch. Phil's favourite was the ghostly warship limping home in the sunset, while she always chose the little black steam train, hurrying through a yellow-grey mist. She picked up her glass and followed the landlord through a door at the side of the bar. There was a buzz of relief from the men behind her and she heard the elaborate orchestral score of their porn film start up again. It sounded like Debussy.

The sheets were clean but cold. Karen sat up in

bed in her blouse, a cardigan round her shoulders. Probably not what the men at the bar would consider foxy, but she locked the door and put the chain on anyway. The room was uniformly yellow with years of cigarette smoke, or maybe it was intentional. Perhaps Dulux had a special colour called Pub Fag Yellow. There was paint peeling from the cornices on the ceiling and the embossed wallpaper was scratched and torn. The bulb in the bedside lamp had blown, so she sat with the stark overhead light on and sipped her wine. Its rough, raw tannins hit the roof of her mouth and sucked at her cheeks. She phoned Max and told him what had happened and that she was safe. He said she should have checked the timetable, which she didn't need to hear. She wished she had a radio, the low mumbling of a documentary or even the shipping forecast, but there was just the sound of the occasional passing car below the window and a swarm of questions buzzing round in her head. She tried to think things through, but nothing would stay put.

Karen had a sudden start, as if a door had banged. She knew she'd been asleep, but she couldn't tell for how long. Her heart was pounding in her ears and the light was still on. Her watch said half past two and she needed the toilet. She crossed the sticky carpet, thankful for her socks, pausing at the shabby sight of herself in the mirror, make-up worn to a smudge on her pale skin and her hair flattened on one side. She realised that Max must see her like this all the time. That was the point of being married. You said what you thought, looked how you wanted to; nothing mattered. At least that's what she'd always believed. She was suddenly overwhelmed with the urge to go home to Max and the children.

## BONFIRE NIGHT: 8.45 a.m.

By quarter to nine, the scrubby brown fields and makeshift fences along the main road had given way to the boundary wall of a new-build estate and Phil was trapped in traffic. For the last five minutes he'd been looking at the words: 'Is your wife as dirty as your van', written in the dust on the back end of a white Luton. He used the opportunity to poke at the jammed cassette player with a biro refill. As the Luton lurched forwards ahead of him, the tape finally slithered free of the machine.

The address he was looking for was on the other side of Doncaster Racecourse. He thought he knew a short cut from his one and only visit to the races. Keith, Stacey's dad, had taken him for a day out and a bit of man-to-man talk, after they'd announced Stacey was pregnant. Phil hadn't needed to get drunk and be mildly threatened by Keith Clegg to do the right thing by his daughter, but he went along with it. The day had turned out OK, he'd lost a tenner and Keith had won fifty quid. The wedding was all planned before the end of the last race.

His memory served him well. His short cut

opened out on to the road on Mackenzie's note. Between a hairdresser's and a pet shop, a narrow entry led to a row of garages. He eased the van up between high red-brick walls and out into a square behind a row of 1960s flats. He turned the music off and waited. Somewhere a siren tried to force its way through the morning traffic. Phil wished it luck. A woman in a navy tracksuit, covered with a floral apron, banged the gate behind her as she came out of the back of the flats. She smiled at Phil and he opened the window.

'You got Mackenzie's stuff?' she said.

'Yup.'

'I'm Carole. Back up to garage number eighteen, will you, love?'

They unloaded the van into the garage with a bit of small talk about the weather and how it was getting much colder at night.

'Can't believe it's Bonfire Night already,' Carole said. 'Doesn't seem five minutes since August Bank Holiday.'

The boxes weren't particularly heavy and Phil could see she liked to work at speed, as if she had plenty of other jobs to get done today. When the van was empty she locked up and thanked him, before disappearing back into the flats with a brisk wave. She was an improvement on the man in Hull, friendly at least. He wondered where Mackenzie found his odd little team. The guys he'd met back on the farm in Moorsby had all been Eastern European. Same as the girls on the cleaning teams. They only cracked a smile when they came into the office for their money. And you never saw them in the village. He suspected the boss didn't want them mixing with the locals. Stacey was right, Johnny Mac had done well for himself, but Phil didn't entirely like the smell of his money. A wave of leaves and paper bags blew along the guttering in front of the garages and Phil climbed back into the van. There was another load waiting for him in Hull.

The sun was low in the sky and failed to reach over the high brick wall, condemning the red freight container to a chilly shade. Len was waiting for Phil in his car. A news broadcast boomed indistinctly from behind the steamed-up windows.

'What took you?' he grunted at Phil, getting out and walking stiffly towards the container without waiting for an answer.

He unlocked a huge padlock and let the heavy bar drop away from the door, clanging against the metal.

'There's another five cases of Panda Pops for Carole and then this lot needs to go in Mr Mackenzie's little hut, d'you know it?'

Phil shook his head.

'I'll draw you a map.' He led Phil further into the container where larger boxes were stacked one on top of another. 'Make a start with these. Don't know why he didn't send you with a bigger van. Still, it's his funeral if we don't get it all shifted in time.'

Phil didn't like to ask what the rush was. He was trying to work out what was in the boxes. At first he thought the picture on the side looked like a television, but then he realised they were microwave ovens. He stacked twelve of them in the back of the van, then lifted in the cases of drinks.

'You better take some of these as well.'

The man was handing him four slimmer boxes. They were surprisingly heavy. He recognised the logo of the Intel processor. Early this morning he hadn't been too bothered by crisps and fizzy drinks, but laptops were a different matter. Phil studied the hand-drawn map and realised the hut wasn't far from Carole's lock-up garage. He decided to do the high-end stuff first; the less time he spent near it, the better.

Just below the Humber Bridge, he pulled over to have a pee. On this stretch of mud, lapped by the Humber Estuary, fag butts and condoms joined a tidemark of dead algae and reed stalks. He sat for a moment facing the water and watched the seabirds swoop and dive into the shallows. He recognised the smaller black-headed gulls among the ugly sharp-eyed herring gulls, but his knowledge of ornithology ended there. His father had tried to teach him about birds on their walks up Telegraph Hill. They used to drive to the village of Lilley and then head out towards a spot on the map called Lilley Hoo. Always the same joke between them: knock, knock. Who's there? Lily. Lily Who? Karen never came; she always stayed to look after Mum. That was his time with his dad. Once Phil hit his teens, he stopped going on the walks, he'd rather spend time with his friends or hide out in the dark fug of his bedroom. He couldn't bear the idea that Holly would be like that one day, embarrassed to be seen out with her dad.

He flicked a new tape into the machine and moved back out into the traffic to the surprising sound of a country track he didn't remember buying. A mournful female vocalist was singing about a tree that had stayed standing because it was strong enough to bend in the wind.

## CHAPTER EIGHT

Karen checked the Sunday morning timetable and realised that she could have lingered over her greasy breakfast with the pot-bellied landlord a bit longer. She would have to kill time wandering the town centre, which was even more deserted than the night before. Somewhere in the distance she thought she could hear a brass band tuning up. A blue pedestrian signpost tipped down a side street. Police station. She was too tired to think, she just wanted to do something, make things happen. She let her feet take her down a glass-strewn pavement and up three steps until she found herself standing at the front desk.

'Excuse me, I'd like to report a missing person.'

The female officer didn't look up. 'Take a seat.'

The officer pressed a buzzer and spoke into a microphone, without lifting her eyes from her paperwork. 'Sean, can you get me a P879. Ta. He'll be with you in a minute. Can I just take your name?'

'Friedman, Karen Friedman.'

'Can you spell that?'

Karen reached in her purse for a business card. 'Here.'

The vinyl-covered bench hadn't been cleaned in a while so she decided to remain standing. The heating was on full blast and there was a stench of sick and bleach. She wished she hadn't eaten so much or at least could have cleaned her teeth. The smell wasn't mixing well with the lingering taste of bacon and sausage. She read the health and safety poster to keep her mind off it, then the Phone Frank poster and the Neighbourhood Watch leaflet, and was just starting on a leaflet about safe sex, when a young male officer appeared through a door to the side of the front desk.

'Hi. My name's Sean, I'm a Community Support Officer. You wish to report a missing person?' He had a gentle smile, which made it hard not to smile back.

'Yes, please.' It sounded so ridiculous, like saying please for an ice cream when you were a kid.

'I'll just ask you to fill out the form. Then one of my colleagues will book it on. OK?'

She nodded.

'Do you need any help with the form at all?'

His pitch gave the impression of the kind of customer-service training those girls in call centres go through, the ones that kept offering her a new mobile phone when she was trying to cook the dinner. He warned her to stick to the facts. Dates, name of person who last saw him, avoid guesswork. She guessed it was Johnny who saw him last, but it could have been anyone. She knew the date was the fifth of November. While she was watching the school firework display with Ben and Sophie, Phil had been ... what? Getting on a plane to Florida with a woman he loved? Or something else?

81

'I'm sorry, Sean, I don't know very much. But I've done the physical description, the date and my contact details.'

'Are you the next of kin?' She should have said no, but she said yes. She felt shabby, as if she was cheating on Stacey. 'Just tick the box and we'll let you know if anything comes up.'

'I've got a picture.'

She opened her handbag and carefully took out a photo of Phil, taken in her father's garden. Her brother was standing next to a miniature weeping cherry tree, which Reg had planted when Phil was born. He used to take the same picture every year, showing how much faster Phil had grown than the tree. This one was taken nearly two years ago. Reg had sent it to Karen with a note to say the tree was finally catching up.

'You'll have to blow it up, make the face a bit clearer,' she said.

'We'll see what we can do. The Missing Persons Unit might do a poster. If not I'll get something up around the station, make sure everyone's keeping an eye out.'

He took the photograph and was checking through the form when an overweight, red-faced man suddenly burst through the door behind them.

'Ah, Percy, you'll do. Can't find a constable for love nor money.'

The desk officer mumbled something and nodded in Karen's direction. She showed him the business card.

'Migrants' advice? This to do with that Chinese girl?' He didn't wait for an answer. 'It'll have to wait. Bit short staffed up here, so now I have to come in on a Sunday to sort out the mess.'

There was an awkward silence, which was broken by the community support officer. 'If you'll excuse me, Mrs Friedman, I'll ask my colleague to book this on. We'll be in touch...'

'That can wait, Percy,' the fat man said.

'It's Denton, sir. Sean Denton.'

'I know. You come with me. The farmer who owns the land behind the lay-by just phoned back, finally. He's been in Doncaster Infirmary for the past six weeks, hip replacement gone nasty. It's on your manor, so you can navigate. I'll pick you up round the front in two minutes, with the scene-of-crime report, if that's not too much bother.'

'Right!' The poor lad jumped up so fast that he dropped his clipboard and Phil's picture slid away across the floor. 'Sorry, I'm so sorry.' Panic-stricken, he gathered everything together, then turned to Karen. 'Sorry about Burger, he's a bit...'

'Of an arse?' That cheered him up. The soft smile was back. 'Why Burger? Except the obvious.'

'King. DCI Barry King.'

'What did he mean about a Chinese girl?'

'Oh.' He seemed to be blushing. 'It's just we found ... I found ... a body. I sort of thought, when you said missing person, that you might have been looking for her.'

'I see. And your boss, Burger? Why did *he* think I was looking for her?'

'Just trying to put two and two together I suppose, and you do look sort of official. For round here anyway.'

'I'll take that as a compliment, I think.'

Sean looked relieved.

'I just can't believe no one's missing her,' he said sadly and then seemed to gather himself. 'We'll be in touch. Or, call us, you know, if you need anything, or if he turns up, obviously.'

Karen didn't want him to go. She touched his arm.

'Look, your Chinese girl, maybe I can help? I could make some enquiries. The guy I work for helps young women who've been trafficked into the UK. Do you think she could have been?'

'It's possible.' The young man spoke quickly, as if he was worried the fat detective might suddenly reappear and shout at him. 'She was a prostitute.' He looked towards the door and was about to say something, but a car horn sounded in the street and he was gone.


# CHAPTER NINE

Burger was telling Sean he was doing well. Could do better if he signed up as proper police; too good for the plastics in his opinion. Sean didn't know what to make of it, thought maybe the boss had been out on the lash last night and wasn't quite sober. Through the scent of Extra Strong Mints he was getting an occasional whiff of stale brandy and Burger was showing an unhealthy disregard of speed limits. Then Sean saw the gate.

'Here!' he shouted.

Burger nearly sent them both through the windscreen as he slammed on the brakes. They'd just passed a pair of wrought-iron gates, at least fifteen foot at their highest point, with the words Lower Brook Farm twisted into the pattern of black rods. The entrance was at odds with the neat fences of the new-build homes on this side of the ring road. Burger backed up at speed, narrowly missing a hooded youth on a tiny BMX bike. He opened the window and made a gesture that Sean could only guess at.

Sean leant out and pressed the buzzer on the intercom. A reedy voice answered and finally the gates swung open.

'It's a bit Addams family.' He started to hum the tune, tapping it out on the glove box. Burger sighed and Sean went quiet.

The drive snaked behind the houses and their postage-stamp gardens until suddenly they were passing open fields. Sean counted at least three security company brand names, alerting intruders to CCTV, dogs and the certainty of prosecution if they trespassed. After a quarter of a mile, they turned on to a wide sweep of gravel in front of a large modern house with a white-pillared porch.

'Right, my turn,' said Burger. 'Name this tune. Tah-tah, na-na-na-na-na-naah! Ta-da! Remember that? No? Too bloody young.' Sean shrugged. *'Dynasty,'* you fool! Bugger me, no culture the young. Let's see if Joan Collins is waiting for us in the bathtub.'

As they got out of the car, a frail old man appeared on the porch leaning on an aluminium walking stick. A crumpled remembrance poppy was stuck at a skewed angle on his lapel. Inside the house a frantic dog was barking.

'Come in. I'll get the kettle on. You lads look like you need a cup of tea.'

Inside, Sean caught his breath. The stench of urine, possibly human, mingled with cigarette smoke and wet animal. A line of yellowing newspaper led across the carpet from the hall to the kitchen. The dog continued to bark.

'Christ Almighty,' Burger muttered. 'I'm going to need my inhaler if we stay too long in here.'

'I think I'll give the tea a miss,' Sean whispered back.

It wasn't that easy. Mr Mayhew insisted on being the perfect host and Sean found himself stirring a cracked mug of milky brown liquid, trying to break down the buttery lumps floating on the surface. Burger asked about the snack bar trailer but Mr Mayhew had launched into his life story, which included the amazing good fortune of being offered what he called 'silly money' to sell half his land for housing.

'Sold all the cows, no money in milk, I saw it coming. Gave up on pigs. I lease a couple of chicken sheds out to a fellow from Epworth. So long as he pays on time, that's all right by me. Knocked the old farmhouse down and built this. Then the wife died. My son keeps telling me I should move out, but he's just after the money, so he can bugger off.'

'The field, Mr Mayhew, up by the ring road.' Burger took his time, as if he were speaking to a child. 'Remember? We left a couple of messages while you were in hospital.'

'Meant to be a straightforward hip replacement,

86

but then I got pneumonia and that MRSA.' He broke into a cough.

'There was a trailer up there. A sort of van, someone was living in it.' Burger said, as soon as the farmer had caught his breath.

'Potatoes. Don't bother myself with them. It's leased out.'

'To the man from Epworth?'

'No, he's chickens. It's the other fellow. Never see him. When we built this house, we cut another road through. The old farm track comes out by the quarry. Didn't want a load of muck past the new house. Had enough of it all my life.'

Sean could hear Burger's breath getting shorter. 'You all right, sir?'

He nodded. 'Need a bit of fresh air. Get a name, a number if you can. Excuse me.' He got to his feet and stumbled back through the hall to the front door.

'He all right?' The old man seemed unfazed by DCI King's departure.

'Bit of asthma.'

A huge ball of black and white fur was settled on a pile of newspapers on the kitchen surface. It opened its eyes and stared at him.

'Mr Mayhew,' Sean pulled his gaze away before the animal hypnotised him, 'there was a snack bar van, with red writing. The model was called a *Motorchef,* it was on your land.'

'Yes, with a dead girl, one of your fellers said so on the phone. Bit odd that. I've never had anyone pay rent on that field for a snack bar van. I've got a little caravan, of course, for the ones that do the picking. The wife and I bought it for holidays.

Lovely orange curtains, she made them herself. We keep it out the back.' He sighed. 'Used to be gypsies, now it's all foreigners. Don't have their own accommodation, that's the drawback, so we have to lay it on. *Motorchef* did you say?'

'Yes sir, does that ring any bells?'

'No. Sounds like a place you'd get on the motorway, not on the Chasebridge bypass.'

Sean asked if he could have a look outside. Mr Mayhew walked painfully to the back door to unlock it, but it was stuck in the frame. As Sean tugged it free, cobwebs broke apart and a spider ran for cover. He took a few steps across the overgrown lawn and looked out at the remains of the farm. The wind seemed to blow straight at him, carrying the smell of chicken shit from a low shed beyond a derelict barn. There was no caravan.

'Funny,' Mr Mayhew said from the doorway. 'Some bugger's nicked it.'

'When did you last see it?'

'Well, it was here when I was took into hospital, I'm sure of that.'

He started to cough. Sean helped him back to his seat in the kitchen. He could feel the rattle of the old man's lungs vibrating through his bony arm.

'Can you tell me the name of the person who rents the far field? They might know something about the trailer.'

'Forsyth. He rents that field.'

'Have you got a number?'

'On the wall by the phone.'

Sean followed where Mayhew pointed his stick. The large cat was eyeing him impassively. Only when he was close enough to read the numbers did it begin to growl, its ears flat and its tail fluffed out.

'Pay no attention to Tiddles. She's expecting.'

Sean found an old envelope and jotted the number down on it. He needed to be out of there. Burger was tooting his horn on the driveway and the smell inside the house was going to make him vomit soon, if the cat didn't get him first.

As he made his way to the door, Mr Mayhew called after him.

'Will you make sure it's reported, my caravan from out the back? See if you can sort out who's nicked it. There's a good lad.'

## CHAPTER TEN

As she turned the corner, Karen checked her messages. There was a text from Max to say he was cooking Sunday lunch. He had sent it at noon and it was now two o'clock. She walked into a silent house. The kitchen looked like foxes had broken in and burgled the place. The stripped chicken carcass lay on its side on the chopping board, the plates and glasses were still on the table, covered with cold, picked-over food, and Arnold, the ginger cat, jumped down when he saw her and skulked away under the boiler.

It was nearly dark when they came back, muddy shoes running through the hall to greet her.

'Take them off! Max! For goodness' sake, they

should take their shoes off on the front step!'

And it unravelled from there. Her voice was too harsh. She heard it too late. Ben started crying and Sophie sulked.

'Welcome home, dear wife.'

Max hung his coat up and went into the front room. She followed him and stood in front of the television.

'Look,' she said, 'I've just cleared up, washed up and there's a slice of cheese-on-toast, turning to rubber on the kitchen table, which I haven't even got round to eating.'

'Big deal,' Max counter-attacked. 'I've had twenty-four hours of looking after the children, cooked a Sunday lunch, which you didn't appear for. I've been running round the park with a kite, like an idiot, when frankly, I would rather have put my feet up and watched the rugby.'

'Stop it, you two!' Sophie walked into the living room. 'You're like a fucking soap opera.'

'Don't swear!' They said together.

Sophie laughed first, then Max joined in. Karen told herself to smile, but she wasn't feeling it. At bedtime, she tried to make it better with a story for Ben. He wanted *Owl Babies*, with its beautiful pictures of wide-eyed owls, who miss their mummy. His hair smelt of shampoo, floppy and dark, soft under her nose.

After turning off Ben's light, she stood in Sophie's doorway, watching her daughter flick through a teen magazine. Sophie had become un-touchable. Karen could sit on the end of her bed, if she was lucky, but only if Sophie was in the mood for a chat. Her skin reflected the pink shade of the bedside light and her lips were red from the wind, like a hand-tinted postcard of a silent starlet. There were girls of Sophie's age on the files at work. Unaccompanied children, who'd slipped through the net, sometimes disappeared altogether. Names, ages, country of origin. Karen shivered. She tried to keep the two worlds apart but they seemed to be getting closer.

'Mum? You can sit down. You're really worried about Uncle Phil, aren't you?' Sophie pulled her earplugs out. The tinny whine of the MP3 player was still audible.

Karen sighed. 'Yes. I am. But...'

'He'll be all right, won't he? I couldn't bear it if anyone else in this family was to die.'

Karen sat on the end of the bed and looked at Sophie. 'Do you think about your sister?'

'Sometimes. But I feel terrible, Mum. I don't really remember what she looked like.'

There was one picture of Cara on the mantelpiece. A tiny silver frame that often disappeared behind greetings cards or the children's artwork. It was not a particularly good likeness. Cara asleep. Gone to sleep. The graveyard euphemism. There was a photo album, but Karen kept it in the back of the desk drawer. She knew its contents by heart: Cara in the hospital, red and slick from the birth, wrapped in blue; Cara's eyes open, dark pools of unknown thought; Cara balanced in Sophie's arms like a piece of precious porcelain; Cara beginning to smile. Whenever she felt strong enough to drill down into her soul – for it was excruciating – she would take it out. It was a beautiful pain actually, one that reminded

91

her she was still alive, still feeling something.

'Mum. You're miles away.' Sophie put down her magazine.

'Remind me tomorrow, and I'll show you the photo album.'

'Of Cara?'

'Yes.' She needed to share it. Perhaps it would release the grip it had on her. She needed to make some space, now there was the potential for a new pain. If Phil wasn't coming back, she would have to let Cara fade out, join the grandmother she never saw, in the shadows where we put those who've been dead the longest.

'Does that mean I don't have to go to school tomorrow?'

'Oh my God, it's Monday tomorrow.' Uniforms, packed lunches, had Max even put the machine on?

By the time she'd finished all the Sunday night chores Max had gone to bed. Karen felt restless. She poured a large glass of red wine and headed for the little study next to the bathroom. She thought about the young PCSO in Doncaster and his confusion that she was something to do with a Chinese girl. She searched the Internet and it was all there, on the website of *The Star*, the South Yorkshire paper: *Mystery of Unknown Woman*, and a subheading, *Tragic Chinese Drug Death*. There was a stiff police request for information about 'a former refreshment vehicle in which the deceased had been living at the time of her death'. She wondered what that meant. The Chinese link was interesting; she might mention it to Jaz or his friend, Charlie Moon.

In bed, Max stirred and then woke fully. He held her tightly to his chest and kissed her head. She knew he wanted sex. She didn't, not really, but it had been a while. Max pulled her on top of him and she hoped she didn't give herself away. She tried hard to concentrate, to banish the faces and voices of her weekend. An image of the fat detective popped into her head. Burger. That was what the young officer had called him. She smiled at the rubbish pun. Max smiled up at her, and she closed her eyes. Eventually she let herself go with it, smoothed by the wine. As long as she kept her eyes closed, she could be held in the spell. But she couldn't resist. Like Lot's wife turning round, the shock of Max's pale skin and his gaze, fixed on her left breast, nearly turned her to salt.

The next morning she was early for work, so she decided to walk. As she passed under Bootham Bar, the sun broke through the cloud and the Minster came into view. She never tired of it, especially at this time of day with nobody around. In the Minster Gardens a sign reminded the public that drinking alcohol was forbidden. She sat on the edge of one of the benches, which was still damp from last night's rain, and watched a man in a quilted anorak, shiny with dirt, begin his day with a long drink of Diamond White. Head back and bottle-up, he almost breathed it in. She wondered if he'd been there all night. The dead girl in Doncaster was a heroin addict. She wondered about Phil. She knew he'd been into drugs, but not that sort. He smoked cannabis and she had to assume he'd done ecstasy, or something like it. He'd been into the dance scene for long enough. It had all passed her by somehow; she hoped it would pass Sophie by too.

Jaz wasn't in the office. She looked at her to-do list and tried to clear a space in her brain for paperwork, but her mind kept slipping off elsewhere. The alcoholic in the park had begun a thread of ideas, which she couldn't switch off. It kept leading her back again to the dead Chinese girl. Finally, Jaz blew in and went straight upstairs. After lunch she decided it was time to test a few ideas out on him.

'Got a minute?'

'Of course.' He gestured to a pile of boxes, where she perched uneasily and began by telling him about the unidentified girl.

'The thing that bothers me is the heroin overdose. I may be way out of line here, but is it a common drug for young women in the Chinese community? I just wondered whether your friend Charlie Moon might be interested, if there's a trafficking link.'

'What else do we know?'

'That she was a sex worker.'

'Do you think she could be connected to the haulage company in Grimsby?'

'That's what I was wondering,' she said. 'Do you think we should ask Moon to see if there's a DNA match between the girl and the samples from the lorries?'

'I always said you had a good nose. Fancy a brew?' He led the way downstairs. 'Do you mind me asking what you were doing down there anyway? Doncaster doesn't strike me as your ideal weekend break location.'

She began to tell him about Phil. He came back to her desk with two mugs.

'And you didn't say anything? Come on, Karen, I could have pulled some strings, I know a few policemen, and women, come to think of it.'

'I know, but ... for all I know, my sister-in-law is right and he's just gone off.'

'*Cherchez la femme?*' He sounded like Inspector Clouseau and Karen laughed despite herself. 'Leave it with me,' he continued. 'I'll have a dig about, Charlie owes me one.' He handed her a coffee and perched on the edge of her desk. 'You could be on to something with the trafficking link. I wonder if the guys in Doncaster have still got the girl, or some of her DNA at least. I hope they haven't cremated her already and burnt the evidence.'

Early in the afternoon, the phone rang.

'Karen? Charlie Moon here. Tell me about your brother.'

Jaz hadn't wasted any time sharing her story. Moon listened briefly, then interrupted. 'You know that the first forty-eight hours is crucial in any missing persons' inquiry?'

'Meaning?'

'Meaning, don't get your hopes up.'

It was as if he had thumped her, hard, in the solar plexus. When she finally breathed in, her throat ached with the effort of trying not to cry.

'I see,' she said. 'Look, while you're on, I want to talk to you about something else.'

95

She coolly discussed the body of the dead woman, a suspected drug overdose, and gave him the name of the police station in Doncaster. She imagined her tone to be measured, professional, while underneath she was screaming: *You bastard. My hopes are all I've got.*

At Doncaster Central, Carly Jayson's huge laugh bounced off the Formica tables of the staff canteen, as Sean did his impression of Burger wheezing his way out of the reeking farmhouse. He liked Carly; she had a good attitude. The other person at the table was Sandy Schofield, a civilian who worked in admin. She and Carly were a couple. Partners in crime, Sandy liked to say. Sandy liked to mother him and Carly treated him like a mate. She could also beat him hands down at pool, which she never failed to remind him.

'And then there was this massive cat.' Sean was enjoying having an audience. 'You should have seen it!'

'Burger's long-lost brother?' Carly said.

The three of them were still laughing when Lizzie Morrison put her tray down on the edge of the table.

'Mind if I join you?'

After so much noise the silence was horrible. Sean broke it. 'No problem.' But as he spoke, Carly was already standing up.

'Got to be off.'

'Me too.' Sandy tidied their empty sandwich packets onto her tray. 'I need to type up some handover notes.'

Sean fingered the label on his water bottle.

He'd finished eating but he had time.

'Catch you later, ladies.' When they'd gone he looked at Lizzie. She was jabbing a fork into a heap of lettuce leaves. 'You all right?'

'Mmm. Fine.'

'Really? You don't sound fine?' He could see the muscle in her cheek pulsing as she chewed on her salad. 'Don't mind Carly, she's just like that.'

'Rude?'

'Just a bit of a tough nut.'

'One of the lads?' She gulped down her water. 'And I'm not.'

'You're Scene of Crime. It's different. I mean it's not personal. It's just a bit us and them in this place.'

'Well I'm not "them" either. The officers in CID don't speak to me because I'm not police and the old-time SOCOs hate me too. It's the graduate-training thing. Posh totty, that's what they think of me.'

Sean didn't know what to say. He wasn't expecting this from Lizzie Morrison: the self-assured, intelligent, my-dad's-on-the-board-of-Doncaster-Rovers-Miss-Morrison. She blew her nose and took a deep breath.

'Forget it. Just had a bad morning, that's all. What were you all laughing about anyway?'

'Not you, just ... a colleague.' She didn't look as if she believed him. 'DCI King, if you must know.'

'That idiot! I wish I'd known, I could have joined in.'

Sean tried to re-tell the trip to Lower Brook Farm. He wanted to make Lizzie laugh, but he couldn't get the timing quite right and she took

97

it all too seriously.

'And you gave the number to Burger?'

'Yes. Why?'

'Did you keep a copy?'

'No. I ... just wrote it on a bit of paper I found by the phone, an old envelope.'

'Why didn't you use your notebook?'

'I didn't think. Sorry.'

'Never mind.' She went back to spearing her lettuce. 'It's just that he should have passed it on to me, if we need to go over the crime scene again. I mean, if we ever find the bloody crime scene. Why would anyone move a catering trailer which is behind a cordon?'

'Someone who doesn't want it found.'

'Is that Burger's line of inquiry?' she said.

'Burger's not bothered about Su-Mai ... I mean, the victim.'

'Because he doesn't think she is a victim. Just a nuisance. Like the second girl. The lab results are back. It's the same batch of heroin.' She met his eyes. 'You said Su-Mai.'

Sean picked at the label on the water bottle. 'Just a name I made up. Can't keep calling her *that Chinese girl*.'

'I've just had an email from a detective I know in the Human Trafficking Service. Said there might be a connection with something they're doing. Interesting?'

'What does Burger say?'

'Nothing. I haven't told him. Let's keep it between the two of us.'

The two of us. He liked the sound of that. He went up to the counter to get them both a cup of coffee. When he got back she was talking on the phone.

'OK. Yeah. OK. And can you call Donald too?' She wrote something in her notebook, her quick fingers gripped so tight round the pen he thought she would snap it. 'OK, I'll be right there.'

He put the cups down.

'Sorry, Sean, I've got to go. There's another body on the Chasebridge estate.'

## BONFIRE NIGHT: 11.30 a.m.

Phil slowed down for the roundabout and took the second turning, away from the estate where Carole had her lock-up garage. He was on a dual carriageway but kept his speed down, watching out for the left turn on Len's hand-drawn map. Level with the flats at the top of Carole's estate, he passed a lay-by where a piece of blue-and-white plastic tape fluttered in the hedge like a kite tail. Just beyond it he spotted the lane. Len had put a letter T on the map and, sure enough, there was the sign, a red-and-white T on a blue background. A dead end. He turned in.

The van jerked as the front wheel swished through a deep puddle. He would have to watch out for more potholes; the road surface hadn't been repaired for years. On either side spindly hedges banked up above the grass verge, stalks of decaying rose-bay willow-herb stood to attention and a dumped fridge had attracted an island of rubbish all around it. The road sloped up, away from the dual carriageway. Where the sun had reached, the frost had melted and there was a surplus of colour: the deep brown of ploughed earth, blood-red berries, and thick green grass were saturated like an old Kodacolor snap. While on the frosted side the colours were calmed and delicate, as if a Christmas-card painter had prepared them.

He almost missed the gateway in Len's instructions and had to put his foot hard on the brake, immediately wishing he hadn't when he heard the boxes shift behind him and thud against the back of the driver's cab. Ahead the lane continued downhill and a pitted and rusty sign warned *Danger: Quarry Workings: Keep Out!* To his right a rough track skirted a line of trees. He put the van into first gear and swung right, up onto the track.

This must have been a proper road once, years ago. The stony surface gave plenty of grip, as long as he kept in the tyre-marked ruts, but it was a bumpy ride. He wondered why Johnny Mackenzie stored all this stock in such a godforsaken place, when his own farmyard was full of barns and outhouses, but as the question formed in his mind, he tried to dismiss the obvious answer.

In the shadow of the trees a small, mucky-white caravan stood looking lost on the edge of a ploughed field. Phil glanced at it as he passed, not wanting to take his eyes off the track for too long in case the wheels caught the slippery mud at its edge. The caravan seemed to be abandoned, faded orange curtains pulled tight at the windows. The track followed the edge of the woods and there in front of him was an old Nissen hut, its corrugated metal hulk painted black and patched up in places with new sheets of metal, like a battle-scarred whale. This was what Len had drawn for him, a simple upturned U-shape, marked on the map as Mackenzie's Hut.

He unlocked the padlock with the key Len had given him and started to unload the van. Carole's trays of drinks had to come out first before he could reach the boxes of microwaves. The ground around him was wet, so he placed the pallets on the floor just inside the hut. It was gloomy in there with no source of electric light, so he propped both doors wide open to see what he was doing. There were three rows of metal shelving units. They were battered and slightly rusty, as if they'd done years of service in a factory or a warehouse. Most of the shelves were empty, but towards the back of the shed a few boxes were stacked on the bottom shelf, covered with clear plastic sheeting. He lifted the edge and saw a label which read Aviators: UV lenses: silver. Sunglasses. Wrong time of year for shifting those. Something caught his eye and he looked up quickly. Just for a moment it seemed as if the light had dimmed: as if someone or something was blocking the door-way. He stood still and listened. There was nothing but the wind, breathing through the leafless trees and a single bird, a thrush he guessed, singing close by. He went outside and looked around but the place seemed deserted.

Phil worked quickly, unloading the boxes from the van into the Nissen hut. It was late morning and he wanted to get out of there and back to Carole's garage as soon as possible, then up to Hull by lunchtime. The bacon sandwich seemed a long time ago. When the van was empty, he lifted the drinks trays back in and slammed the van doors. He pulled the metal doors of the hut closed and clicked the padlock shut, tugging at it once to check it was locked. He turned to the driver's door and that was when he saw her.

On the step of the caravan a girl was standing with her arms folded over a long dark coat. She was about fifty yards from him but in the quiet air her voice carried clearly.

'You want cup of tea? I have made for you.' Foreign, maybe Polish, he wasn't sure.

A rook took off from the top of a Scots pine and circled, barking a greeting or a warning. He walked across to the caravan and took the warm mug in his hands.

'Sorry. No milk.' The girl said, reaching inside the caravan for her own mug. She leant against the door, waiting for him to taste it.

He took a sip. The tea was black and sweet.

'Thank you,' he said. 'I need this.' And he meant it: not least for the shock of seeing this thin young woman watching him, and the realisation that she'd been watching him since he arrived.

'So, you work for Mr Mackenzie?' she said.

He nodded. 'Do you know him?'

'Of course.'

He followed her gaze out over the field.

'You work here?' he said and pictured her picking potatoes like her ancestors in the Polish countryside.

'Yes,' she said. 'I work here.'

It seemed miles from anywhere and there was no sign of a car or even a bicycle. The tea was cooling in his mug but he felt reluctant to drink up and leave. The girl continued to watch him with her incredibly green eyes, ringed with hazel. Her hair was bright red. He was no expert, but he guessed it was dyed. He drained the mug and handed it to her.

'That was great. I'd better go.'

'OK,' she shrugged.

She was still staring at him as he walked back to the van and got in. He turned the engine over and put it in reverse, he didn't fancy backing all the way down to the quarry road, so he pulled forward towards the trees in order to turn round. He shifted into reverse again and put his foot on the accelerator but the van didn't move. A fountain of mud was being thrown up from the spinning front tyres.

'Shit!' The rear wheels were still on the stony track but the front wheels were on the soft, wet grass. He pulled on the handbrake and got out to take a look. The girl was coming over and he was relieved to see she wasn't laughing at him.

'You want I push?' she said.

She didn't look strong enough.

'Can you drive?' he said, but she shook her head. 'Maybe if I show you what to do, then I can push and you can put your foot on the pedals and steer.'

'Is very dangerous. Through the trees is quarry side. Is very steep.'

'You'll be going backwards, so it'll be OK.'

It was about ten metres to the edge of the trees

103

and he would be in front of the van. If it lurched forwards instead of backwards, he'd have to jump clear and hope she could stop it in time.

She looked doubtful but came closer. He helped her up into the driver's seat.

'Put your left foot on the clutch, that pedal, OK? Now I'm going to move the gear stick. That's reverse; don't change it, whatever you do. Keep your left foot down. Then put your right foot on the accelerator and bring your left foot up when I say go, but not before. Got it?'

She nodded, her jaw clenched with concentration and he was distracted for a moment by the line of bone that traced her cheek. He would have liked to run his finger along it.

'So?' she said, 'I'm ready.'

He went to the front of the van and braced himself, hands above the radiator grille. He could see her through the windscreen, behind a reflection of spindly-armed trees and a cloudless sky, staring straight ahead as if she were preparing for a cavalry charge.

'Ready and go!'

The engine whirred and the mud sprayed in his face, but as he put all his weight into the van, it lurched back, stalled and stopped with all four wheels back on the track.

'We did it!' she called.

'Yes, we did.' He wiped a fleck of earth from his lip and went to help her down. She laughed at him, exhilarated by her success.

'Is very powerful, to make an engine to go. I would like to drive, I think.'

'You should learn.'

She lifted her hand and he almost flinched, but then she wiped his cheek with her fingertips. He felt a pulse in his groin and tried to ignore it. She took his hand and jumped down.

'I'll be back this way later on,' he said. 'I've got another load of stuff to bring down, so if you need anything?'

'OK.' she said. 'Yes. Something to eat. I am so bored with cup of soup.'

She asked for a sandwich and he promised he'd be back. The van rattled more than ever on the track and it was a relief to pull onto the smooth surface of the dual carriageway. He decided to risk the cassette player again and pulled a new tape out of his bag. He turned at the third round-about onto the motorway and put his foot down as Jackie Wilson's 'I Get The Sweetest Feeling' filled the van with sound.

## CHAPTER ELEVEN

Florence Moyo sat in the boardroom with her hands on the table in front of her, fingers gripping the sides as if she was holding on to a ledge.

'There are some kind people in our church,' she said, 'but it is not enough. My husband is ashamed that we have to accept charity. He doesn't know I am here. Please, is there anything you can do to speed things up?'

Jaz looked at his notes and then at Mrs Moyo. 'We're doing everything we can. It's complicated.

The Home Office thinks that everyone should apply for asylum as soon as they arrive at the port of entry.'

'We were told not to. We were told we would be sent back if we did that.'

Karen knew from Mr Moyo's testimony that they'd used an agent, paid a lot of money for so-called help, which had turned out to be worthless. Jaz told her they might have got asylum from Zimbabwe if they'd gone through the proper channels, but the borrowed passport counted against them.

'We're going to have to find a way to prove you are not, in fact, South African. We'll have to explain why you didn't have your own papers.' Jaz's voice was calm and gentle, but Florence Moyo was restless. 'If Mr Moyo wants me to go through it again with him?'

'He's gone to find work, with my daughter. A man has told him there is some work.'

It was illegal for them to work, but Karen understood they had to eat.

'I thought Elizabeth was at school?' she said.

'She's nearly sixteen.' Florence Moyo sounded defensive. 'Look, if we play by your rules, we will starve.'

Jaz put his hand into his inside pocket. 'There might be some funding you can apply for but, meanwhile, I'd rather your daughter was able to stay in school, please, let me help.' He took three twenty-pound notes out of his wallet. 'Just a loan.'

Florence Moyo got to her feet unsteadily. She seemed to sway for a moment, her eyes fixed on the opposite wall. Then she walked out of the office with her head held high. Jaz folded the money and put it back in his jacket.

At the school gates Karen was the last of the Year Two parents to pick up.

'There's Mummy, at *last!*' Mrs Leith forced a smile. Ben ran to Karen and fished her hand out of her coat pocket, gripping it in his own.

'I'm on a new book. The dog's not in this one. What's for tea?'

'Good. Or bad, if you like the dog. Fish fingers?'

'Yeah!'

She held Ben's hand as they crossed the road. He was telling her about an argument with his best friend but she didn't hear the words, just the cues to nod or shake her head. She was thinking about Mrs Moyo and trying to imagine what she must be feeling. Florence Moyo had said she would do anything to keep her family safe. Since Karen had come back from her visit to Stacey, she'd done nothing more about trying to find Phil. That was useless, pathetic, when she had none of the problems Mrs Moyo had to face.

'...anyway,' Ben was saying, 'it can't be true, because you are the biggest mummy at school. You're almost as big as Mr Evans and he's the headteacher.'

'Tallest, you mean I'm the tallest. Biggest makes me sound...'

'Fat?'

'Cheeky boy!' She laughed and pretended to chase him. Just now, if anyone were watching, they would think what a jolly mum she was, a catalogue mum, kicking up the dead leaves, her corduroy skirt matching his dark-red scarf. They thundered down the pavement and arrived together, breathless, at the front door.

When Ben was safely in front of children's TV, she went into the kitchen and picked up the phone. The girl at Doncaster Central Police Station left her on hold for seven minutes. She counted it on the kitchen clock. She should have been onto this sooner. Charlie Moon was right, a thirty-two-year-old man, with all his faculties, was not a priority case, so she was going to have to be pushy. The line let out an intermittent beep and an electronic voice reminded her she was on hold and thanked her for waiting. She wondered if they'd put any posters up yet or whether the Missing Persons Unit had decided to feature Phil in one of their newspaper campaigns. She'd seen them on screens in the doctor's waiting room and in the Post Office queue. She might suggest that to the desk sergeant at Doncaster, if she ever came back on the line.

*Leave it. Let them get on with their job.* Max's voice was in her head and maybe he was right. Except that she felt something gnawing away inside her and it was always the same question. She thought about the young support officer she'd met in Doncaster worrying about a dead Chinese girl. *I can't believe no one's looking for her.* But what if someone was, just as she was looking for Phil? A woman's voice came back on the line to tell her that there was no further information and a colleague would be in contact regarding the poster campaign in due course. She looked up The Volunteer Arms on the Internet and phoned Jackie. Would she put up missing posters? There was a silence and then, very kindly, very gently, Jackie said no. There was no point, everyone in the village knew Phil and if they'd seen him they would have said. If he turned up, or if she heard anything, she'd certainly let Karen know. It seemed that everyone, except Karen, believed it was entirely plausible that he'd run off with another woman. She stared out at a bank of grey clouds above the house next door and tried to imagine Phil in Florida. She liked to think he would have let them know if he was going abroad, but she couldn't be sure. He didn't even tell their father when he'd got married to Stacey. Just phoned up one day: *By the way, guess what I did at the weekend.* Maybe the others were right and she should just leave it, wait for him to get in touch and get on with her life.

Max came home late that evening, long after the children were in bed, and found her googling local newspapers for North Lincolnshire and South Yorkshire.

'Can I get on there?'

'Just a minute...'

'No, I haven't got a minute. Look, Karen. I need to check some details for tomorrow. We're pitching for the Ptarmigan Project.'

'I'm just checking Saturday's *Star.*'

'You've had all day. I'm sorry, but you'll just have to leave it.'

'Isn't a ptarmigan a kind of bird?'

'In this case, they're a Scottish development consortium and they have a very big shopping centre in the offing.' His voice was rising. The muscles in his neck seemed to be battling for control of his vocal cords, veins standing out with the effort. 'A shopping centre which I'd quite like to design, so that my employers continue to pay me, so that I can put bread in the mouths of my children. Please, I won't ask you again. Will you leave all this amateur sleuthing and get off my computer. Now!'

She sat very still and watched the screen blur. She wasn't aware that she was crying until she blinked and her cheeks ran with tears. She wanted to say something about not waking the children, but she couldn't speak. If he'd tried to hold her or just put his hands on her shoulders, things might have been different, but he didn't.

'They're my children too. And Phil is my brother.'

'For God's sake, Karen, just leave it alone! You can't magic him up. He'll come back when he's good and ready. Now, move.'

As she got up, he stepped aside to let her get to the door. He went straight to the desk and logged himself on. Karen walked out onto the landing and stood for a moment, waiting for him to apologise, until she realised he wasn't going to.

The next morning, she walked the children to school and came home to the silence of the house. She filled it with the sound of the vacuum cleaner and Radio Two in every room. She'd never liked housework, but today she wanted to do it: dusting and polishing, wiping marks off the paintwork. After an hour, she sat down on the stairs, sweating and breathless. She felt an overwhelming desire to get on top of everything, to straighten it all out. A small drift of dust behind one of the banister rails caught her eye and she rubbed it away with her fingertip. Lives could be like that. There one minute, gone the next. Like Cara's, which had hardly begun, and the Chinese girl, who couldn't have had much of a life before the heroin took her out of it.

Over the next hour, she worked more slowly. She retuned the radio in the bedroom to Radio Four. It was a drama about a woman dying of cancer. She started the ironing. Up here, the sound of the street was muffled, and the dormer window looked out at a sky of aeroplanes and birds. The iron nosed under the pleat of Sophie's skirt and the steam rose to tickle her nostrils. The woman on the radio talked about her chemotherapy. Karen felt a rush behind her eyes and knew that if she let herself cry again, she might not be able to stop.

'Sod this!'

Her voice sent the cat leaping off the bed in surprise. He looked at her uncertainly, his body clock whirring towards the possibility of feeding time. He dodged her feet as she pounded down the stairs to the study. She chewed the jagged edge of a broken fingernail while she waited for the computer to get going, then she put Johnny Mackenzie's name into the search bar. Just to see.

# CHAPTER TWELVE

Sean passed the door of the Crime Scene Investigation Office and saw Lizzie at the far end, almost hidden by a huge spider plant on her desk. The rest of the office was empty. He tiptoed up to the plant to surprise her but before he could say 'boo', she parted the leaves and said 'hi'.

'You trying to do camouflage or what?' he asked.

She laughed. Nice. He hadn't seen her laugh much. 'Figured that if I sit at the back and hide behind the plant, they won't know I'm here and then they might not take the piss.'

'Good plan. I used to do that at school, without the plant obviously. And it was the teachers taking the piss in my case.'

'Fancy a coffee?' she said.

'Canteen coffee? Not much. But if you've got time, we could nip out. There's an Italian greasy spoon off Duke Street.'

'Sounds lovely,' she said sarcastically.

'No, seriously, they have a proper coffee machine, cappuccino and that, but half the price of Starbucks.'

'I'm not being funny, Sean, but can I meet you there? Rather than actually walk out of the building with a member of the opposite sex. I don't want to give anyone any more ammunition to shoot me down.'

Sean nodded and left the office. He passed a

couple of CID blokes in the corridor and asked them if they knew where DCI King was. They grunted in reply. He was about to say 'what?' when he realised that it had actually been a grunt like a pig. Funny joke time again. Well it was all right for them, they didn't have to go out there everyday and deal with dog shit on their shoes. He felt like slamming the door shut behind him, but he didn't.

The Venetian Piazza Café was in a side street next to a charity shop. They sat at the back, away from the window.

'I feel like a snout. Meeting in secret.'

She laughed for half a second, before her face went serious again. 'What did you think about the news in this morning's briefing?'

He shuffled in his seat. 'Missed it. My bus was late. I heard it was another overdose.'

'That's what the autopsy says. The theory is that the body gets used to a certain level, so if it's purer than usual it can be toxic. Su-Mai and the victim in Balby had taken something that was almost a hundred per cent. This latest girl had a methadone prescription, so she should have been weaning herself off, but it's beginning to look like it was the same stuff that killed the other two.'

They went quiet as another customer came in and ordered a sandwich. Sean leant forward. 'Was she on the game too?'

Lizzie shook her head. 'Young mum with three kids.'

He felt a chill creep up the back of his neck.

'There's a connection between all three.' Lizzie laid out three paper packets of sugar on the table. 'First girl is from overseas, she's on the game and she's found here. The second is on the other side of town, but also foreign and a prostitute. Then number three, found a few hundred yards from number one on your manor.' She ripped the ends of the sugar packets and let the grains fall over the table. 'Number one and number two are stuffed full of nearly pure heroin and a pick and mix of male DNA. Number three, same heroin, but only one recent sexual partner. I don't know, maybe she was just unlucky.'

'Why are you telling me all this?' Sean's head felt tight, like he had a migraine coming.

'It helps me to think out loud. And I can trust you.'

She looked gorgeous. He rubbed his temples and forced himself to focus on what she was saying.

'Now this guy from the HTS is asking for a sample of Su-Mai's DNA,' she said.

'HTS?'

'Human Trafficking Service.'

'So we might find out who Su-Mai really is?'

'Or at least where she's from and how she got here.'

Sean had a vision of his sheet of flipchart paper filled with names, dates, an address, a photograph of a family with a little girl in its centre. He wondered what it would be like, telling her mother, through an interpreter perhaps, that she had died peacefully on a sunny day, with the sound of birdsong in her ears, or the sound of the bypass at any rate.

'Can you do that?' he said. 'Send her DNA off to another unit?'

'I'll have to get authorisation, and I need to think about how to get round Burger Barry. I just don't want him saying no to me again, it's getting boring.'

'You'll think of something.' He meant it. There was just something about her that instilled confidence, even when she said she was being picked on. She didn't make out that she was a victim; just made it sound like an irritation, something that got in the way.

'Girl number three, what was she called, by the way?'

'Taneesha McManus, known to her friends and family as Neesha.'

Sean spent the rest of the day on the Chasebridge estate, listening to Carly's unbroken monologue about the state of her house, which she'd bought off the council and wished she could give back. It was damp, the windows rattled and the new wallpaper wouldn't stick. He felt numb. A pile of flowers had appeared at the foot of one of the blocks near the ring road. They watched a thin young man in a hoody circle the estate on a BMX, standing up on the pedals, his tracksuit trousers hanging low around his hips. Sean squinted and tried to work out if he knew him, but he couldn't tell. These lads all looked the same. They didn't dress to be different; they dressed to be invisible.

When he got home, he looked at the sheet of flipchart paper on his, wall. He'd added a newspaper cutting: *Tragic Refugee Girl Found by Flatmate*. The picture was the same over-exposed snap of both of them, crammed together in a photo booth, which had been pinned on the incident board. You could see she'd been pretty. Then he got out a blue pen and drew a new line for Taneesha McManus. He didn't have a photo of her, just a picture of the flowers, but he knew what she looked like. She was the only one of the three he'd seen alive. He could still see her bitten-down fingernails as she snatched the leaflet from him, and her skinny legs, goosebumped in the cold.

The Key Stage One assembly at Chasebridge Community Primary School was an easy-to-please sort of audience. They laughed at Sean's jokes and put their hands up nicely at question time. He could have told them anything and they would have believed him. But he didn't. He stuck to the script that he and Carly had been given: community policing, business as usual. They weren't there to talk about the heroin problem, just to be a reassuring presence. Keeping things positive was supposed to help flush out those with information to share.

A little boy, with a smear of something ketchup-coloured on his chin, asked if Sean and Carly carried guns. A small girl wanted to know if they were married. There was barely stifled laughter from a couple of the teachers.

When it was over, Carly wanted to slip off to have a word with her son Daniel's teacher. He was suffering from stress over his SATs revision and she wanted to know if they could lay off him a bit. Sean said he'd get the bus back into town, if she wanted to come back in the car. He was on a split shift, with time to kill, so he was easy. As he came out of the school gates, he nearly collided with someone on a bike, riding on the pavement.

'Hey, steady on!'

The other guy flicked him the V-sign and rode off. Sean was still trying to place him, when the bike spun round and came back. Sean stood his ground until the last moment then stepped off the kerb, just as the other man skidded to a halt, his face uncomfortably close to Sean's.

'Divvo Denton isn't it? You still look like a twat.' He spat on the floor and let out a shrill, false laugh. 'Remember me?'

Sean stood still, wishing he wasn't on his own. He had a taste like metal in his mouth. Lee Stubbs. Same year at school, different universe. Sean had avoided him for years. He'd handed over some dinner money in Year Seven, everyone did, then he'd kept well away. He was surprised Stubbs even knew his name.

'I remember you,' he said quietly.

'Yeah? Well you can fuck off, copper!'

Stubbs turned his bike back up the hill and as he did so, his profile was framed by his hood. A woman hurried past. She looked over her shoulder, took in Sean's uniform and pulled her coat tightly around her. It was a pity the parents weren't as trusting as the children. Further up the hill, Stubbs was hovering on his bike, waiting for the woman.

Sean heard a car draw up alongside him, and instinctively stepped back with his hand on his radio. The passenger window lowered and a familiar voice said, 'Hop in.'

'Lizzie? What are you doing here?'

'Looking for you.'

He stooped to get into the passenger seat and fastened his seat belt.

'You missed my performance for the kids.'

'Never mind. You can do it again while we're driving. You got half an hour?'

'Sure, where are we going?' He didn't really care. Anywhere that wasn't here would make him happy right now.

'Forsyth Agrico. It's a farming contractor based out near Thorne. They lease the land at Lower Brook Farm.'

'Did Burger give you the number?'

'No need. I just looked them up.'

Forsyth Agrico was based in a converted filling station. Lizzie pulled up where the pumps would have been and they went into a bright reception area, subdivided from the original shop. A middle-aged woman in a flower-patterned blouse, topped off by a huge floppy bow, smiled up at them from behind the desk.

'We'd like to speak to Mr Forsyth, if that's possible.' The woman took in Lizzie's accent and Sean's uniform and paled slightly.

'Just one moment, I'll see if he's available.' She got up from her chair and backed out through a door behind the desk, keeping them in her sights, as if they might do something unexpected.

'It's a shame you haven't got a warrant card. That would make him more available.'

'Thanks for nothing,' Sean replied. 'I could say the same about you.'

'It would be handy. But why don't you get one? Only a few weeks' training, you'd be great as a–'

'Proper copper? No thanks, I'm all right as I am.'

Sean was grateful that this conversation didn't have to go any further. The only useful qualification he had was what his nan called his boyish grin. He used it to good effect when Mr Forsyth appeared.

'How can I help you?' Forsyth returned Sean's smile with soft wet lips, but his eyes narrowed like a cat's.

'Is there somewhere we can have a chat?' Lizzie looked around the reception area. It was clear that she didn't want to talk here, where floppy-bow woman would be listening.

Forsyth led them into an office and offered Lizzie a chair while Sean remained standing. She explained the issue of the woman in the catering trailer and Sean filled in some of the details about his visit to Stanley Mayhew.

'So how can I help?'

Sean couldn't decide whether the guy was being stupid on purpose.

'You rent the fields, the crop, potatoes or whatever,' he said, 'and you bring in the people to pick them, and they're the people, according to Stanley Mayhew, who live temporarily on his land.'

'But we've got no one up there at the moment,' Forsyth interrupted him. 'It's the wrong time of year. It's all earlies on that field, nice little salad potatoes. That's what people want these days.'

'OK, but when you did have someone up there for the early potato harvest,' Lizzie's voice was brittle, she was losing patience, 'was there a catering trailer there and was anyone living in it?'

'No idea. You'd have to ask the guy that brings in the pickers. I use agencies.'

'Could you give us a name?'

Forsyth's smile dropped. He rubbed his plump hands together.

'Now let me think, I'm not sure I can remember, we have a lot of contracts and a lot of competitors too, you see, and I don't like to just, you know, divulge that sort of information.'

'I could come back with a search warrant.' Lizzie sounded like she meant it, but Sean was hoping Forsyth wasn't going to hold her to it.

'That won't be necessary.' Forsyth scribbled something on a compliments slip, which he handed to Lizzie. 'The agency I used this autumn was called Exchange Labour. There's the number. The fellow's name is Mackenzie, Johnny Mackenzie.'

## CHAPTER THIRTEEN

When her phone rang, Karen was in the kitchen, cooking dinner. She dropped the knife she'd been using to cut parsley and fumbled with wet hands in the pocket of her apron. She didn't give herself time to look at the screen.

'Hello, Karen Friedman speaking.'

'Are you free on Friday?' It was Jaz. 'I thought we'd have a work's outing.'

'Oh.' It was like a wave, building and breaking. The hope it might be news of Phil, the rush of adrenaline crashed and washed out of her, leaving a sour taste in her mouth.

'There's a folk band on,' Jaz was saying. 'Charlie reckons they're good. He's going to get a few guys from his work to come along.'

'Sure, why not?' Apart from a million reasons, but none of them formed into words. She told herself she really needed to get out more, and she needed to stop grabbing the phone like this every time it rang.

On Friday, she arrived at The Brown Cow at seven-thirty. It was a tiny Victorian pub on the corner of a street near the river. She opened the door and the sound of a fiddle drew her in. There were three musicians sitting at a corner table by the fire, playing something fast and folky to an audience scattered round the room. People were drinking and talking, breaking off to applaud when a tune found its way to the end. She was relieved to see Jaz at the bar.

'I've bagged the snug,' he said. 'Bit quieter in there. Why don't you go through?'

He went to get the drinks while Karen tried to relax. The snug lived up to its name, a tiny room with just two tables and dark, wooden-panelled walls. A woman in jeans and a leather jacket appeared in the doorway.

'Hi, you must be Karen. Jaz said I'd find you here. Natalie Drummond, by the way.'

She had a Northern Irish accent and a bright smile. They shook hands. Natalie was in the Vice Squad and said she'd done some work with the Human Trafficking Service.

'With your man Charlie Moon, trying to get through to the girls who are on the game.'

By the time Jaz came back from the bar, Karen and Natalie were deep in conversation about the issues of trafficked women.

'The problem is, you've got to prove they've been coerced,' Natalie was saying, 'because you have to accept that for some women, it's a choice.'

Jaz was struggling to balance two glasses of wine and a pint. Natalie took one of the glasses with a smile, which was returned by a boyish grin from Jaz. It was an expression Karen had never seen in the office. She had a sinking feeling. When she was a teenager, it was called playing gooseberry. Hopefully some others would be along soon.

An impossibly fast jig was being played in the next room. Karen decided she would give the two of them time alone, so she mouthed that she was going to the ladies' and slipped out of the snug. In the main body of the pub all eyes were on the three musicians and Karen found herself hypnotised too. She leant against a wooden shelf in the panelled wall and watched. It didn't seem possible that the fiddle players' fingers could move that fast and still be making the right notes. She thought of Phil and the times she'd seen him play. It hadn't been often, not often enough she realised. But she'd been fascinated by the way his trombone could make such an amazing range of sounds and when he played guitar, it had actually made her want to weep. Mind you, just about anything could do that at the moment. Even Max had noticed. He'd suggested she talk to a shrink, but that wasn't going to make any difference.

She didn't see Charlie Moon until he was next to her. He was speaking but his voice was drowned out. She pointed to the snug and hoped he didn't interrupt the lovebirds' private moment too soon, while she went to the ladies' and contrived to spend as long in there as she could. She wondered how soon she could go home without appearing rude, but as she washed her hands and tidied her hair in the mirror, she told herself to make the best of it. After all, she was out, without the kids, and the music was all right. Max was working late and Trisha from next door was babysitting. She could give it another hour for form's sake then do a runner.

A second glass of wine helped. Back in the snug Natalie was rattling off a string of anecdotes about the things she'd seen in brothels.

'...and the poor wee lass was laid out, chocolate sauce all over her chest, while this great big fellow was on his knees licking it off.'

Karen could see why Jaz had chosen the privacy of the back room. Halfway through her third glass Karen remembered she hadn't eaten much all day. She'd picked at a cheese sandwich at lunchtime, but her appetite had failed her. Now the wine was working on her muscles and she wondered if she might just fall asleep. Her toes tapped lazily under the table to the rhythm of a bodhrán, while she watched Jaz smiling and nodding at everything Natalie said. Charlie didn't say anything at all. From the other room she could hear feet pounding and shuffling across the wooden floor.

Suddenly Charlie nudged her arm. 'Fancy a dance?'

Before she had time to think about it, she was on her feet, being guided through to the main bar.

'Thought we should let them get on with it.' Charlie was almost shouting to be heard. 'Don't know why they feel the need to drag their friends out to witness the bleeding obvious, but I think he's still telling himself they're just mates.'

That clarified a lot about the whole set-up of the evening. A set-up, that was exactly what it was, and she was the stooge, Charlie too. Well, she thought, she was here now, half-cut on cheap pub wine and she might as well make the most of it. So she and Charlie danced, bumping limbs and treading on toes, in a vaguely Celtic reel. When the song ended, they collapsed onto two seats in the main bar. She realised he was laughing and it had the most incredible effect on his face. The tight lines around his eyes lifted and she found herself smiling back.

'I hope you're not laughing at me!'

'God no, Karen, I'm laughing at myself and my two left feet. I'm sorry.'

'I'm going to have to get something to eat.' She drained her glass and the wine stuck in her throat like acid.

'One more dance?' he said. 'Then I'll take you to a little place I know. We can get something to soak up the booze.'

On her next trip to the loo she slurped some water from the tap, trying to sober up. She'd have to go soon, she really would. But it was ten o'clock by the time they left the warmth behind them and she stood on the edge of the pavement swallowing cold air. Her head was unsteady on her shoulders and she was trying not to feel sick.

He led the way down the river path, back into the city centre. Walking sobered her and she started to wonder if Max would be worried. Charlie was quiet, only swearing under his breath as his foot slipped in goose muck. She didn't have much to say either, so they listened to the water slapping against the stone of the bank and the distant voices of nightclubbers on the bridge. They cut through the Coppergate Centre and came out at All Saints' Church by a kebab van, where he bought her a large portion of chips.

'My treat,' he said.

'Is this it? Classy joint.'

They sat on the wall behind the church, and ate in silence, licking chip fat off their fingers. Her legs and arms began to feel more solid, although she knew she was still drunk. He asked her if she was all right and she said yes, she was fine.

'And you're a much nicer man than I thought you were.' It sounded childish, and the fact that she was slurring didn't help. 'No, I didn't mean that.'

'Yes you did,' he sighed. 'I'm not always the most sympathetic person in the world, I know that.'

'You said it was a waste of time, after forty-eight hours.' He didn't reply. 'That was my brother you were talking about, how would you like it if your brother...?'

But she couldn't carry on because tears were streaming down her face. He put his hand on her shoulder and held her steady, as if she would rock off the wall.

125

'Tell me about it,' he said.

She took a deep breath and told him all she knew, about her visit to Doncaster, about the lack of any clues anywhere and the fact that Stacey didn't even seem to care. He questioned her gently about Stacey's version of events and why was it so hard to believe that Phil had gone off with another woman?

'How much do we ever know about one another? Especially our families,' he said. 'Just because you knew someone in the past, doesn't mean you can understand what they're doing now.'

'It doesn't fit.' She wiped her nose on a ragged tissue she found in her pocket. 'That's all. It just doesn't feel right, do you know what I mean?'

'I know exactly what you mean. But having a hunch isn't enough. In my line of work I need something more definite.'

'I think about him all the time. Even when I'm thinking about something else, it's there in the background, like a dull hum that I can't switch off.'

'You seem to be coping really well. On the surface anyway.'

'I'm just drowning the hum out with stuff, work stuff, family stuff. So long as I'm busy.'

She was shivering and he helped her down from the wall, offering her his coat, but she refused. As they walked towards the taxi rank, the wind pushed against them and a group of drunken young men almost collided with her, but Charlie pulled her out of their path just in time.

'Steady.'

126

His arm stayed round her shoulder for a second longer than was necessary. When it was gone, she could still feel its weight and warmth. She turned away and a fine spray of rain brought her round, back to herself: Karen Friedman, married mother of two, who shouldn't be out this late with a man she hardly knew.

They reached the line of taxis waiting with their engines running like purring cats, and she wondered if the drivers enjoyed their work or hated having to scoop up the casualties of the pubs and clubs.

'Will you be OK?' Charlie asked.

'I'm fine. What about you? Do you have far to go?' It had only just occurred to her that she didn't even know where he lived.

'Sheffield. But I'm on Jaz's couch tonight. I should be in time for last orders if I set off back to the Brown Cow.'

She hesitated before saying goodbye. How were they supposed to do this? He took her shoulders and looked directly into her eyes.

'If you need any help, looking for your brother, I'll do what I can. I'd like to help you, Karen. I'm sorry about what I said the other day. I'll go to Doncaster, if you want me to, ask some questions, find out what they're doing about Phil.'

'Thank you.' She meant it. It was like handing over a heavy load, her shoulders lifted.

He kissed her lightly on the cheek and then she was in the taxi, giving the name of her road. Against the window, she watched her double-blurred reflection against a moving backcloth of streetlights and shop lights. She was tired, more

127

than tired. A sagging, limb-dragging heaviness forced her eyes shut. She lingered on the edge of sleep, replaying her evening over and over again.

## BONFIRE NIGHT: 12.20 p.m.

Phil was approaching the first motorway junction out of Doncaster. The fuel gauge was on red, so he slowed for the slip road and tried to shift down a gear, but the gearbox had a mind of its own. The engine roared and decelerated as it found second instead of fourth. In the mirror he could see a lorry bearing down on him, the driver's face and waving fist clearly visible. Phil swore and tried again, forcing the gear stick into place just in time to jerk away from the lorry before it was on top of him. He heard something slide across the floor of the van behind him and he remembered the cases of Panda Pops.

'Bloody hell.' He wasn't going to get to Hull before lunchtime; Len would have to wait. There was a supermarket just off the motorway. He decided to fill up the van and get something to eat then he could double-back and deliver the drinks to Carole.

In the supermarket he hesitated over the choice of sandwiches. His phone buzzed in his pocket with a text from Johnny Mackenzie. Phil read it and rang the office number. It was the answer machine. He left a message to say that everything was fine and he was on his way to Carole's with the drinks. He looked back at the rows of plastic triangles and wondered if the girl in the caravan would like mayonnaise or not. It was weird to be standing here, trying to choose a sandwich for someone he'd barely exchanged two words with, but she seemed so vulnerable stuck in the middle of nowhere. He went for the cheese ploughman's – it would suit the landscape if nothing else – an iced Danish and a can of Coke. While he was waiting at the till, he picked up a packet of sparklers for Holly. If he got back in time, they could go and watch the fireworks at the pub together.

Carole was waiting for him at the garages, talking to a skinny boy on a BMX bike.

'Give us a hand, Lee,' she said. 'My back's knackered.'

'Nah, I've got a delivery.' The boy nodded up towards the dual carriageway. 'A little something for a lady in a caravan.'

On closer inspection, Phil saw that the youth was older than he'd first thought. Despite the underdeveloped body, he had stubble on his face.

'Near the quarry?' Phil said and the youth nodded. 'I'm on the way up there myself. I can drop something off for you. Take it as payment, if you've got time to give us a hand with these.'

The young man peered at Phil from under the oversized brim of his baseball cap.

'What's your business with her?' he said.

'I offered to take her a sandwich for her lunch.'

'That foreign lass?' His eyes seemed fixed on a point somewhere inside Phil's head. The way he said foreign was like someone saying turd or filth.

'Yeah. She's foreign.'

'Hang on.'

The young man seemed to have forgotten there was some kind of deal here and rode off on the bike, standing high on the pedals. Carole shrugged and took the first case of drinks out herself, leaving the rest for Phil. She was locking up the garage and Phil was about to get back in the van, when Lee reappeared.

'Here,' he thrust a padded envelope at Phil. 'Give this to your little friend by the quarry. Something to cheer her up. If she likes it, there's more where that came from.'

Once he was in the van and Carole and the boy were out of sight, Phil looked in the envelope. Five years ago he might have asked the boy for a quarter of blow or some cocaine to tide him over, but he was finished with all that now. He let out a whistle between his teeth. So, the girl was a potato picker who didn't drive and was about to have her lunch delivered with a couple of wraps of heroin.

The sun had risen just enough to filter through the tops of the trees, melting the last of the frost on the lane up to the quarry. Phil parked the van and knocked on the caravan door. She opened it straightaway, with her long coat wrapped tight around her.

'Oh. Hello, driver boy. You came again.'

'With lunch, as requested.' He held up a pink and white plastic bag but she was looking at the envelope. She took the package and turned it over in her hand, frowning.

'You better come in.'

Phil stooped under the low doorway and stood up again carefully, taking in the neat interior, the carefully made bed at one end and the tiny table with its upholstered seats to the right of the door. He put the plastic bag on the table.

She tucked the envelope in the back of a locker above the small sink and took out two plates. A gas heater was doing its best to warm the damp air. Phil folded himself into one of the seats and watched her unpack the picnic. He broke the silence first.

'So you said you work for Mackenzie.'

She nodded.

'On this farm? Potato picking?'

If she hesitated, he didn't notice.

'Yes. Yes, you have it right. It is to do with vegetables.' She laughed and put her hand up to her mouth to stop a tiny piece of cheese escaping. 'And what about you, driver boy? You Mister Mackenzie's right-hand man?'

'No. I'm a musician. I play trombone, a bit of guitar too, when I can get a gig.'

'Of course. Naturally you are poor musician and take any job. I understand.'

That was nice. Simple. She said it like she meant it. There was none of the *are-you-going-to-be-famous-have-you-made-any-records* nonsense he usually had to put up with.

'So. You meet skinny boy? You like him? I do not like him. He is pig. So, driver boy. You have name? I think, also, you are lunch boy now.'

'Phil. Short for Philip. And no, I don't know the skinny boy, I met him for the first time about ten minutes ago.' He noticed she had nearly finished

131

her sandwich and he'd barely started his. He pushed the iced Danish towards her. He didn't know what he'd expected, but a little gratitude wouldn't have gone amiss

'OK. And normally you work for Mr Mackenzie, Philip?' She exaggerated the 'f' sound. It was nice, like someone playing a flute that second before the note kicks in.

'Sometimes. I paint his properties or I work in the office. Nothing like today. Today's not normal.'

'Not normal to have lunch with pretty girl? Shame!'

'Not normal to deliver drugs to pretty girl in caravan. No.'

She didn't register any surprise but took a large bite of her sandwich and looked out of the murky plastic window towards the field. There wasn't much to see. It was a mess of stubble stalks and stones between muddy furrows.

'Mr Mackenzie doesn't like to get hands dirty. I am here two weeks and he does not come to see I settle in, like he promise. Look!' She turned her gaze back into the caravan, as if it were a palace, which Johnny was missing out on. 'I clean everything. New sheets, nice candles, but Johnny Mackenzie does not even bring pretty girl cup of coffee. Always someone else to do work.'

He looked towards the bed and noticed that the quilt cover had an Aztec pattern in reds and blues. Like she said, it looked brand new. A mobile phone let out a text alert and she checked her pocket, reading the text with a frown.

'I may be out of my depth here, but you seem...' he tried not to sound judgemental but she met his look with those incredible green eyes and he faltered. 'I don't know ... what I mean is, you seem too together. To be a smackhead.'

'Me? No. It's not for me, it's for a friend.' She put her slim hand over his and left it there for a moment. 'Look it's long story. I tell you another time. But you have to go now. I have to get ready for work.'

'Will I see you again?' He didn't mean it to sound like a chat-up line, but it was too late, the words were out there, hanging in the air between them.

She smiled. 'I hope so. But I don't know.'

When she leant forward to kiss him on the cheek, he smelt her cigarettes and perfume, a tang of sweet and citrus that left him feeling about fifteen years old. Other women didn't normally have this effect on him. He thought he'd become immune with age and with parenthood but, as they'd established, today wasn't a normal day.

'Wrap up warm,' he said. 'It's going to be cold in the fields.'

'Goodbye, Fffillip.' He thought she was about to laugh then, but the door closed and he was walking back to the van, trying to shrug off the feeling of the kiss burning a guilty little hole in his cheek.

# CHAPTER FOURTEEN

Carly Jayson swung the car into the space marked PCSO Vehicle at a speed that Sean couldn't believe was either safe or accurate. When he winced, she just laughed her big laugh.

'Cheer up, flower. Fancy a game of pool when we're done? I'll buy you a pint to make up for my crap driving.'

'Yeah, go on.'

As he followed her into the police station, Lizzie Morrison was coming through the double doors towards them.

'Sean. Can I have a word?'

'Catch you in a minute, Carly.'

'Whatever.'

She raised an eyebrow behind Lizzie's back and let the door swing shut behind her.

'What's up?' he said. 'I daren't keep Carly waiting.'

'I asked Rick Houghton if he could get me the original charge sheets for Flora Ishmaili. You know Rick? He's a DI in Drugs. Anyway Vice are supposed to have picked her up three times, but one of them's missing.'

'The overdose vic in Balby? Why would anyone take the charge sheet?'

'I don't know. It could just be a mistake. But there's something else, she was picked up on the street two years ago, then nothing else until two weeks before she died. Most of the street girls are in and out all the time. I want to know where she was in between.'

'Is that actually part of your remit?'

'Not really, but I'm beginning to feel like nobody's actually bothered about these girls except us.'

Us. That was nice. He could have kissed her. A second later, he couldn't believe he'd even thought it and blushed to the roots of his hair.

The nearest pub was round the corner from the police station. It had two pool tables in a large room at the back. Carly had brought a couple of mates along, Rick Houghton and another DI called Steve. Sean recognised him as the second Drug Squad detective he'd overheard in the gents, the day of the briefing after Flora Ishmaili had been found dead.

'Been helping old ladies across the road then?' Steve said, looking at Sean.

'Fuck off!' Carly stood her ground, pool cue at the ready. 'You need us PCSOs and you know it. We're your eyes and ears on the ground.'

'Eugh! Sounds nasty,' Steve said.

'Course we need you, don't take any notice of Steve,' Rick said. 'What you having?'

Sean went with him to get a round from the bar. While they waited, he looked at the pictures on the wall, vaguely familiar from the art room at school, dingy things with smeary paint to show the sky was full of weather.

'You work the Chasebridge estate?' Rick asked.

'Yeah, with Carly.'

'You know a lot of people down there?'

'I grew up there, so yeah, some, by sight.'

'We arrested a guy up there a few months back. Major dealer but we think he's been replaced. I wondered if you'd seen anyone new around.'

From somewhere behind him a fruit machine paid out. The clattering of coins seemed to go on forever.

'Lee Stubbs.' Sean said.

'Sorry?' Rick paid for the drinks, but Sean was still staring at the paintings beside the bar.

'A feller I keep seeing on the Chasebridge estate. I knew him at school. Right headcase. Got chucked out for sniffing the oil paints in Art. Goes around on a BMX. I think he knew the third victim. I saw her with someone who looked very like him.'

'Nature abhors a vacuum.'

'What d'you mean?'

'We had a feeling someone had taken over the business when we pulled our guy,' Rick said and took a long drink from the top of his pint. 'Either one of his associates or a smaller player could be exploiting a gap in the market. If he's an amateur, it could explain why such strong gear's getting out there. Are you on duty tomorrow?'

'Yeah.'

'I'll get you detailed to ride with us. See if you can point him out.'

'OK.' Sean picked up two pints of lager. 'We'd better get these drinks back to Carly and Steve.'

'Yep. Steve's nasty when he's thirsty,' Rick grinned.

At eight-thirty the next morning, a black Ford Focus was parked opposite Chasebridge Community Primary School. Steve and Rick were up front, with Sean in the back watching families walking their children up to the school gates. Some kids ran ahead, others were being tugged along, a few were yelled at to *get in that school or I'll batter you.* A shouting match broke out between two mothers. Sean would have preferred to be out there, hovering nearby, not intervening yet, but just letting them know someone was in the vicinity in case it got any uglier. But he was trapped behind tinted glass, watching, waiting. By ten to nine, the tide had turned and the adults were walking away.

'Follow her.'

Sean pointed out the woman he'd seen after his talk at the school. He had a hunch he knew who she was meeting. They waited for her to go round the corner, then moved the car forward. In Darwin Road, she stopped to lean on a lamp post and took out her phone. Then she carried on walking as she sent a text, struggling against the slope in high heels. She turned towards a block of flats, next to the one where flowers for Taneesha McManus were already beginning to wilt. Across the top line of brickwork, large white capital letters spelt out EAGLE MOUNT TWO. They didn't have to wait long before the thin frame of a man on a tiny bike appeared on the crest of the hill. He plummeted down the grassy slope, skidding sideways as he hit the Tarmac. Even from a distance, Sean was sure.

'That's Lee Stubbs.'

'Delivery boy.' Steve dropped the Mars Bar

137

he'd been eating onto Rick's lap and put his foot down. 'Let's go.'

Stubbs must have sensed that a shiny new motor, clean and undented, could only mean one thing. As the car began to move, he lifted the front wheel and turned his bike, like a rearing horse, onto the pavement. He set off across the grass towards the slabbed path between the housing blocks. Steve drew the Ford level, just as Stubbs slipped round a bollard between the buildings. Rick jumped out.

'Get the car round the back!'

Sean shouted directions to Steve, but he didn't think they had much hope. The blocks, Eagle Mounts One, Two, Three and Four, were arranged around a square patch of grass and paving. Stubbs could take any one of four exits and each opened onto a different street. It was impossible to get a car round faster than a bike because each road had a barrier to stop joyriders. They spotted Rick running out through the gap between Eagle Mounts One and Four. He waved them away and turned back to the centre. On the second entry road, facing Eagle Mount Two, they had better luck. Stubbs was coming straight towards them. He leapt onto the pavement and whizzed past, as Steve swore and turned the car around.

'Bloody genius, whoever named these. The postie must have a right job.'

Out of the rear window, Sean could see Rick running down the hill, away from the blocks. He jumped the low fence around the recreation ground and cut a diagonal path through the children's play area. A woman pushing a toddler on a swing didn't even look up. Then Rick was back on the street, forcing Stubbs into a U-turn.

'He's gone left. We've got him now! There's a row of lock-ups by the shops, it's a dead-end.' Sean was thrown back in his seat as Steve took the corner.

When they pulled up at the far end of the entry road, Lee Stubbs was leaning against a metal garage door. He spat on the ground and waited.

'I'm saying nowt without a solicitor.'

Stubbs stared out of the car window with his baseball hat and hood pulled low over his face, silent until they got back to the station. Only when Rick bundled him out of the car, did he finally make eye contact with Sean.

'I'll see you,' he said, before he was led towards the custody suite downstairs. Sean went in the opposite direction to find Carly. He heard raised voices behind him and looked back over his shoulder. Burger was coming through the swing doors at the head of the stairs. He had his hand on Steve's arm.

'Leave it with me, son,' Burger said. Steve didn't look like he appreciated being called son or having his arm touched, but he was keeping his mouth shut. 'I know the lad. I'm sure we can sort it out without needing to get into too much paperwork.'

Sean would have liked to hear more but the vibe between Steve and Burger told him to make himself scarce. Half an hour later, Sean passed the interview room. Through the one-way glass he could see Stubbs on the other side of the table. He seemed to be talking quietly to someone who was standing, just out of view. There was no sign of a solicitor and the lights on the tape recorder were off.

'It's not the flipping zoo, Denton.' He hadn't heard the door open and suddenly Burger was standing there with a face like a slapped arse. 'Instead of gawping, get this lad a cup of tea.'

When he got back from the canteen, Burger was gone and Lee Stubbs was sitting with his chair pushed back and his feet up on the table.

'Anywhere round here you can get a bag of crisps?' Stubbs asked.

'There's a vending machine.'

'Get us one then.'

'They're sixty pence.'

'Then I'll have to owe you. I've nowt on me.'

Sean shrugged. 'Sorry, mate, I've got no change.'

'Never mind. I'll be on my way any minute now.'

'Yeah?' Sean tried not to sound surprised.

'Did you think I was going to get locked up for riding me bike on the pavement?' Stubbs sneered.

'No, I...'

'You're a twat, you always were, and you're even more of one in that uniform. You're not even a real copper, are you Denton?'

Carly put her head round the door.

'What's up?'

Sean hoped she hadn't heard the last bit; he didn't want her losing her job for assault on a suspect. Not on his account.

'This a Mr Stubbs?'

Lee sucked his teeth and tried his best to look hard. 'Who wants to know?'

'Well if it is, you can show him off the premises.'

'I'd be delighted.'

Stubbs slouched down the corridor ahead of him, rolling his hips as if he was a Los Angeles gangster, not a puny white boy from the edge of Doncaster. Then he stopped. He was looking at a poster on the wall.

'I've seen him.'

It was the photograph of Mrs Friedman's brother, which Sean had enlarged on the photocopier.

'When?'

Lee Stubbs sucked his teeth. 'Let me see. That would have been Bonfire Night. Busy night. Lots of parties. He did some business with me. A little package. D'you get me?'

Sean thought he probably did get him. 'We might have to ask you some more questions about that.'

'Yeah, well, your man knows where I live. But I wouldn't bother. I can't tell you no more than what I just have. In fact, I never told you nothing. We never spoke. That's it.'

Five minutes later, Sean was upstairs looking out over the car park. He saw three people walking away from the building, Lee Stubbs, a middle-aged woman with square shoulders and blonde bobbed hair and DCI Barry King. The woman had her arm linked with Lee's and, as he watched, Burger put his arm round the woman's shoulders. She stopped and pointed her key fob at a dark-blue BMW. King opened the door for her. He was saying something through the window as she drove away. The car had a personalised number plate. Sean squinted but he couldn't make out

141

what it was meant to say. He just kept saying the letters over and over so they fixed in his head.

He slipped into one of the admin offices and found Sandy, who did him a DVLA search. 'Stella Stubbs, 47 Linden Avenue.'

'Stubbs? His mum.'

'What were you expecting, pet?'

'Don't know.'

Burger obviously knew the woman, knew her well. Linden Avenue. It was on that estate with the posh new houses, just before they'd swerved off down the drive to Lower Brook Farm. Burger had stuck the twos up at a boy on a bike. Or had he?

'How come Stubbs walked?' he asked Sandy.

'You haven't seen Steve? He was in here, fuming. The lad had nothing on him apparently and Burger overruled him, said that there wasn't enough evidence to book him, let alone keep him.'

'He must have ditched his stash while we were following. You don't make that much effort to get away if you've got nothing to hide.'

'Burger's said he's not going to authorise a team to search the whole of the Chasebridge estate.'

Had Burger stuck the twos up? Or had he waved?

'It'll be pointless now, anyway,' said Sean. 'Lee Stubbs will be way ahead of us.'

'Oh, Sean,' Lizzie put her head round the door, 'I thought I heard your voice.' Sandy switched from the DVLA screen back to a document she was typing.

'If you've got a minute,' Lizzie said, 'there's something I'd like you to look at.'

Sean thanked Sandy and excused himself.

# CHAPTER FIFTEEN

Karen dialled the Moyos' number again in case she'd made a mistake. There was still no reply. She'd been trying to contact them for two days to tell them that a date had been scheduled for their appeal hearing. She was going to have to go to the house.

She jostled the tourists and Christmas shoppers, pulling her handbag close and tightening her scarf. A bitter wind cut round the corner of the Minster. As people passed her, the air smelt of perfume and alcohol. Max had been out every night for at least ten days; schmoozing or being schmoozed by clients. His firm had offices in Leeds, Edinburgh and London, so for several nights he didn't come home at all. Outside office hours, she'd stayed in, decorating the house and writing Christmas cards. In her address book, under H, Phil's name was there in blue biro: Holroyd Reg, Holroyd, Philip. Nothing from Phil. No card, no phone call. There was a heaviness in her stomach that made her dread the postman and she felt exhausted every time she picked up the mail from the mat.

The address was off Leeman Road, behind the station. She crossed the river and turned towards the Railway Museum. She hadn't heard from Charlie Moon. The night at the Brown Cow was almost a month ago and she was beginning to think she'd made a fool of herself, or maybe he thought he had. Now, it was the children's final day at school and her last chance to pick up any presents without them seeing.

The Moyos' house was a two-up, two-down terrace in need of a lick of paint. There was a *To Let* sign in the window, and through the empty glass she could see that the house was empty, no furniture or curtains left. She peered through the letterbox and saw a heap of pizza menus and free sheets cascading across the hall carpet. She wondered if they could postpone the hearing, or whether they would have to let it go. Jaz would be furious; he really felt they had a chance of winning.

She was glad the wind was behind her, as she made her way back into the city centre. Outside Debenhams a young Santa was collecting money for a homeless charity. She remembered when Sophie was little, and she was pregnant with Cara, they used to pass a homeless man on their way to the mother and toddler group, behind the back door of the Co-op. He had a filthy white beard and straggly hair and Sophie thought he was Santa. One day he was gone and, when he reappeared a week later, he'd been shaved and shorn. Sophie was devastated. What had they done to her Father Christmas? This young man looked even less like Santa than that old tramp; she couldn't imagine any child being fooled by his costume. As she put her hand in her pocket for some change, she felt her phone vibrate. Number withheld.

'Happy Christmas!' A deep voice with a hint of the valleys.

'Charlie? It's a bit early, there's another week.'

144

'Are you annoyed? You sound annoyed.'

'No, I'm fine.' It didn't come out quite right.

'Look, I'm sorry, you've got every right to be annoyed. I said I'd help you with your brother.'

'It's fine, really.'

'Where are you?' he said.

'Outside Debenhams.'

'Are you going into the RAMA office?'

'I've finished for the day.' The skinny Santa shook his bucket in her direction. 'I was just going to do a bit of last-minute shopping.'

'I think I've found something for you,' Charlie said. 'I've got to pop in and see Jaz but afterwards, tell you what, we'll have lunch. I'll meet you at the Italian on the river.'

Karen looked at her watch. It was noon. She had time.

'OK.'

The restaurant was packed. The maître d', a tall grey-haired Italian, greeted her with a smile.

'I'm meeting a friend.' He showed her to a table for two in a dark corner of the restaurant. She had nothing to hide, but somehow she felt grateful for his discretion.

'Sorry I'm late.'

Charlie Moon unwound his scarf and dropped his coat into the hands of a waiter who appeared behind him. He seemed quite at home. She'd never been inside this place and she'd been expecting a pizza joint, but one look at the clients told her it was a great deal more exclusive than that; definitely a step up from the kebab van at All Saints' Church.

'There's been a sighting of Phil,' Charlie said, the second he sat down.

Karen felt dizzy. 'When?'

He explained about a man on a bike and a chase and the PCSO. She pictured the young officer. He'd remembered her and she was grateful.

'When did this drug dealer say he'd seen Phil?'

'Bonfire Night.'

She'd lost her appetite now and when the waiter appeared to take their order she couldn't decide.

'Just a salad, I think, I'm not very hungry.'

'I'll have the linguine and a half bottle of Chianti.' He waited for the waiter to move away. 'It seems that Stubbs is denying that he said anything to the PCSO. He's probably woken up to the fact that it doesn't look good if he's on record admitting he can identify one of his customers.'

'So why say it to Sean Denton in the first place?'

'Denton got the impression that Lee Stubbs was showing off.'

The wine arrived and he filled her glass without asking. It stemmed the flow of questions she had, but which she knew he couldn't answer. They talked shop for a while. The trial of the Grimsby lorry owner, Xhoui Li, was coming up and he was busy trying to chase the forensic lab to secure an expert witness.

'He's playing hard to get, Mr Li. Every time the CPS provides an interpreter, he claims it's the wrong dialect.'

'Was Doncaster part of your target area or did you just go there on a whim?'

'Bit of both,' he smiled and the tension left the muscles in his face.

She finished her salad and, after another glass of wine, decided she needed something else to soak up the alcohol. She ordered tiramisu and when it came it was beautiful: creamy, bittersweet and a texture that melted on her tongue.

'Oh my God, have you tried this?' Without thinking, she passed him a spoonful. He hesitated and then closed his mouth around the spoon. He shut his eyes. When he opened them again, she had to look away.

Suddenly it was three o'clock and she remembered Ben. If she wasn't quick he'd be waiting with Mrs Leith again, arms full of cardboard robins and advent calendars covered in cotton wool. She reached into her purse and took out a twenty.

'I've got to dash.'

He waved her money away. 'I'll get this.'

Within minutes they were outside again and she was wishing him a Happy Christmas.

'And thank you, for lunch and for finding out about Phil, and the guy who recognised him. It's not really sunk in.'

She reached out to shake Charlie's hand, not wanting him to embrace her, not in broad daylight in this small city where everyone knew everyone else, and yet wanting more than anything to be held in those arms and press her face into the soft down of his puffa jacket. He handed her a small white envelope. Beautiful fingers, she thought. She wanted to kiss them, but she didn't.

On the bus, she tried to shake off the torpor of the lunchtime wine. She pulled Charlie's envelope out of her bag and opened it. It was a card with a bunch of snowdrops on the front. Inside

147

Charlie had written in rapid biro: *A Very Happy Christmas – Phone if you need anything – C* and there was a mobile number. That 'C' could mean anything, anyone. He must have known she was going home to someone who might ask.

That evening Karen watched Sophie singing in the school concert at the Minster. It was gone ten when they walked back up the street and Sophie was sulking, three paces behind, because they'd argued on the way home about the length of her skirt. Karen opened the front door and heard an unmistakable yelp. The first time she heard that laugh, she thought Trisha had choked on a pretzel. After eight months of living next door to her, she'd almost got used to it.

She tidied her hair in the hall mirror, wiped stray eyeliner from under her eyes and rubbed colour into her cheeks. Sophie put her head round the door of the living room, said a cursory hello and stomped off upstairs. Trisha and her husband Paul were sprawled on the sofa with Paul's laptop, showing Max a slideshow of their holiday in Thailand. Karen heard Trisha say that the beaches were, 'a bit scruffy, you know, a bit washed up.' Then she yelped again at her own pun. Paul turned to Max and said in a stage whisper that the girls in the bars more than made up for it. A Buddhist temple appeared on the screen, lit in a sunset glow. From where Karen stood in the doorway, its deep reds, reflecting off a gold dome, were flattened out into a blue-black negative.

'Hi, Trisha. Paul. Nice holiday?'

'There you are.' Max looked up from the sofa.

'There's some pasta for you.'

She went into the kitchen and closed the door. She wasn't in the mood for holiday snaps. Max had plated up her food and she slid it into the microwave. She eased her feet out of her shoes and wished she could stay in the kitchen until they left, but she knew Max would be critical about her lack of manners and she hadn't got the energy for another argument. He had a lot in common with Paul, a divorce lawyer serving the upper end of the market. Theirs was a world of profit and loss and us and them. It must be easy, she thought, to see things in such simple terms if you're on the winning side. She thought about all the losers: the unnamed Chinese girl and the Thai girls who serviced the tourist trade. It was the sort of thing she could probably talk to Charlie about. A shudder rippled through her, like an aftershock or maybe a warning tremor and she wondered if there was such a thing as a before-shock. The microwave pinged and she took the steaming bowl to the table. There was fresh chilli in the sauce and plenty of garlic. It tasted good. Surprisingly good, considering Max was usually a 'can't cook, won't cook' kind of guy. Then she spotted an unfamiliar pan on the bob and realised Trisha must have brought it over.

She finished her food and took her glass of wine back to the front room. They were talking about football and Trisha was flicking through the magazine from the Sunday paper, she looked up at Karen.

'You OK?'

'Yeah, better with some food inside me.'

149

'Any news?' Trisha said. 'I mean about your brother?'

'No, none at all.'

Karen wished she hadn't asked. She couldn't stop thinking about the drug dealer who'd recognised Phil from the poster. She took a gulp of wine and as it entered her bloodstream, pictures of the day replayed through her mind. Not just pictures either, the taste of the tiramisu, the warmth of Charlie's skin when they shook hands outside the restaurant. She hadn't wanted to let go.

'...it's not happening.' Trisha lowered her voice and Karen realised she'd missed the first part of what Trisha had said. 'Paul's got to go for some tests and then me. But I bet it's me, I mean he's already got the twins from his first marriage, so it's bound to be my fault.'

'Oh?'

'He's found a really good man, very high success rate. I just don't know if I can face all that prodding about and the hormones make you go really fat.'

'You poor things.'

'I know and some people just seem to pop them out and then they can't look after them properly. You hear such terrible stories of babies dying from neglect.'

Karen watched Trisha open and shut her mouth like a fish, as if her words could return to her unspoken.

'Oh, God, Karen! That came out all wrong, I didn't mean... I never thought...'

'Time to go, babe, I've got to get on a plane to Frankfurt tomorrow.'

'I'll ring you, Trish,' Karen was saying. She didn't want her to leave now, halfway through this conversation. They would never be best friends but they got on all right, muddling along on the surface. The cold air from the open front door raised the tiny hairs on one side of her face and she shivered. Trisha kissed her other cheek.

## BONFIRE NIGHT: 2.45 p.m.

Driving east, Phil saw how the colour was fading from the sky. The day had barely warmed up before it was starting to cool again. The heater in the van competed with the music and finally he turned them both off and just listened to the engine. He flicked the side lights on, although it wasn't quite three o'clock. He reckoned he'd need full headlights soon.

He turned onto Clive Sullivan Way as the traffic was starting to slow into an endless trail of red tail lights. He wondered what time he would make it home. Stacey would have to take Holly with her to the pub if he was late. He didn't like his daughter sitting on the bar being treated like a doll by the regulars, while her mother worked. It wasn't healthy. He'd rather be there himself, see the fireworks and get Holly home in good time for bed. The little café on the industrial estate was closed. Just beyond it a man was sitting on a bench, reading a newspaper. As Phil drew level with him, the man jumped up and waved the newspaper above

151

his head. It was Len. Phil pulled up and waited for him to catch up.

'Where the fuck have you been?' Len's face was reddening and Phil could smell whisky on his breath. 'I've been sat there for an hour.'

'Sorry, mate.'

'I'm not your mate,' Len said and climbed in, stretching across to switch the heater on full, 'and I'm nithered.'

Phil waited for him to do his seat belt up, but it didn't look as if Len was going to bother, so he moved off in the direction of the freight container at the back of the concrete sheds. Above the noise of the fan heater Phil asked him why he hadn't stayed in his car.

'Had to move it out. Plod's been sniffing around. Two constables. I thought this might happen if we didn't get a move on. They'll probably come back with a warrant. You'll need to stay off the motorway on the way back to Donny.'

Great, Phil thought, that would make him even later. The rising heat in the van and the smell of Len's breath began to creep over him like a series of new anxieties. He'd made a decision several hours ago not to ask too much, but now he was beginning to worry about what he'd say if he did get stopped. He wasn't sure that ignorance was any defence if he'd a van full of knock-off laptops.

'Get as close in as you can,' Len said. 'We don't want to be seen from the end of the road.'

Phil straightened the van up in the narrow space in front of the container, leaving just enough room to open its doors. It would be a squeeze for him and Len to get the boxes into the back of the van, but he wasn't going to argue. They worked quickly, each carrying four or five laptop boxes in a stack. Phil stopped to take his jacket off and Len barked at him to get a move on. He wasn't laughing now and the gold tooth stayed hidden.

It was getting hard to see inside the container but as Phil moved further towards the back he was aware of several competing smells. The most dominant was a strong smell of over-ripe oranges, musty and acrid as if some of them had started to rot. But there was another smell, more human, like a bedroom that hasn't been aired. It reminded him of the staff cabin on the ferry. He'd shared it with the Abba cover band's drummer: a man with only one pair of socks. He couldn't see to the back of the container because there was a wall of pallets, stacked with shallow cardboard boxes. This was the source of the rotting fruit.

'Bit late for this lot, isn't it?' he said over his shoulder to Len, who'd just come back from the van for another load.

'Leave that,' he snapped at Phil. 'It's none of your business.'

'It's only fruit. Calm down!' Phil laughed. When he turned round, Len was standing in the entrance of the container, arms by his sides and fists tight as if he was squaring up for a fight.

'I can't make out if you're a fool or just playing at it,' Len growled, 'but you keep your mouth shut from now on and do exactly what I tell you.'

Phil held up his hands in submission. He decided that when he got home he would look in the paper for a proper job. He'd had enough of being part of Mackenzie's empire; it stank.

He worked silently until the last box was in the van. He shut the rear doors carefully, taking care not to slam them, although there seemed to be no one around to notice. Then he locked up and waited for Len. He could hear him shuffling around inside the container but he was taking his time. Phil went to see if he needed any help and was struck by a new smell. Something was smouldering. He walked slowly, making as little noise as possible, into the container. He couldn't see Len at first, but then he noticed light filtering through the wall of fruit boxes. He went closer and put his eye up to a gap where the corner of a box was crushed inward. Through a tiny triangle of space he could see an area of about eleven foot square with nothing in it except a pile of sleeping bags. The light was coming from a flame, which was curling up over a blue nylon cover. Len was holding his cigarette lighter against the fabric of another bag but he was struggling to get the flame to take hold. A part of Phil's brain wanted to tell Len that they were probably fire-retardant so he might have a job with just a lighter, then something else clicked in and Phil felt sick. Someone had been living here, sleeping here. The other smell, of unwashed bodies in an airless room, made sense now. No wonder Len didn't want Phil anywhere near the fruit boxes, they were a screen, so highly pungent that even a port-side sniffer dog wouldn't know there were people in the container. Phil crept back out and stood by the van for a moment. Fuck Len, he could find his own way back, he wanted no more to do with this. He would get rid of the laptops at Mackenzie's shed and go home.

# CHAPTER SIXTEEN

Sean stepped off the bus and turned up the collar of his jacket against the wind. His uniform was at his nan's house. He was on his own time now. There was a parade of shops, shuttered against the dark, some of them closed for good. A couple of takeaways lit up the pavement before the Balby Post Office and General Store. It was seven-thirty in the evening and there was nobody around. He pulled a piece of paper out of his jeans pocket and unfolded it. He studied the blurred letters but the printout from his camera phone wasn't great. He checked the street sign, Derby Street, and traced the letters on the paper carefully with his finger. This was definitely it.

There were two doorbells at number seventeen. He pressed the top one and waited. Nothing happened. If he hadn't been looking up when he pressed it the second time, he wouldn't have seen her. A slight shift of the curtain revealed half a pale face and an eye at the upstairs window. Then the curtain dropped. He rang again. This time a light came on and he heard footsteps on the stairs. The front door was opened on its security chain. A woman stood back from the gap.

'What you want?' Husky, a hint of foreign. Sean had rehearsed what he wanted to say.

'I'm a friend of Flora's. Is she here?'

'No.'

'When will she be back? I can wait.'

She came forward and looked at him, then slipped the chain off and opened the door a little wider. Her foot was behind it. She looked ready to kick it shut again.

'You say you are friend of Flora?'

'Yes.'

'Where you know her from?'

'Used to see her now and again, have a drink and that.'

'You are punter?'

Sean had his story. He hoped it was going to work. 'No, I'm part of a church group. We try to help, where we can. You know. We just struck up a friendship. She's hasn't been around for a while, I was...'

'You can't see her. She's dead.'

'Dead?' Sean hoped he sounded convincing. 'God, that's terrible. How?'

'How you think?'

'I can't imagine, she was so young ... was she ill?'

The door opened a little wider. She was framed by the light behind her, a slim woman with dyed red hair and pale green eyes, a long brown cardigan pulled round her waist over her skinny jeans.

'You better come in, church boy.'

He followed her up the stairs. The flat seemed bare. No television, a battered settee, but no table or chairs. A suitcase was open on the floor, half-packed.

'Sit please. I can't offer you drink, I just sold kettle.' Then to Sean's surprise, she laughed. 'Just like home.'

'Sorry?'

'My home in Pristina. There was nothing left. My father sell everything for drink of brandy. My clothes even.'

'I see.'

'Do you, church boy? It's shame you not a punter, I could use some money now.'

'Tell me what happened to Flora.'

'Overdose. Heroin.'

'Were you with her when she died?'

'No, she is dead when I come. You think I sit and watch my friend die? You very unkind, church boy.'

What was he trying to do? He'd thought he'd find some answers but he just had more questions. This woman didn't look like an addict, her skin was clear and she was a normal weight, but maybe she knew who her friend's supplier was.

'Where did she, I mean how did she, get her stuff?'

'You really from church or from police?' The woman fixed him with her wide eyes.

'Look, I'm sorry. I had no business coming here.' He stood up. 'I don't even know your name.'

'Arieta.'

'Arieta.' He shook her hand; it was cold. 'Thank you for telling me about Flora. It must have been terrible to lose your friend. If there's anything I can do.'

'OK. Yes, you drive me to train station. I lie on my back for bloody weeks to buy ticket. I sell everything, now I go.'

She flattened the pile of clothes in the suitcase and closed it.

'I came on the bus,' Sean looked down at his

trainers, 'but I can get your bus fare into town, if that's any good.'

As she stood up, she was laughing. 'I run off into sunset with knight in shining armour on number fifteen bus. It is not a movie, no?'

'Not a movie.' Sean smiled. 'Let me take your case.'

She was twitchy as they stood at the bus stop. Her eyes flicked up and down the quiet street and she stood back in the shadows when a car passed. They didn't speak. Even when the bus came and he paid both fares, she just went to sit in the corner of the back seat, with her suitcase on her lap. Beyond the bus windows, traffic went by, people walked their dogs and the houses were lit up against the dark evening. She watched it all as if she was drinking it in. They were almost in the town centre when he summoned up the courage to ask her another question.

'Who are you running from?'

She leant her forehead against the glass.

'Nobody must run. Nobody should leave,' she mumbled.

'What did you say?'

But she just stared out of the window at the late shoppers and early clubbers struggling against the wind.

They came to a standstill inside the bus station. He offered to take the case but she held it tightly. She looked more nervous than ever as they walked the short distance to the railway station.

'Where are you going to go?'

'Away from here. Far as I can.'

'And then what? How are you going to live?'

'Same as before. Always men to pay for sex.'

'Please, let me help.'

'You and your church, what can you do?'

Sean wished he really did have a church backing him up: some kind old ladies who'd donate this girl some clothes, maybe a vicar who'd offer her a room in return for some housekeeping. The only kind old lady he knew was his nan, and she wouldn't thank him for describing her like that.

There was a queue at the booking office so they went to the automatic ticket machine. She didn't want to hang about. Together they looked at the A to Z of station names, and Sean explained where each one was. She wanted a big city and he suggested Birmingham.

'No way. That is where I start. Internet bride to man with teeth like a horse. Find another.'

She looked over her shoulder and froze. Then she dropped to her knees and started tugging at the zip on the suitcase. She lifted the lid and hid behind it.

'Stand there, no there!' she hissed. 'So legs cover me. And look normal.'

How could he look normal with a woman's head and torso disappearing into a suitcase between him and the ticket machine?

'Who are we hiding from?'

'Sh! Don't speak. Look, on ramp. With pram.'

A mousy brown ponytail bounced over the hood of a light-blue tracksuit. The buggy was top of the range, black with wheels like a mini mountain bike. Then the girl pushing it was gone, out of sight, around the corner to the platforms.

'Who was that?'

'She look all friendly, nice girl. But she work for Miss Estelle. She hang around. Talk to lonely girls, offer them job in massage parlour, offer them nice little something to take their mind off bad feelings. She's going on platforms now to sniff out sad girls too late to go home.'

'Who's Miss Estelle?'

'You don't want to know.'

No, he did want to know. That was the whole point. 'Arieta, who is she?'

'She runs All Star Massage Parlour. She is bitch.'

Sean took her arm and pulled her to her feet. 'Come on.'

The lid of the suitcase fell shut and without letting go of her, he leant down, tugged the zip closed and picked up the case. He propelled her across the forecourt, but she tried to twist her arm out of his grip.

'Look,' he held tight, 'I don't want to make a scene, and of course it's your life. But that girl's on the platform, and if you're as scared of her as I think you are, you don't want to go that way. So what are you going to do?'

She made a grab for her bag, but he spun it behind him. It was surprisingly light. As if her whole life only weighed a couple of kilos.

'You have to trust me,' he hissed.

'OK, church boy, I don't have choices. But where are you taking me? I have right to know. Otherwise I scream. OK?'

'My nan's. Grandmother. You understand?'

He felt the muscles in her arm relax. She let him lead her outside to the taxi rank, where he

160

was relieved to see there was no queue. He gave the address to the driver and took out his phone.

'Lizzie? Can you get over to my nan's place, 12 Clement Grove? I've got someone I think you should meet.'

Maureen looked at the woman on the doorstep. She looked at her grandson, and waited for an explanation.

'Nan, this is Arieta, she needs our help. This is Maureen, my grandmother.'

'I see. Well you better come in.' Behind the girl's back, Maureen raised one plucked eyebrow at him.

She offered the girl a cup of tea and the three of them sat at the kitchen table. Silence. This felt wrong, really wrong. Bringing work home and not just flipchart paper and a bit of Blu Tack.

'Someone's coming to talk to you, Arieta. Someone who can help.'

'From church?'

Sean rubbed a spot on the vinyl tablecloth.

'What's she on about?' Maureen sat back in her chair and looked from the girl to Sean, as if she was watching a tennis match. Sean cleared his throat.

'Wait there. Don't go anywhere, OK? I just need to get something from upstairs.'

When he came down with the flipchart paper, they hadn't moved. He wondered if they'd said anything at all or just sat listening to the rush of the gas boiler.

'I need to explain something.' He paused, positioning himself between Arieta and the door

161

in case she ran. 'I don't go to church, I'm sorry that wasn't true. I work for the police, but I'm just a PCSO. Do you know what that is?' She sat still, looking at him, her back straight. He spread the chart out across the table. 'I work in the community, keep an eye on things and, well, there's been a few things going on round here that you might be able to help with.'

The strange, dead image of Su-Mai lay at the centre. Arieta held the handle of her mug tight, but her face gave nothing away.

'You knew Flora of course.' He touched the newspaper cutting lightly, watching her for any sign of emotion. 'But did you know this girl? Su-Mai isn't her real name, but we don't know what it is. Maybe you can help?'

He should have waited for Lizzie. She would have known how to do this properly. Arieta hadn't taken her coat off. She sat with her suitcase by her side, her eyes darting to the back door.

'And this girl,' Maureen tapped the picture of Taneesha McManus, 'was a pretty little thing. I remember her when she was tiny. Her mum went off the rails too. I knew her nana, nice woman, she used to do my hair.'

The doorbell rang into the silence and all three of them flinched. As Sean got up, he saw Maureen lay her hand on Arieta's.

'It'll be all right, love. My Sean will make sure you won't come to any harm.'

Arieta met her eyes. Her spine softened and she released her grip on the mug.

The bolts to the front door were stiff; everyone else came round the back at his nan's. When he

162

finally got it open, Lizzie stood on the doorstep in the same smart coat he'd seen her wearing at the football ground. She seemed to have grown three inches and he caught a glimpse of some pricey-looking black fabric poking out from under her coat.

'Sorry, were you...?'

'Out? Yup. Charity dinner at the racecourse. Don't worry, it was very dull. I had to get a lift from Guy because I didn't have the car and even if I had, I'm over the limit. Sean, whatever you've got for me, I'm definitely not on duty.' Over her shoulder he could see a silver Audi TT parked at the kerb. 'It's OK. He'll wait. He's very good like that.'

'Is he? Where did you find one ready house-trained?'

'Don't be mean. You've met Guy, haven't you? He was at Doncaster Rovers with me, on firework night. He's their marketing manager. Friend of my dad's.'

He didn't want to hear about her chauffeur, or her date, or whoever he was. She seemed to have forgotten that on firework night he'd been on duty and not exactly one of her party.

'Come on in.'

She stepped into the hall and he saw her glance quickly around, taking in the purple and green walls that his nan had asked him to paint the way she'd seen them on a makeover show. The laminate floor he'd laid last summer looked cheap and ragged already, especially where he hadn't lined it up flush under the skirting. Her heels struck it like lead shot on plastic as she made her

163

way towards the kitchen.

'Wait.' He needed to fill her in on Arieta's story.

She listened, glancing every now and then at the framed poster of Elvis, which had pride of place in the hall. He guessed they had proper artists on the walls at her house.

'OK,' she said, when he'd told her what he knew, 'let's talk to her, but we'll have to get someone else involved if she tells us anything material. You know that.'

Maureen offered to take Lizzie's coat but she decided to keep it on. When she undid it, he could see the beads and sequins of a strapless evening dress.

It didn't go well. Maureen watched the proceedings, her lips tight. He could tell that Lizzie's accent got her back up, while Arieta's response to most of Lizzie's questions was a shrug. It was only when she was asked again about Su-Mai that Arieta paused, looking at the picture.

'There was Chinese girl. It could be her. She went a little before.'

'Before?' Lizzie said. 'Before what?'

'Before I am offered new job and I leave Miss Estelle. Couple of weeks before maybe.'

'Was she a heroin addict too, like Flora?'

Again the shrug. Then nothing. Her shoulders sank and she stared into the empty mug. Lizzie shifted in her seat and he could hear the rustling of whatever stiff material her skirt was made of. She took a business card out of her little beaded handbag.

'Here's my number. If you think of anything,

call me.'

The card lay on the table while Arieta carried on staring into her mug. He saw Lizzie to the door.

'Sorry if that was a bit if a waste of time,' he said.

'These things happen. Guy understands.'

'Yeah. I'm sure he knows you wouldn't be seen dead in this neighbourhood unless it was a work matter.' He tried to sound offhand, like it could be a joke, but it didn't come out like that.

'What's up? You seem touchy.'

'No I'm not.' It came out too fast and, even to his ears, he sounded like a five-year-old answering back.

'Whatever you say.'

She went to open the door but it had stuck in the frame. He leant forward to pull it free. Her skirt brushed his knee and he wanted to cry out. Their faces were close enough to touch noses and she was looking hard at him, like she was reading his thoughts. He saw the moment in her eyes when she understood and pulled away as the door opened.

'We're just friends, Sean.'

'You and Guy?' Pointless, but worth a try.

'You and me. Aren't we?'

'Of course.'

When she'd gone, he wanted to smash his head against the door. He settled for giving it a hard kick.

'Sean? Everything all right?'

'Door's sticking, just making sure it's properly shut.'

165

He went upstairs to the bathroom and washed his face. He lifted his head and looked in the shaving mirror. She was so out of his league. Why had he ever imagined anything else? He could hear the Audi revving up and the sound of its engine trailing away down the street.

He came back downstairs. Maureen was sitting on the sofa in the front room holding Arieta's hand and telling her again not to worry, everything would be all right. He stood in the doorway and was just about to say something, when the girl turned to Maureen and started to cry, speaking quickly between blowing her nose and wiping her running mascara. He stepped back and listened at the open door.

She was talking about how she'd fled her alcoholic father to marry the man in Birmingham. She'd met him on the Internet. After six months he'd become possessive and violent, so she ran away. She got to the railway station and jumped on a train. When the guard finally asked for her ticket, she was just outside Doncaster. She got thrown off and sat on a bench for what seemed like hours, until the young girl with the pram offered her a cigarette. She went with the girl, who said she knew someone who could give her a job with a room above the business: a massage parlour.

'Not nice job. First massage with extras. Then upstairs. Not nice but it pays. Soon I don't care.'

When she hesitated, Sean could hear his nan quietly encouraging her to go on. She never sounded shocked. Arieta was telling her how Flora was already working at the massage parlour. Although she'd come from Kosovo ten years before,

166

she still spoke Albanian.

'Refugee girl. Very sad story. Fighting with foster parents, then running away.'

Her friend was getting more and more dependent on heroin and couldn't earn enough to keep herself going. Arieta stayed clean.

'You won't believe, but I never do drugs, only a little bit of drink. You have to do something, to get through the day.'

She had worked for both of them, trying to put a bit by all the time. The madam was nasty, she said, and took too much of the girls' money. She ripped them off when they needed to score.

'Always there was something we had to pay, rent for bed, cleaning costs and her percentage.'

She thought Flora was going to die, so she got them both out of Miss Estelle's place. She found Flora the flat and paid the first month's rent for her with what she'd saved. Her friend promised her she was going to get clean and Arieta believed her. She took another 'situation' as she put it, but it went wrong, very wrong. She went back to her friend Flora but the other girl was still using, a few days later she was dead. Sean heard her blow her nose and try to say something else, but she was sobbing too hard to speak.

This was all hearsay. But if they *could* check it out, find the massage parlour, maybe find someone else willing to talk and if he could persuade Arieta to stay with them a little longer, maybe she would learn to trust him and then he might find out more. Maureen was speaking now. Sean backed away into the kitchen as he heard her getting to her feet. She went upstairs and came down with sheets and blankets.

'Fix us a hot water bottle will you, love?' She put her head round the kitchen door. 'She's exhausted, poor thing. You and me, we'll have a talk about this in the morning.'

## CHAPTER SEVENTEEN

Karen took her father's bag at the door. The journey had washed the colour from his face.

'I would have been perfectly all right in my own home.' He tugged at his scarf and she fumbled him out of his coat.

'You can't be on your own at Christmas, espeially this year.'

'I've managed before.'

'I'm sorry, Dad.'

'What for? Not your fault.'

Ben wandered out of the living room, trying to balance a light sabre on his nose. 'What's not Mum's fault?'

'Nothing, Ben. Careful, you'll drop it!'

She took the bag upstairs while Reg went for a smoke. He didn't argue about being sent out into the garden. She sat on the spare bed and poked her fingers in and out of the crevices of the candlewick bedspread.

'Happy bloody Christmas,' she said to herself.

She came down to find Reg looking at the cards on the mantelpiece. He picked up each one and checked the writing.

'Just wondered if you'd heard from him.' He dropped one, like a small boy caught snooping. A Victorian family fell to the floor.

'Don't you think I'd have told you?'

'Of course.' He rubbed at the papery skin that hung loose around his jawline. 'I'm sorry.'

Charlie's card was hidden towards the back. She had thought twice about putting it out with the others, but then decided it would look more suspicious if Max came across a card tucked out of sight in a drawer. This way it could be explained as a card from a friend at work or the children's school. 'C' could easily be a Cathy or a Claire.

Christmas Day played out in slow motion. At ten o'clock, Max opened a bottle of champagne. By eleven, Karen was peeling sprouts with heavy arms and legs like dead tree trunks. From the living room the whine of something battery-operated started and stopped, started and stopped. And stopped. She counted the seconds of silence until Ben's wail cut through the air.

'You've broken it! Mummeeeee! Sophie's broken it!'

'Shall I try and have a word?' Reg put down the tea towel he was holding and went towards the hall. He turned in the doorway. 'Takes me right back to you and your brother at...'

But the words didn't come. He cleared his throat and shook his head.

'Don't worry, Dad, I'll sort it. Is Max in there?'

'Upstairs on the computer. Mind if I pop out to stretch my legs? Need a bit of fresh air. I'll just walk round the block. Back in a tick.'

She found him later in the park, hunched on a bench watching a squirrel on the edge of a litter bin. The squirrel saw her coming and glared at her fiercely, as if she was the thief.

'Come on, Dad.'

'Just wish we knew,' he said quietly. 'Even if ... even if he is dead. It would be easier knowing.' He got up slowly, taking her hand to steady himself. 'You get used to the idea that you're there to protect your children, Karen. Then you have to get used to the idea that you can't.'

When she opened the front door, they were greeted by the smell of burning and Max flapping a tea towel around the kitchen.

'Shit! I kept watching them. Then I forgot. Sprouts. Little buggers have burnt to the bottom of the pan.'

'For God's sake, Max, can't you even cook a simple vegetable?'

He turned then, a wooden spoon in his hand, his bald skull red. He didn't need to be told how to cook, it wasn't his fault if he'd had to go and sort the children out because they were fighting again. And where had she been? Her father didn't need fussing over like a half-wit.

'If you hadn't been messing around on the computer, then you would have noticed the sprouts.'

'Pull yourself together, Karen. You and I both know what's going on here.'

'Do we?'

In the silence turkey fat spat against the insides of the hot oven.

'You've got to let it go,' Max's voice softened.

170

'What? What do I have to let go?'

'This business with Phil. This is your family, me, the children. We need you here. You can't do it all, something has to give.' He put the wooden spoon down. Wiping his hands on his blue-and-white apron, he hesitated, as if he wasn't sure whether to hug her. 'You don't need to work too, you know, we're doing all right. If you need more time for your dad, well that's OK, but perhaps you shouldn't try to cram work in too. That's all I'm trying to say.'

Karen held her breath. Part of her wanted to give in, give up. He turned away and ran the water into the sink to wash his hands. He seemed to have forgotten the impulse to hold her. Perhaps she'd imagined it. He dried his hands on the towel and folded it neatly over the radiator.

When the meal was finally on the table, Max did most of the talking. He did most of the drinking too. He filled every silence with attempts to draw Reg into conversation, including telling him about the Ptarmigan Project, a vast out-of-town shopping mall he was designing. According to Max it would regenerate a community blighted by high unemployment.

'What was there before?' Reg asked, a dry shred of turkey halfway to his mouth. Karen watched. It was like the beginning of a car crash, the moment when one notices that the light is red, that the car is still moving, that the road is not entirely clear. Max saw nothing.

'Load of old factories. Terrible mess really.'

'Factories, eh? Where people worked. Mmm... Skilled labour.' He chewed slowly. 'What do those

171

working men and women do in the new shopping centre? Window shop? Shelf stack?'

While Max launched further into his sales pitch, Karen watched her father's jaw tighten. Her husband finally remembered to whom he was talking, and just before the moment of impact, steered drunkenly in another direction. They were saved from further disaster by Max's phone.

'Does he ever turn it off?' Reg muttered, not quietly enough.

'Text from Trisha and Paul,' Max said. 'Happy Christmas! They're having lunch at Middlewood Hall. They took Trisha's mum and dad.'

Later, while Karen washed up, her father stood outside the back door with his pipe. As the sweet smell of smoke reached her, she felt like a little girl again, ready to throw her arms round his legs and be swung up into the air. When he came back in, there was a drip on the end of his nose. He hadn't felt it. She handed him a piece of kitchen towel and wished he wasn't getting older.

'I suppose you'd rather be at Middlewood Hall too,' he said, 'if you didn't have your poor old dad staying. I bet they don't burn the sprouts.'

'I bet they do. They probably call it Bruxelles Brulées and charge extra.'

He almost laughed, but it came out as a sigh.

'I don't know what to think, Karen,' he cleared his throat. 'I haven't felt very close to your brother for the last few years. But every Christmas, he did at least send a card, pick up the phone.'

'I know.' She put her arm round his tweedy shoulders.

172

They were in bed early. Max turned away from her, his nose in a new book about men and their ties.

'We should have goose next year. Everyone has goose.' And then, almost immediately, he was snoring and the book slid to the floor.

On her bedside table her mobile phone was plugged into its charger. She turned it on. There were no messages. She thought about tiptoeing downstairs to get Charlie's card. She could text him a Happy Christmas, but he was probably with someone. She didn't want to cause any trouble.

## BONFIRE NIGHT: 4.30 p.m.

Phil turned off the dual carriageway and slowed into the narrow lane towards the quarry. The light was almost gone and he flicked his headlights on to full beam, startling a rabbit, which froze before turning and scarpering with a flick of its white tail. Where the lane dipped down towards the quarry itself, the trees and bushes appeared blacker. Beyond them an endless darkness looked like it could suck in an unwary traveller. He laughed at how easily he could scare himself, but he couldn't wait to get the stock in the shed and be on his way home.

He veered right onto the track and noticed a glow leaking through the caravan's thin curtains. There was another car parked in front, a dark-green Vauxhall Astra. He cut the van engine and

173

got out, leaving the lights on. He circled the empty car. There was a grey suit jacket hanging from the handle above the rear window. Phil tapped on the door of the caravan and it was opened immediately. The girl was wearing a long baggy T-shirt and her legs were bare.

'Hello again.' She smiled as if she was pleased to see him. He was confused for a moment.

'I thought you'd be at work,' he said.

A man's voice from inside the caravan called out, 'Eh! What's going on?'

'I am at work.' The smile fell. 'I've got to go now.'

She closed the door. Phil stood for a moment, looking at the scratched plastic window, frosted with condensation trapped behind a dirty orange curtain. A drop of water detached itself and ran like a tear towards a greenish strip of rubber sealant.

'You thick bugger,' he muttered to himself. 'Potato picking in November?'

He turned back to his van. The last cup of coffee had made its way through his system and he needed to pee. He liberally sprayed the near-side wheel of the Astra and was reminded of the neighbours' cats marking territory in his dad's suburban garden.

Over beyond the dual carriageway the haze, which lit up the ragged edge of the Chasebridge estate, was interrupted by a sudden burst of bright green; like a flower head spitting stars. It was the first firework, sent up early as dusk turned to evening. He rolled a cigarette and walked along the field edge, watching the skyline for the next

174

firework. The whole situation in the caravan made him feel sick. Another burst of colour, a cluster of purple and gold exploding above the streetlights. He lit his cigarette and drew on it, pinpointing the moment when the nicotine rush claimed that quiet spot in the centre of his brain. Then he heard someone cry out.

Phil turned back towards the caravan. His boots ground the loose stones of the track, picking up a rhythm until he was running. The cold metal catch sprang under his fingers, the door so flimsy that it bounced as he flung it back. Then he was inside. A tea-light in a saucer on the edge of the sink cast shadows over a landscape of two dirty cups, nesting on the plates they'd eaten their sandwiches off at lunchtime. Beyond this was another tableau, framed by the sweating walls of the van itself, candlelit and frozen at Phil's entrance. The girl was on the far corner of the bed, her mouth gagged with a pair of tights, her wrists tied with a man's leather belt and hooked above her head on the edge of the curtain pelmet. She was naked. A dark-haired man, fully dressed in a shirt and tie but with his trousers round his ankles, stood leaning forward, his hands taking his weight. Phil was reminded of the stance of a mountain gorilla. The man turned and his mouth opened but no sound came. He tried to grab at the waistband of his trousers but Phil was already on him, his right fist raised, and then dropped square into the man's face. Something under his knuckle seemed to crumple. Cartilage, bone maybe. The man was sprawled backwards on the bed and then someone was screaming. It was the girl, the tights in her hand, the belt hanging empty on the edge of the pelmet. She threw herself at Phil.

'What you doing? Stop it!'

She was pushing him backwards towards the sink. His back hit the edge of the unit and he felt the pile of crockery slide away. Cups and plates landed and shattered on the floor. The blood was spreading across the man's face. He seemed to forget about his trousers as he felt for his nose.

'You fucking bitch!' he shouted. 'That's your game, is it? Well you're not going to rob me, you and your fucking pimp!'

The man picked up a broken plate from the floor and then he was on his feet, lunging forwards in that tiny space; the light of the candles flickering off the sharp edge of the china.

## CHAPTER EIGHTEEN

The Doncaster Central Police Christmas party was well underway in the room above the New Moon Chinese Restaurant. Sean was on his third JD and Coke when Sandy Schofield dragged him onto the dance floor, singing at the top of her voice.

'All I want for Christmas is you!'

'You could give Mariah Carey a run for her money,' Sean said.

'Is it Mariah Carey?' Sandy shouted. 'I thought it was whatsisname. Oh I've forgotten.' She did a twirl and crashed into Carly.

'It is Mariah Carey,' Carly said. 'It's a cover. What's up, Sean? Dancing with my missus?'

'What did she call me?' Sandy asked.

They were good-humoured enough, but the drink was flowing.

'Go on, Sean,' Carly had a wicked look in her eyes, 'can't you find someone your own age?'

'Course I can, watch me now!' He spun round and spotted Lizzie by the buffet. 'Miss Morrison, are you dancing?'

He didn't wait for an answer, but took Lizzie by the arm and drew her onto the sticky dance floor. She was saying something, but he couldn't hear over the music. He reached round her waist in what he imagined was a ballroom hold.

'Don't be an arsehole, Sean,' she shouted. 'It doesn't suit you.'

Then she made a move so fast and hard with her hands that he thought his arm was going to come out of its socket.

Carly came to his rescue and led him to the bar. 'That was a nifty move. Kansetsu-waza, if I'm not much mistaken.'

'Sounds like something off the buffet.' He rubbed his wrist.

'It's jiu-jitsu. I must ask her where she trains.' Carly said. 'And you were being an arsehole.'

'Should I apologise? I should, shouldn't I?'

But he was saved the trouble by the appearance in the doorway of a man in a very slick pinstripe suit. Lizzie flashed a hard smile at no one in particular, wished them all a happy Christmas and left with the suit.

'Who was that?' Sandy joined them at the bar.

177

'Nice-looking feller. That her bloke?'

'That's Guy of the Rovers. He drives an Audi TT.' And he's a wanker, Sean said to himself, and ordered another JD and Coke.

At 12 Clement Grove, Arieta had taken up residence on the settee. Since she'd arrived, she'd woken early, tidied her bedclothes into a neat pile, opened the curtains and was usually reading a magazine at the kitchen table by the time Sean or Maureen were up. She usually offered him a coffee and would have cooked him breakfast, if he'd let her. She talked about the weather or something she'd seen on TV, but she wouldn't tell him any more about her life. She seemed content to live from day to day, watching television with Maureen and doing the crosswords in the puzzle magazines that filled the coffee table. She hadn't left the house, apart from standing in the back garden to have a cigarette. It was as if she was waiting for something, a sign that it was safe to move on. She appeared to have forgiven him for his play-acting and claimed to have known all along that he wasn't from a church.

'Too nice-looking,' she said.

On Christmas morning, he discovered she'd helped Maureen pack his stocking. She bounced up and down on the sofa as he opened it.

'If I had little brother, he would be like you.'

The last thing out of the old football sock – after the sweets and the apple and the satsuma, the playing cards and the joke book – wrapped so tightly he thought it was just more tissue paper, was a small square of fine cotton lacework. When he held it up to the light, he could see it was a picture of a goose.

'One day I fly south again, like goose. You have something to remember me by. It is only small because I have little time. But I remember what my grandmother taught me.'

'It's lovely.' He had no idea what he was supposed to do with it but Maureen came to his rescue. She'd bought him a postcard frame that fitted it perfectly, the delicate white pattern set off against the black card background.

They divided the turkey roast between the three of them and Arieta cried into her sherry because she said she was so happy.

On Boxing Day he was back on duty. He polished his left shoe until it shone; picked up the right shoe and held it close to his face. He'd already cleaned it, but there was a little mark, just off-centre near the toe. He spat and rubbed, as if having clean shoes would make pacing the estate any more enticing. He took the hi-vis jacket from the back of the kitchen chair. Police Community Support Officer in big silver letters on a blue background. He liked it when people called him officer. It didn't happen often, but ever since he'd found Su-Mai, he'd begun to feel like a real policeman. Now, though, he wondered if having Arieta in his house could get him into trouble, fired even. But he couldn't throw her back out onto the street, wouldn't be able to even if he wanted to. Maureen would never allow it.

'Got your warm socks on, love?' Maureen wrapped her dressing gown tightly around her.

'It's going to be cold out there. There was a hard frost last night.'

She wasn't wrong. It was bitter. He walked fast to keep his feet warm and his toes from going numb. He wished he had someone to talk to, but Carly had been called in for a meeting to question her conduct on Christmas Eve. By her own admission she'd shoved a teenager who'd been giving her lip. Sean hadn't seen the incident, but he imagined the lad was asking for it. Today he'd have to be the Lone Ranger again, walking the mean streets of the estate.

He checked his watch. Just gone eight o'clock in the morning. Nice and quiet. No one about. This lull between Christmas and New Year felt like a truce in the middle of a battle. He took the road up towards the recreation ground and sat down for a breather on a low concrete wall that skirted the corner of the Eagle Mount blocks. A dog was snuffling through ripped bin bags against the wall opposite. It seemed to sense him watching and returned his stare. He whistled to see what it would do, but it ignored him and turned back to the bags. A window opened on the first floor and someone threw a shoe down in the dog's direction.

'Fuck off, Ruby, you little bastard! Declan, get that bloody dog in, she's after the turkey bones.'

Within a minute a door slammed and Declan appeared from the flats. Sean stood up and crossed over.

'Hello there, having a good holiday?'

'S'all right.' The boy peered up at him. 'You were the one when we found that lass, weren't you?'

'Yes, you did a good job there, son.'

'Yeah? And I've found summat else.'

He didn't say any more, but concentrated on trying to pull Ruby away from the bin bag. The dog braced her back legs and engaged him in a tug of war.

'Do you want a hand?'

'All right.'

Sean got hold of the dog's collar with both hands behind her neck, hoping she wouldn't be able to bite him at that angle. Together they tugged her towards the back door of the block. As they got close, the dog finally relaxed, and Declan managed to shut her inside. They heard her claws skitter on the concrete stairs;

'She knows where to go. She'll bark at the door and they'll let her in, if they feel like it.' He turned back to Sean, a grin playing across his face. 'Aren't you going to ask me?'

'OK then, what have you found?' Sean sighed.

'There's a caravan in the quarry.'

'Oh?'

'Might have been nicked.'

Sean thought of old Mr Mayhew and how he'd agreed to help him find his missing caravan.

'Go on then, let's have a look.'

When Sean was a kid the quarry was still functioning. The lorries hurtled back and forth along the narrow lane, coating the brambles with a fine yellow dust. It must have closed down eight or nine years ago. Now grasses and thistles punctured the Tarmac. A hoar frost made it almost beautiful, if it hadn't been for the bin bags and the old tyres, carpets and fridges piled up in

181

mounds under the hawthorn hedge at either side.

'Not a good day,' had been the response of the operator when he called it in. She pointed out that half the station was still on holiday, so maybe he should just have a look and then radio back if it looked like the stolen caravan. He looked down at Declan, trying to match his footsteps with a frown of concentration on his small face. The boy's legs struck out ahead of him like a tin soldier. Chasebridge kids were either overweight or underweight. There was no in-between. Declan was one of the skinny type with hard cheekbones and large eyes glowering under a choppy fringe. It was a quiet day; it couldn't do any harm to give the boy a bit of positive attention. PCSOs were meant to be role models; that's what the training manual said. The lane climbed past a potato field. Through a broken wooden gate, Sean could see the ring road on the other side. Downhill and around the next bend was the entrance to the quarry itself. The gate there was a sturdy, five-bar metal construction with a large chain and padlock. Sean was wondering whether to climb or vault over it, when Declan tugged at his sleeve.

'This way. There's a guard dog through there.'

He steered Sean off the lane to the right and on to a path that snaked steeply up from the base of the quarry and round the side. They ducked under self-seeded sycamores with spindly trunks. The ground was rocky now and the trees hung on with shallow roots. Sean guessed they must be nearly at the top of the quarry but it was hard to see the edge beneath the undergrowth. He was glad that Declan was in front.

182

'Careful here,' he said and gestured to Sean to stay back. The path seemed to crumble away to their left and they were forced to tuck up behind a tree that Sean didn't dare hold on to for support.

'Nearly there. Look!'

When Sean looked down, he saw the rock below them falling away in a sheer vertical cliff, punctuated by scrubby plants that had rooted where it didn't seem possible. At the foot of the cliff was a patch of short trees and bushes surrounding a pool of dark water, from which the back end of a caravan stuck up like an enormous ducktail.

'I need to get a closer look,' Sean said. He listened hard, but there was no sound other than the wind in the trees and the dull hum of the ring road behind them. 'Are you sure about the guard dog?'

'There's a sign,' Declan said. 'It's got a picture of a snarly toothed German shepherd on it.'

Sean thought the guard dog was long gone and the sign probably dated back to when the quarry was last in use.

'We'll be OK. Come on, let's go.'

They made their way down to the edge of the quarry yard. Two graffiti-covered buildings stood silently, their windows boarded up. Beyond the yard, nothing disturbed the surface of the water.

'You come up here a lot?' Sean asked.

The boy shrugged.

'I used to,' Sean said, 'when I was about your age. It was busier then.'

Declan peered at him, as if he didn't believe Sean had ever been a kid. Yet there was only ten years between them.

'Got freaked out the last time,' Declan said.

'By the dog?'

'No. Up there,' Declan whispered. 'There was a ghost.' He pointed up to the edge of the quarry, in the direction of the viewpoint they'd just left. A couple of metres from where they'd been standing a pattern of destruction scarred the low trees and undergrowth from the lip of the quarry to where the caravan had come to rest in the water.

'No such thing as ghosts,' Sean said. They were walking round the edge of the pool now, its water dark and bottomless.

'There was lights flickering in that caravan. It was parked under the trees up there. Brandon saw it too. He nearly shat himself. I told my brother and he said it were another prozzie in there. But I think it was something else.'

'When was this?'

The boy shrugged. They'd reached the caravan. Its wheels had caught on the muddy edge of the pool so only one end was submerged. Sean's feet slid in the clay at the water's edge and he wished he was wearing rubber boots, not his uniform black shoes. Through the murky rear window, he could see an orangey coloured fabric.

'Bingo!' Mr Mayhew's caravan. Not that it would be much use to him now.

Declan stood on tiptoe next to him, peering through the plastic window.

'What's that?' He was pointing at a shape, slumped in the corner of the bed.

'Shit!' Sean's voice carried clearly across the still water, the 't' bouncing back for a split-second from the quarry walls. It was the body of a man.

It didn't seem that anyone was in a hurry to get the body out, but finally Lizzie Morrison arrived with a couple of burly looking guys in SOCO uniforms. She greeted Sean with a nod as they all struggled into their white suits. He noticed that she didn't offer him a smile.

'OK.' Lizzie turned to her two colleagues. 'Let's have a look inside. I'm not getting frostbite waiting for CID.'

She and the SOCOs put on waders and gloves while Sean stood back. Lizzie was clearly following procedure this time. One of the two SOCOs asked him to keep the scene secure. 'Twenty metres distance and no bystanders please.'

That meant Declan. He walked with him to the edge of the quarry yard and made him promise not to bring any of his mates back up here to rubber-neck.

Sean kept a low profile at the station. He wouldn't have minded a bit of praise, but the general consensus was that it was really bad timing on his part, when everyone had been enjoying a bit of family time over the festive season. A team had to be pulled in from across the region to examine the caravan and now every spare corner was given over to temporary office space. The body of an unknown male had gone to the morgue to wait for Huggins, the senior pathologist, to get back from a family Christmas in Aberdeen. The quarry, the field and the track from the bypass were all subject to fingertip searches. The proximity of two bodies could be a coincidence but had to be explored, so the lay-by was being scrutinised again too. Anyone who could be found was brought in to lend a hand. Sean found himself shuffling across the potato field next to Carly.

'Have you been forgiven?' Sean asked.

'For shoving a little scrote who deserved it?' she said. 'We'll see. I don't reckon anyone's going to give me a disciplinary while there's a panic on. They'll probably just send me on a course.'

Blue-and-white tape marked off the place where the caravan had been, before someone had seen fit to shove it over the edge of the quarry. Sean watched a detective constable following the stony track around the low trees, which marked the lip of the quarry, eyes to the ground, until he stopped and stood up straight. He was looking at a black Nissen hut. It wasn't visible from the lane, or Sean would have noticed it when he walked up with Declan, but he recognised it. When he was a kid they used to hide in there. It was full of hay bales back then, when this field was covered with grazing sheep. Someone had repaired it with a section of new corrugated metal along one side and its steel doors were wide open. The detective constable got out his notebook and started to write.

When he got back to the station after a two-hour stint, Sean went straight to the gents. The cold air and too much coffee was playing hell with his system. As he came out, the door of the ladies opened and he was face-to-face with Lizzie. She was shaking water off her hands and her face was damp too.

'That's better!' Her tone was brisk. 'I don't feel like the smell's attached to me any more.'

186

'Right.'

None of the words struggling to form into an order in his head seemed like the sort of thing she'd want to hear. He waited for her to fill the silence but she was walking away down the corridor. He didn't want it to look like he was deliberately following her, but he needed to go in the same direction, so he took out his phone and walked slowly, composing a text to Maureen to say what time he'd be home. His nan wasn't likely to pick it up any time soon. She only turned on her phone when it suited her; generally believing it was for emergencies, not day-to-day communication, but it gave him something to do.

'Oh, Sean,' Lizzie turned and he looked up at her, his heart lifting in the same moment. 'Did you know, the file on Su-Mai is definitely going to be reopened?'

'Really?'

'Apparently the Chief Superintendent's spitting feathers about the original investigation. He's on a skiing holiday in Austria with his family, trying to get a flight back as we speak. I wouldn't like to be in Burger's shoes.'

'They wouldn't fit.'

'Yawn, the old ones are not the best ones.' But the corner of her mouth definitely twitched. Maybe he'd be forgiven for manhandling her on the dance floor.

In the Ops Room, Sandy Schofield was typing up the scene-of-crime notes.

'Something here for you, Sean, love, something on your body, or should I say your second body.' Recognition at last, even if it was only from

187

Sandy. 'They found a phone, did you know that? In the caravan. Says here that *the mobile phone has a splintered fascia, as if it had received a heavy blow.* Now why would someone want to hit a phone?'

'What if the phone was used to hit the vic?'

'There'd be splinters of the phone fascia on the body and it doesn't say that here. Not visible anyhow. We'll have to see what comes out in the post-mortem.'

Sean looked over her shoulder at the report. There was an estimate of how long the body had been there: two to three months.

'That all they've got?'

'So far, until the post-mortem's done and all the lab reports come back. No wallet, no driving licence. He was quite well preserved, it says here. The way he was lying kept him in the dry end of the van, out of the water. And there's this bit in the notes, just about to type it in; they've been on to the phone company, last call made to the phone at 10.00 a.m., November 5th, from a landline with a North Lincolnshire STD code.'

Sean had a hunch that was the same date as the last known sighting of Mrs Friedman's brother, who came from North Lincolnshire. It was also the day Donald was supposed to visit the catering trailer to dust for prints, but he was a day late and found it vanished. Was it a coincidence? Maybe if Burger hadn't been so quick to write off Su-Mai, this second death wouldn't have happened. He only had Declan's brother's word for it so far, but he had a feeling that this new caravan was operating the same trade as Su-Mai's refreshment bar. When he got upstairs to the CID office, he

188

didn't bother knocking. Barry King looked like he was about to tell him to push off, but Sean didn't give him the chance.

'I think I can ID this morning's caravan victim. I'll bet you he's called Philip Holroyd and he's from Moorsby-on-Humber.'

The detective looked at Sean and shifted his chewing gum from one cheek to the other.

'Nice one, Columbo, that would explain why the mobile phone we found by the body was registered to a Philip Holroyd of Moorsby-on-bloody-Humber.'

'Oh. You know.'

'Yup.' Burger looked at his screen. 'We'll need to get the grieving loved ones to have a look at him, get a definite ID. I've got the landline number linked to the mobile contract. I'll enjoy telling them what their dirty fucking relative was up to when he met his maker.'

'So it's true?'

'What is?' Burger looked up.

'The boy at the quarry said there was a prostitute...'

'In the van? Mmm...' Burger stabbed a fat finger towards his computer screen. 'Just seen it in the forensic report.'

Sean looked at him for a moment, his belly rolling over his belt where it pushed against the buttons of his shirt. Something didn't hang together, and not just Burger's outfit, but Sean couldn't quite put his finger on what it was. He decided that he wanted to be the one to break it to the man's sister. It wasn't protocol, but he felt he owed it to her. He also wanted to tell her he'd been there himself, put two and two together and pretty much confirmed the ID. He didn't want to overstep the mark, as his nan would say, but this was still his case, no doubt about it. His case and his body.

## CHAPTER NINETEEN

When she heard the familiar voice on the other end of the phone, she couldn't place it at first. She was standing at the breakfast bar in the kitchen, wiping up a milky trail of cereal.

'Mrs Friedman?'

He told her his name and that he was phoning from the police station in Doncaster, then she realised what was coming.

'A body has been found.'

Not a man, Karen thought, just a body. Sean Denton was still speaking, something about a mobile phone. She remembered ticking a box, giving her name as next of kin. He was saying they were waiting for positive identification.

'Where is he?'

'The mortuary at Doncaster Royal Infirmary.'

Pinpricks of light danced around her eyes. She took a sharp breath and held on to the side of the kitchen counter and let her legs lower her onto a stool.

'I...'

'Mrs Friedman? I know this must come as a shock to you.'

'It's OK... I'm still here... Just trying to take it in.' Her voice was like lead in her ears. 'I'll come. I'll identify him.'

She blinked hard, tried to think in some normal way: practical thoughts about the house, the cat, husband, children. The order was wrong. Max first. Max was at work, dealing with the next stage of the shopping-centre project. He was essential to the shopping centre project, but no use to her. No use at all. Children. She'd have to make arrangements for the children.

'I can come tomorrow? Or it could be today?'

'Well, it would be helpful to have an identification as soon as possible,' he said.

'Of course.'

'And, Mrs Friedman, if there is anything I can do to help, please let me know.'

In the clock-ticking quiet of the kitchen, a draught caught a silver streamer, it waved sadly from where Sophie had draped it over the window frame. Karen needed to call her father, but not yet. Let him have a few more minutes or hours of believing Phil was out there somewhere, living a new life. She should ring Stacey. They hadn't spoken to each other since November. Why had she given her name as next of kin, not Stacey's? She couldn't remember. It didn't matter now; by the time she got through, Stacey already knew.

'Thanks for ringing, Karen, but the police have telephoned.' Stacey's voice was controlled. 'I didn't realise you'd reported him missing, but I suppose I'm glad you did... No, you don't need to come, I'll go over this afternoon.'

'Will you be OK?'

191

'I don't know.' Stacey hesitated. 'I'll take a friend. The policeman said it might be a bit unpleasant.'

'I'm sure…'

'No, I mean because he's been there some time, where they found him.'

Sean Denton hadn't mentioned that. A second wave of knowledge hit her. Phil wasn't just dead. He'd been dead all along.

'Do they know what happened?'

'Not yet. They'll do a post-mortem. And an inquest, I suppose.'

'Have you told Holly?' Silence. Then Stacey spoke in a different tone, like she was explaining something to a very small child.

'Holly thinks he's gone away. I think that's for the best, don't you?'

Karen looked at the clock, it wasn't yet ten. 'If you can wait for me, I'd like to come with you. I could be in Doncaster by lunchtime, no problem.'

'There's no need…'

'Stacey, look, he's my brother…'

'Well…'

'You could pick me up at the station,' Karen said. 'I'll phone from the train, let you know what time it's getting in.'

Then she was rushing, grabbing her handbag, finding her purse, knocking over Christmas cards in her clumsiness. The snowdrops on a green background caught her eye. She picked up Charlie's card and shoved it in her bag. She let herself out of the back door and tapped on next-door's kitchen window. Trisha was all smiles and understanding, happy to help. She hugged Karen

192

and said, 'you poor thing', over and over until Karen thought she would scream. Trisha suggested that Ben and Sophie could sleep over, but Karen insisted she'd be back for them tonight.

She stepped off the train at Doncaster Station and pulled her coat closer against the bitter wind. As the crowd thinned out, onto other platforms and down the stairs, she looked for Stacey. She wasn't waiting at platform level, so Karen followed the signs to the exit and into the open air, where a line of taxis and private cars jostled for space at the pick-up point. After twenty minutes it was clear that Stacey wasn't coming. Karen couldn't understand it. She'd left a message on Stacey's mobile from the train but there'd been no response. There was no queue for taxis. Karen got into a white mini-cab and asked for the hospital.

The automatic doors swished her into an overheated foyer, where the air hummed with low voices and the squeak of wheelchairs on linoleum. Karen tried to shake off the memory of spending so many hours waiting for her mother in hospitals. She checked a map for directions. At the mortuary, there was a young woman in uniform behind the desk, a nurse or some kind of orderly, Karen wasn't sure. Fair, straight hair tucked behind her ears, she didn't look old enough to be dealing with the dead.

'How may I help you?'

Karen gave her name and Phil's. The woman frowned and asked Karen to wait a moment. She disappeared through a set of double doors, panelled with opaque glass, and returned some minutes later.

'I'm sorry to have kept you waiting. It seems you may have had an unnecessary, journey. Mr Holroyd has already been positively identified by his wife and the body's been transferred to pathology.'

'I don't understand... I'm his sister, she was going to wait for me...'

'I'm so sorry.'

'Please, I really need to see him.' Karen's hands were on the desk, tensed, as if she was clawing her way towards the young woman. They didn't seem to belong to her.

'I know this is a stressful time but, please, you must understand. We have to follow procedure.'

Karen wandered back through endless corridors feeling numb and nauseous. The sun had gone behind a tall building, leaving a haze of purple light outside the sealed world of the hospital. Beyond the glass doors the cold was a shock for the second time that day. She walked quickly, in what she hoped was the direction of the station. She started to warm up. Stacey's phone was still switched to voicemail and she gave up leaving messages. When her own phone rang, she pounced on it. It was Max. He'd come home early and wanted to know where she was and where the hell the children were. Karen stood still and looked around her.

'I'm outside Netto in Doncaster. The children are at Trisha's. Phone me again when you've checked your messages.'

She cut him off and started walking again, not certain that this was even the right road, but she was past caring. If she kept going she wouldn't scream. Sweat was prickling her armpits. She remembered that she hadn't phoned her dad. Maybe she would get Stacey to do that too, since she'd decided to take over. She turned the corner and the railway station was suddenly there in front of her, sooner than she was expecting. She quickened her pace and scanned the departure board: two minutes to get to Platform Five. She wasn't going to get stuck in this shitty town again. Her legs felt like lead as she ran, but she made it to the train and jumped on board as the whistle blew and threw herself into the first empty seat, gasping for breath, while the station slipped away.

Max hadn't rung back. She wondered if she should check whether he had picked up the children. The anger she felt towards him was frightening. She tried to tell herself that it wasn't his fault; just ironic that this would be the one day he came home early, to find life going on without him. She toyed with her phone, checking backwards and forwards through her contacts for someone to talk to. She looked out of the window. There was something odd. They passed a town of new houses with an old castle on a hill. This wasn't on the way to York. The train stopped at a station she didn't recognise, then announced that the next station would be Sheffield.

She looked out at flat rectangles of land, piled with mountains of brick and twisted metal. It had started to rain. One windowless factory was still standing, its jagged roof open to the sky. The feeling of wanting to scream gripped her again. She had managed everything up until now. She had listened to the young officer, the nurse too.

She could have screamed at them, but she didn't. She held herself back, but now she was trapped in this tin box on wheels, going the wrong way through a place that looked as if it had been broken by giants, and the only person she could scream at was herself for getting on the wrong bastard train. There was a packet of tissues at the bottom of her handbag. She put her hand in and scrabbled around for them, not caring that her pens and lipstick were falling out on the seat beside her. She needed to smother what was trying to get out of her.

Her hand caught against the corner of something stiff. She pulled out a Christmas card: green background, hand-painted snowdrops. Did she put this in her bag this morning? She couldn't remember doing it. There was a phone number. The train was going to Sheffield. He lived in Sheffield. He might be there now. She punched the number in.

'Hello?'

'Charlie?' She didn't wait for him to reply. Her words tumbled out: about Phil, about the hospital and Stacey, that she was on the wrong train and was on her way to Sheffield by mistake. 'I can't believe it, that he's dead. I needed to see for myself, I'm sorry...'

She kept apologising for laying all this on him, but she didn't know anyone else she could talk to. She caught her breath and heard Charlie saying he would be there and what time did the train come in? He would be there. He would be there.

In the dark press of winter coats, she saw him

straight away, pushing down the stairs to meet her. She tried to hurry towards him, but it was crowded and her legs were heavy, like in a dream where she couldn't run. When he wrapped his arms around her and held her against his chest, she felt the vibration of his voice, calming, soothing.

They walked quickly along the wet streets, as cars slicked past through the darkening afternoon.

'It's not far,' he said, as they turned a corner into a narrow square of new flats with glass balconies. He led her up a flight of concrete stairs, which opened on to a corridor of front doors; each painted a flat matt, primary colour. They stopped at a red one. He started to apologise that his flat was only small, as he fumbled for his keys. Once inside, he took her coat and she wandered like a sleepwalker into a kitchen with a fitted wooden table and bench. Some disconnected part of her brain was marvelling at the clever use of the tight space. There appeared to be a bathroom to the left of the front door and then one other room, which looked like a combined bedroom and sitting room. It was neat and square, with a high ceiling. She couldn't imagine how Charlie's long limbs survived without constantly bumping into the furniture.

Books lined two walls and the third was taken up by a magnificent wooden structure. It was a bed on stilts, high enough for an adult to stand underneath. In the centre of the remaining space, a battered brown leather sofa was strewn with notepads and books, which spilt over onto a red

197

Persian rug.

He put his arms round her waist and she turned to face him. He kissed her, very gently, first on the forehead, then the bridge of her nose and her cheeks until they found each other's mouths. His fingers moved under her shirt, finger to rib, bone to bone. She undid his trousers, and rolled his jeans down over his thighs. Somehow they tripped, still two-thirds dressed, to the sofa. She gathered him beneath her and they didn't come apart, even when they slid onto the floor.

When it was over, they lay on the rug among the books and papers. He reached back to the sofa for a blanket, and pulled it across them. They didn't speak for a long time. Then from somewhere outside, she heard the muffled chimes of a church clock. She counted six and checked her watch.

'You OK?' he whispered.

'I had no idea what time it was...'

'Do you need to go?'

'I don't know. No, actually I thought it was later. But I think I need to eat something.'

He disentangled himself from her and the blanket, kissed her hair and stood up. He did up his trousers and walked towards the kitchen.

'I think I could conjure something up. Omelette?'

'Sounds great.'

She could hear him in the next room, clattering pans, chopping something, whisking up the eggs. The smell coming from the kitchen was good and she felt calm. It shouldn't be like this. She rubbed her knuckles into her temples. She ought to feel terrible. But it was as if she had split in two. Somewhere another Karen had a dead brother, a husband and children at home. While in this cube of a room, with its bed on stilts and its battered brown sofa, the present Karen Friedman was glowing from the touch and the taste and the sheer ache of having made love to Charlie Moon. She looked at her bag and told herself to put her hand in for her phone. She had no idea what she was going to say.

Max had already sent a text. *All back home, let me know your ETA. Shall I keep dinner?*

She texted back: *Train's running late, don't wait up.* As she leant into the sofa and pulled her clothes straight, she wondered when she would start feeling guilty.

They sat at right angles at the tiny table in the corner of the kitchen. He watched her as she plunged her fork into the spongy egg. The omelette was packed with mushrooms and potatoes, and seasoned with gritty black pepper and paprika. Her tongue felt alive.

'You can cook.'

'I can cook, I can read a book...' He laughed. 'I used to read those Dr Seuss books all the time to Sam, my son. You end up thinking in rhymes.'

'Do you like *Green Eggs and Ham?*'

'It was Sam's favourite.'

'Sophie loved *Hands, Hands, Fingers, Thumb* – it's got all these crazy monkeys drumming...' Her voice trailed off. They'd broken the spell. Their children were in the room, in the middle of the table between them.

He broke the silence. 'Can I get you something

to drink?'

'Just coffee.' She needed to have her wits about her to get home.

He had his back to her, reaching into cupboards for cups and the coffee jug.

'Is Sophie your daughter?'

If they'd been fully naked, it would have been obvious that she was a mother. The stretch marks were like tree rings, aging her belly with each pregnancy.

'Yes, she's eleven. And my son Ben is six.' She kept Cara hidden; she was not ready to talk about her. It was not her body, but her dead baby, which seemed like too much of a betrayal of Max.

'You have a husband?' He put the coffee cups on the table and poured a strong black stream of steaming liquid.

'Yes.'

'I thought perhaps you did. So I didn't ask.'

'What about you?'

'Divorced three years ago, hence the studio flat. Louise still lives in London with Sam.'

'Would it have made a difference, if you had asked earlier, I mean?'

He looked into his cup, stirring the sugar into a whirlpool. 'It might have done. But sometimes we choose not to know things.'

There was the sound of cutlery on china as they ate. Outside a tram went over the points. She knew it couldn't last.

'I'm going to have to go.'

'I'll walk you to the station. I don't want you getting lost.' She was happy to let him worry about her. That felt good too.

It was ten o'clock by the time she got home. There was a light on in the dormer window of their bedroom, but the fairy lights on the Christmas tree were off. Its ghostly shape watched her through the bay window as she found her key. She calculated how many steps would get her to the first-floor bathroom. She needed a shower. She'd just bolted the bathroom door when she heard Max on the stairs.

'That you, Karen?'

'Yes, shh, don't wake the kids, I'll be up in a minute.'

'You OK? Trisha told me ... about Phil. Look I'm sorry I was a bit...'

'I'm all right. I'll just have a wee and clean my teeth.' That was stupid. How could she run the shower without him hearing it? Especially as she was normally a morning shower person. She would have to use the train journey as her excuse.

He was asleep when she got upstairs. Her skin felt clean, her hair too wet to lie down straight away. She turned off the light and sat upright in the dark, listening to the rise and fall of his breathing and the clicking of the cooling radiator, feeling the memory of Charlie's lips on her lips and his hands on her breasts. In the stillness, she felt something lurch up inside her. She thought she was going to be sick. But it was a sound that was trying to get out. She covered her mouth to smother the moan, and found herself sobbing into her hands.

# CHAPTER TWENTY

By the end of the second day, the buzz at Doncaster Central had begun to die down. Most of the officers who'd been pulled in from their annual leave had gone home to their families. The forensic team had come back in when it got too dark. In the morning they would start cataloguing their evidence. When old Mr Mayhew called, there was nobody left except Sean to tell him that yes, his caravan had been recovered, and no, he couldn't have it back just yet; it was evidence in a murder inquiry. When the last stragglers signed out at nine o'clock and headed home to their families, it was just Sean, Lizzie and DI Rick Houghton, from the Drug Squad, who didn't have a better offer. Rick asked Sean to join them before Lizzie had a chance to object. They sat in the furthest corner of the pub, away from the bar, and compared notes.

'So, you found it on a shelf?' Rick was saying, when Sean came back from the bar with the drinks.

Lizzie nodded. 'Completely dry. A Jiffy bag with two wraps of heroin. Hadn't been touched.'

'What about the vic, was he a user?' Sean said.

'Not according to Huggins.' Lizzie stirred her gin and tonic thoughtfully. 'They're waiting for blood tests, but there weren't any marks.'

'Maybe,' Sean said, 'it belonged to whoever was

202

working there.'

A man at the pool table let out a volley of swearing as his target ball veered wide of the pocket. Rick turned and gave the man a look, but Lizzie ignored him. She was fixed on Sean.

'What do you mean, working there?'

'The caravan,' he spoke slowly, not wanting to shout over the pub noise, 'it was a brothel, wasn't it? Like the snack bar trailer.'

'What makes you think that?'

Sean told her about Declan's brother's comment. 'And anyway, Burger said it was in the forensic report.'

She was staring at him now.

'What's this?' Rick said. 'How come I haven't seen it? Drug Squad has an interest in this too.'

'Sean?'

'Yesterday, Burger said...' but he ran out of words. He looked into his pint glass and remembered Sandy saying there wasn't much else, and something about waiting for test results. It had taken him three minutes to get upstairs to Burger's office. At that point there couldn't have been a mention of a brothel in any forensic report. Burger had made a mistake.

Lizzie pushed her drink away. 'I'm going to need a clear head to think this through.'

Rick looked at her quizzically. 'Anything you want to share?'

'Possibly. If what Sean says is right, I'll need check the vic's DNA against the semen samples from the catering trailer.'

Rick sighed. 'You'll have a job. DCI King authorised the disposal of all the evidence in the

Chinese girl's case. Straightforward OD. Nothing to investigate. All we've got is the written notes on her blood samples and a bit of hair that we sent off for a toxicology test.'

Lizzie looked stunned. 'Even though he knew that I ... oh, shit. No, he didn't know. I wonder if my authorisation got through in time? You see, Rick, I was following something up, some DNA with the catering trailer girl, it had a link with the Human Trafficking Service, but I kept it quiet.'

'Why keep it quiet?' Rick asked.

'Because I don't like him. And I know that sounds unprofessional, but ever since I started here, Burger's been meddling in my work. Do you think I'm going to be in trouble?'

Sean wasn't sure he should even be listening to this conversation, but he was part of it now. He couldn't unlearn what he knew.

'I've been around this station for a few years,' said Rick, 'and you could say, I've been waiting for most of those years for a moment like this.' He took a mouthful of beer and swilled it behind his teeth, before continuing. 'I think it might be the right time to have a chat with the Chief Superintendent. He's coming in first thing tomorrow.'

They sat in silence for a while. Sean's glass was empty, so he offered to buy another round.

'Always the gentleman,' Lizzie said brightly. 'Mine's an orange juice.'

'Gentleman? Well, makes a change from me being an arsehole, I suppose.' He meant it to sound light-hearted, like he was taking the mick out of himself, but it didn't come out right. She coloured instantly and looked like she was ready to slap him.

'Am I missing something?' Rick said. Sean and Lizzie both looked away. 'Actually, I think it's my round. You two have been very helpful, as it goes.'

He went up to the bar, leaving them sitting in silence, Sean cursing himself for being such an idiot.

'Look. I'm sorry about the party. I was drunk.' He rushed the words out, aware they sounded insincere. Since the things he really wanted to say to her couldn't be said, everything else seemed false.

'Don't worry about it.' She shrugged. The pool player pocketed the red and cheered himself on, as if he'd won the championship.

'So,' Rick said, when he got back to the table, 'let's stop work now, shall we? Did everyone have a nice Christmas?'

Sean mumbled something about it being all right.

'How about you, Lizzie?' Rick said. 'Big family do?'

'Actually it was grim. My parents rowed and my younger brother announced he was leaving university after one term to get a job as a diving instructor in the Maldives. I spent the whole day going from room to room, trying to get everyone to pull themselves together.'

Sean pictured her house, big enough to have plenty of rooms for everyone to sulk in separately. He tried to shake off the fact that he minded. It was pointless being jealous of her. He'd save that for Guy of the Rovers; he had to admit he was jealous of him.

'What about your Christmas, Rick?' she said,

205

giving Rick that lovely smile, the smile that had once fooled Sean into thinking she actually liked him.

'It was my turn to have the kids on Christmas Eve,' Rick said, 'and the wife had them Christmas and Boxing Day. I didn't mind; I spent the whole day in my pyjamas watching TV and eating and drinking what I wanted, when I wanted.'

'Sounds bliss!' Lizzie raised her glass. 'I was *so* relieved to get the call yesterday. I couldn't stand another day with them, if I'm honest.'

'Me too,' Sean said. 'I never thought of my nan as the fussing type, but now I've got two women trying to look after me, I'm beginning to feel smothered.'

'Two women?' Rick winked at him. 'Something you're not telling us?'

Lizzie kicked him under the table. They were supposed to be keeping Arieta secret. It was a nice kick though. A kick that meant they were a team again.

'Friend of my nan's is staying on the couch,' Sean said quickly. 'Double trouble.'

Arieta was still awake when he got back. So was Maureen. They were playing cards at the kitchen table, betting with matches.

'There you are, love, fancy a brew?'

'No, ta.'

'What about a snack? Carole came round again. She had a load more of those crisps with the Paki writing. Dirt cheap, she wanted rid of them, I think. I bought a whole box. I know you like them and Arieta's partial too.'

206

'Very nice,' Arieta said, licking salt off her fingers. 'Like at home. Spicy. You want?'

'Arabic writing, Nan, not Paki. And no, thanks, I'm going up. I'm done in.'

'Is it true they found a body?' Maureen said without looking up from her cards. 'They were talking about it in the paper shop at lunchtime.'

Arieta was dealing a fresh hand, two piles, face down.

'Yeah, it was in a caravan, belonged to that farmer I went to see. It turned up in the quarry, not half a mile from the farm. It had been on his land all along.'

Arieta's hand hesitated and a card hovered in the air. She brought it down slowly on the table.

'Damn. I lose count. I start again.'

His alarm called him out of a very deep sleep at seven the next morning. It was unusual to find the kitchen still in darkness. He put some bread in the toaster and flicked the kettle on.

As he made his way along his normal route, up through the Chasebridge estate, he stopped. There was a BMX bike leant up against the frame of one of the swings on the recreation ground. He could see why it had been dumped; the front wheel was buckled. It wasn't that particular bike that interested him though; it was Lee Stubbs. Stubbs had remembered Philip Holroyd's face and, more than that, he'd recalled the exact date he'd seen him. Bonfire Night. *Busy night. Lots of parties. He did some business with me. A little package. D'you get me?* Oh, yes, I've got you now, you little shite. He took out his phone and dialled.

'Lizzie, hi! Look I think it was Stubbs, Lee Stubbs, who sold the heroin that was in the caravan. He sold it to Philip Holroyd the day he went missing. He as good as told me.'

'Jesus, Sean, don't you sleep?' She sounded like she was chewing something, he tried to visualise what she had for breakfast. 'What are you saying? Stubbs is linked to the girl on the Chasebridge estate and to Holroyd?'

'Must be. I saw him with Taneesha McManus. We just need to link him to Flora Ishmaili and I bet we could get him for Su-Mai as well.'

She said she would mention it to Rick. Meanwhile she had something for him in return. The forensic sample for Human Trafficking had got to the lab before Burger had the chance to get rid of all the Su-Mai evidence, and the result was back. There was an ongoing case against a haulier based in Grimsby and it was ninety-nine per cent certain that their girl was in one of his lorries at some point.

Sean sat down on the wall of the rec and adjusted the phone against his ear to hear her better.

'Which means?'

'It means she was trafficked, and DCI Moon from HTS is coming over from Sheffield. He needs live witnesses, though, not dead ones. I think we should introduce him to Arieta. Maybe she'll open up to him.'

'What about Burger, what's he up to?'

'You haven't heard? He's off the case, pending an internal investigation. Rick Houghton's been brought in, as acting DCI in charge.'

The coloured lines on Sean's chart were beginning to connect. When he got home, he would put a bit more detail on. He'd picked out a nice purple marker from the stationary cupboard. That would do for the Chinese connection.

'Are you still there?' Lizzie asked.

'Yeah, sorry. Just thinking.'

'Well, don't overdo it.'

She sounded kinder than she had done for a while. He wasn't going to read too much into it this time, he promised himself. He rang off and turned the corner at Eagle Mount One. A pair of seagulls were circling the top of the block. As he quickened his pace, his phone began to vibrate in his vest pocket. He took it out and was surprised to see his nan's number on the screen.

'She's gone.' Maureen's voice sounded like she'd been crying.

'Arieta?'

'Taken her suitcase. Like she was never here. I know she wanted to go home, back to Kosovo but, Sean, she hadn't got enough money for that. I was putting a bit by for her, but she didn't know.'

'I'm coming back.'

He texted Lizzie with the news and set off down the hill at a run, walking only when he had no breath left. His phone pinged with an incoming text as he turned the corner into Clement Grove.

*Massive pain in neck, Sean. You'll have to find her. LM*

# CHAPTER TWENTY-ONE

Karen stood in Paul and Trisha's kitchen with a drink in her hand. It was New Year's Eve.

'Manhattan Iced Tea.' A man whose name she couldn't remember, in a pink V-necked jumper, was enthusiastically shaking another cocktail. 'Good, isn't it?'

She couldn't say. Everything tasted the same. She tried to smile. He must be the only person here who didn't know that she was the tragic neighbour whose brother had just been found dead. She preferred his ignorance to the pitying looks she was getting from the others. They didn't speak to her. Just squeezed out a pained smile and moved on to someone whose presence wasn't going to bring them down. She found sanctuary in the kitchen, where at least she could hear the music. *Once in a Lifetime* by Talking Heads was playing.

'Love this song!' The man did a little dance with the cocktail shaker. 'It's the story of my life.'

She smiled for real then. From the recesses of memory she had a feeling his name was Gavin and they had been introduced about two hours ago. It wasn't just the Manhattan Iced Tea, but nothing would stick. Grief was like childbirth, where memory was slippery. At quarter past eleven, Max appeared in the kitchen doorway carrying their coats. She had just started on a

Gin Sling, courtesy of Gavin.

'Are you coming?' It seemed a bit early to be leaving, especially as she was having such a good time. Max read her bemused look. 'To hear the Minster bells?'

Of course. 'Where are the children?' She was slurring a little.

'Sophie's coming, and Ben's asleep under Paul's desk on the landing. I'll wake him up, he wouldn't want to miss it.'

She put her glass down beside the sink. There was a bit of her that was still functioning. She would take Ben home. That would be the best thing for him, and for her too. The thought of being hugged and kissed by strangers on a damp street at midnight made her feel queasy.

'Thank you for the drinks, Gavin, you'd make a great anaesthetist.'

He bowed extravagantly. 'Glad to be of service.'

Max glowered at him. She had to turn away. A cocktail-induced smile was snaking across her face.

Ben didn't wake. She took off his shoes and tucked him into bed. When she came downstairs, Arnold the cat shifted on the sofa and rearranged himself on her lap. She put the television on and flicked channels until she found a movie that was halfway through. It was a western that she'd seen before, but she couldn't remember the title. She was drifting off to sleep when her mobile vibrated in her pocket. She answered it without looking.

'Hello?'

'Happy New Year,' Charlie said. Then she was

fully awake. 'Is this OK? I just wanted to...'

'It's great.' She muted the television and let the bullets fly across the Mexican village in silence. 'Everyone's gone to hear the bells.'

'You OK?'

'I'm OK.'

'I want to see you,' he said, 'tomorrow.'

She wanted to see him now, feel him holding her, but she didn't say it. The conversation turned to practical matters. A place, a time; he would pick her up from outside RAMA's office. She'd find some excuse, a New Year's Day walk, a ramble of some kind. If she left early enough the children wouldn't be awake, so there would be no question of them coming too. She hoped she could get away with telling Max that she'd mentioned it ages ago and he must have forgotten.

She put the phone down and stared at the muted film. There was a man lying in the dust on the street, his gun falling out of his hand. The phone rang again.

'Happy New Year, Mummy! We've been trying to get through for ages!'

She walked out of the house at eight o'clock the next morning. The note on the kitchen table said she'd gone for a walk to clear her head and she might have a look round the January sales. She was thinking, as she walked into town, how sleazy it all was, but how little she'd had to lie. Her head really did feel as if someone had wrung all the moisture from her brain and left it clattering around her skull like a walnut.

Outside the office, she turned her back on the

dead eyes of the china dolls in the shop window. She realised that she didn't know what car he drove. In the end there was no mistaking it. When a black, new-style VW Beetle pulled up, there wasn't another soul in sight.

They drove east towards the coast, through a world empty of people.

'I brought a picnic,' he said. 'Did you have breakfast?'

'Just coffee. When did you have time to sleep?'

'I didn't much, but I'm used to it. I used to do a lot of surveillance work. The mechanism's pretty fucked to be honest.'

At Bridlington, he parked on the front, facing a grey-green sea and a piercing blue sky. The wind rocked the car.

'I've been asking a few questions around Doncaster police station,' he said.

'About Phil?'

He nodded. 'About where he was found. There's something you need to know.'

'Are you allowed to do that? I mean if it's not your case?'

'Told them it was for a colleague. That's sort of true. RAMA are becoming a very important partner to the HTS.' He squeezed her thigh and left his hand there. She folded her own hands around it.

'Another half-truth,' she said. 'I'm getting good at those too.'

A pair of herring gulls hovered overhead. They appeared to be flying backwards as the wind took them.

'We could spend all day discussing the morality

213

of my intelligence techniques,' Charlie said, 'but do you want to know what I found out?'

She knew from his tone that it was something that she didn't want to hear. 'Keep it for later, Charlie. Just shut up for now and kiss me instead.'

He held her head in his hands and kissed her cheeks and all around her mouth before their lips met and their tongues played in and out. She climbed across into his lap, pulling at his belt and opened his fly.

'We should be careful,' he said.

'I've got a coil, it's OK.' She kissed his forehead. 'Or did you mean having sex in a car in broad daylight?'

Later, when the children were tucked up, she sat in bed in her pyjamas, looking at the pictures in a gardening magazine. The words were too hard, as if there wasn't space in her brain for them. When Max came in, she tightened her grip on the magazine, like a knight in chain mail, holding her shield. But it wasn't necessary. Max hadn't tried to start anything since the news of Phil's death. After Cara died, they didn't make love for weeks. Finally something had shifted and when they'd begun to have sex again, she remembered Max completely losing himself in her. As if it was therapy. A twinge of guilt tugged inside her. Maybe that's what she was doing with Charlie. She glanced up. Max was getting undressed with his back to her. Folding his trousers neatly over the back of the chair. She saw the tight ropes of muscle on either side of his spine. Saw them, that was all. She felt nothing.

# CHAPTER TWENTY-TWO

An inquest had been opened and adjourned to release the body for the funeral. It was booked for noon on a day that dawned suitably grey. The cemetery car park was packed. Karen and Reg got out of the car and looked around them. It quickly became apparent that most of the vehicles belonged to the mourners from the previous funeral; clusters of stout women and stooped men, nodding in recognition of a life well lived, appraising one another surreptitiously to see who would be next. A gust of damp air blew across the rows of new graves, neatly laid out on the right, while to the left of the gravel path, the chaotic beauty of crumbling old monuments was overgrown with ivy.

She tried to prepare her face. Civil but friendly? Sad but in control?

'What's up, love?'

'Sorry?'

'You're pulling faces. Is it heartburn?' Reg asked. 'Runs in the family.' He jiggled in his pocket for his packet of antacids. 'I keep them handy for special occasions.'

'Oh, Dad!' She laughed, somewhere on the edge of hysteria and despair. 'I was trying, I don't know, to get the right face on.'

'Well there you go. If you can't laugh, what can you do? And Philip's not here to be offended.' Reg wasn't taken in by the chapel or the stone angels. 'An expensive way of making ourselves feel better. The dead don't care. When you go, you go.'

Karen linked her arm into his and together they crunched up the path to the chapel. She spotted Jackie from The Volunteer Arms next to a big man in a flat cap – presumably Stan. An overweight woman in a tweed coat stood near them, holding Holly by the hand. Although they were still a couple of hundred yards away, Holly spotted them and broke free.

'Grandad!' She ran at full tilt, with the tweed-coat woman puffing behind, unable to keep up. This must be Stacey's mother. Her hair was tightly permed and the damp air had sent it off into sprigs of wiry antennae all over her head.

'Holly! Come back! I'm so sorry!' She called to them. Her shrill voice carried in the wind. 'Her grandad's parking the car. She's got mixed up.'

By the time Holly had wrapped her arms round Reg's legs, Stacey's mother had realised her mistake.

'Oh, I see,' she peered at him as if he were infectious. 'Mr Holroyd is it? My name's Clegg, I'm Holly's nana.'

Karen wondered if she was wearing an invisibility cloak. Mrs Clegg was doing her best to ignore her entirely. Holly looked up at her and there was a flicker of recognition, followed by a cherubic smile. By the time they got back up to the chapel, everyone else had gone in. Everyone else consisted of Jackie and Stan, Stacey and three slightly embarrassed-looking blokes, drinking pals from the pub maybe. A couple came in, both in their early twenties, at a guess. She wore a smart camel coat and he looked uncomfortable in a suit. She knew him from somewhere. Mrs Clegg took her daughter's arm and propelled her to the front row of seats. Holly let go of Reg's hand and skipped after them, while Jackie and Stan hovered awkwardly and settled a couple of rows behind Stacey.

'Let's sit at the back,' whispered Reg, slightly too loudly, 'in case we need a breath of fresh air.'

He'd got his hand firmly gripped around the pipe in his pocket. She guided him to the back row of seats, which had an uninterrupted view down the centre aisle to the plain pine coffin. The door to the outside was just in front of them, to their right. From this vantage point they saw two people come in after the vicar had started his preamble. An older man, red in the face, with windswept hair, who was busy tucking a hip flask into his pocket and another man, shorter and wearing a charcoal Crombie. She recognised him immediately. It was Johnny Mackenzie.

It was clear that this vicar had never met her brother. He'd been provided with a limited biography but had managed to get even that wrong. She winced at references to Philip's virtuosity on the trumpet.

'We note with sorrow that one should be taken so suddenly from his wife, Stacey, and his daughter, Haley.' Reg spluttered and Holly could be heard from the front.

'Nana, who's *Haley?*'

Karen wished they could all stop being so ridiculous; this was not what Phil would have wanted. How could he have been married to a woman who had arranged him such a crap funeral? Then she shivered to think what Max might consider appropriate if she didn't leave clear instructions. And if she got run over by a bus tomorrow, who would tell Charlie? Would he find out in time to come to her funeral? Without warning, she started crying, as much for herself as for Phil. Maybe that was what Reg meant; we do it for ourselves, not for the dead.

She wondered what Charlie was doing now. He'd texted her after their trip to the coast. *Can I call you?*

She'd replied: *Don't know, I'll call you, if that's OK.* She'd ignored two more texts and then he seemed to give up.

When the committal was over, Reg and Karen stumbled back out into the light. Nobody explained what would happen next. Jackie walked over to her.

'Karen?' She squeezed her arm. 'Such a sad business, and to be found like that.'

'Hi, this is my father, Reg Holroyd. Dad, this is Jackie. She runs the pub in Moorsby.'

'Pleased to meet you.' He shook her hand with a slightly formal bow.

'Are you coming to the graveside for the interment?' Jackie offered, but Reg looked horrified.

'For some reason I thought it was a cremation,' Reg said. 'I don't know why. It's just that it usually is.' He was already filling his pipe with tobacco and shuffling in his pocket for a box of matches. 'You seem to me, Jackie, to be a delightful human being, and in usual circumstances I would be

218

pleased to accompany you on a walk among these...' he waved the pipe across the vista of gravestones, 'monuments to human frailty. But I cannot, and will not, stand by any longer to see the discarded carcass of my only son, worthlessly immortalised by the carping of a man in a dress.'

He turned out of the wind and puffed furiously at the pipe, until it gave him the nourishment he needed.

Jackie prodded a bit of gravel with her foot. 'I thought, well, I mean, Stacey said, that the request for burial came from your side. A family tradition.'

Karen knew she should have warned her father, but she hadn't found the right opportunity. Charlie had tried to explain that the pathologists would have taken everything they needed before they released the body, but she was haunted by something Jaz had said, ages ago, something about not burning the evidence. Stacey had agreed, as long as Karen was footing the extra cost.

'We're having a few sandwiches, back at The Volunteer Arms,' Jackie cut through her thoughts. 'I don't know if you'll feel ... well, it's up to you.'

She shrugged and scuttled off to join Stan and the small party who were shuffling between two tall yews towards a part of the cemetery where the newly dug graves gaped open, ready for the dead. Karen watched them go. There was a strange atmosphere of the right thing being done here, but something was missing. It felt like a funeral to which everyone had come grudgingly. She had mourned Phil frequently over the past few weeks, long before she'd accepted he wasn't coming back, but she still felt a piercing sense of loss. They may not have been very close as adults, but he'd taken with him the shared memories of their childhood and of their mum. She couldn't see her sorrow matched by the other mourners, except maybe in her father's gruff defensiveness.

It was probably a mistake to go to The Volunteer Arms, but Reg had decided that he must be there for Holly's sake. He said that with Phil gone, he was Holly's only link to her real family. Karen didn't argue with him, although she was sure Mrs Clegg had some views about who the 'real' grandparents were. They got lost and arrived long after the rest of the sparse congregation. They spotted the funeral party in the back room. Framed by dark wood and the brass of the hand pumps, Stacey's dad was sitting up at the bar, staring into his drink. Behind him were the three men from the chapel. As Reg and Karen approached from the main bar, they could clearly hear one of the young men sharing a joke with his friend.

'Way to go! I mean, I wouldn't mind a bit of that as my last rites!'

'You sick fucker.'

Stacey's father suddenly noticed Karen and Reg and hissed at the young men to shut up. It was too late. Reg had a look that Karen remembered from her childhood.

'Perhaps you'd like to explain that comment?'

'What the...?'

'My name is Reg Holroyd. If you were talking about my son, whom we are mourning here, I would like you to elucidate a little.'

The young man looked nervously at Karen.

Then, as if he had a sore throat, choked on the words, 'Men's talk.'

'Oh, you don't need to worry about my daughter, she's a feminist.'

Stacey's father finally came to the rescue. 'Keith Clegg.' He offered a hand by way of introduction. 'Let me get you a drink, and then perhaps there's a few things you ought to know. Bugger off, you lot. You've had your fill. What'll you have Mr Holroyd?'

He took Karen and Reg over to a small table, and when they'd got a drink in front of them, he began to explain the delicate matter of Phil's body being found in a caravan, believed by police to be some sort of mobile brothel.

'They're saying the cause of death was a head injury. Of course the full inquest will go into much more detail. At the moment they're looking into why the caravan was dumped in the quarry.'

Karen shaped a tiny lake of spilt white wine with her fingertip. Charlie had explained it to her the day they went to Bridlington, but she'd kept it to herself. She was relieved that Keith Clegg was the one to tell her father, and felt a tiny stab of shame that she hadn't found the words herself. She watched Reg nod his head, his eyes hooded with tired skin.

'Shouldn't the police be asking more questions?' Reg cleared his throat, but his voice was still gravelly.

'I expect they are, but they don't do anything in a hurry.'

Of course, the police. Karen realised where she'd seen the young man in the chapel, un-

221

comfortable in his suit beside the girl in the camel coat. It was Sean, the PCSO from Doncaster. She wished she'd realised, she would have spoken to him. It was kind of him to come and pay his respects, and to drag his girlfriend along. He'd tried to help and it had all been for nothing.

The three of them sat in silence, until Keith pushed his stool back and walked over to a table against the wall where some sandwiches had been laid out. 'Here, grab a handful of these. You'll need them on your drive home. I better catch up with the missus. Holly didn't last long, my wife took her home.'

'I was hoping to see her.' Reg seemed to come back from a dream.

'Any time, mate, any time. Stay in touch.' He scrawled a phone number on the back of a beer mat and thrust it at Reg. 'Bloody sad business, especially for the littl'un.'

They were left alone in the back room. Father and daughter and an oval platter of stiffening ham sandwiches. Reg sighed deeply and pushed them away.

'Nice thought. But I think I'll give them a miss.'

## CHAPTER TWENTY-THREE

Maureen was sitting at the kitchen table staring at a puzzle magazine, a cold mug of tea beside her.

'Any news?' She looked up as Sean came through the back door.

He shook his head. 'I think she's long gone, Nan, I'm sorry.'

'Takes me back to when we lost your mam. Played cards even better than Arieta. I think that's why I took to that girl. She had such a look of your mam, when she was nearer your age.'

Sean didn't remember much about his mother. She was twenty-eight when she died of a brain haemorrhage. So bringing Arieta back here had stirred all that up for his nan. Nice one, Sean. There was so much more he wanted to tell her, so much he had to keep to himself. But he meant what he said about Arieta. It had been three weeks. She'd be far away by now. He'd checked the railway station and the bus station. He'd checked the flat in Balby, but there was no hint of her anywhere. Yesterday he thought he saw the girl she was afraid of, the one from the station. She was coming out of Poundland on the high street.

'You know what, Nan? I think I've been looking for the wrong person.'

Maureen didn't look up.

At the railway station Sean stood with his back to the ticket machine, scanning everyone who came in and out. After twenty minutes, he went to the platforms. He checked where the trains were headed and where they'd started. The platform for the Edinburgh-to-London line revealed nothing.

There was a four-carriage train waiting on Platform Three. It had just come the slow way from Hull, via Brough, Gilberdyke and Goole. There she was, wandering slowly up the platform, checking out the benches and peering into the windows of the Pumpkin Café. Skinny, with a tight ponytail that pulled her hair back from her face, she was pushing the black pram with a baby in it. He waited. It was his day off and he had plenty of time.

She gave up her quest after an hour. He could hear the baby starting to cry. She pushed it out in front, as if the distance of her arms would be enough to stop the sound reaching her. Sean followed. She walked quickly and within fifteen minutes she was turning off Nether Hall Road. The narrow pavement gave way to old red-brick frontages that had once been warehouses or small factories. Their black doors were labelled with a splash of colour: Alley Cats, Zoom and the How Hi. Sean had been to a couple of these nightclubs; he couldn't be sure which, they were so similar. He'd never really noticed the building on the corner. It must have been a corner shop, when the clubs were still factories. An orange and black sign, glowing faintly from a dim bulb somewhere inside the frame, announced the All Star Massage Parlour. The girl went to the side door and let herself in with a key.

The front of the shop was on the corner of two streets, Carter Street, where the nightclubs were, and Nelson Road, a street of terraced houses that ended abruptly in a breezeblock wall, spray-painted with a mess of tags. Sean checked both, in case he was being observed, before trying the door. It was locked. There was no information about opening times; maybe you had to make an appointment. Then he saw the bell, black plastic set in the purple gloss doorframe. His hands were hot and his finger made a sweaty print on the button.

The door was opened by the ponytail girl. He hoped she hadn't spotted him earlier.

'Yeah?'

'I've come for a massage.'

'Got an appointment?'

'No, I'm in town with my work, fancied a bit of company.'

He had no idea if that's what you said, but she seemed to think it was plausible, because she opened the door and let him into a small, harshly lit reception area with three doors opening off it. He gripped the keys in his pocket and tried not to jiggle them. He didn't want to seem nervous, or would it matter? Maybe blokes who visited prostitutes were nervous. There must be a first time for everybody, but perhaps that was usually late at night, pissed-up and cheered on by the lads. The girl opened one of the three doors and asked him to go in and wait. She said there would be someone down in a minute. The room was cold and smelt sickly, a mixture of baby lotion, antiseptic and a strong floral perfume. He hadn't known what to expect, but it was a surprise to see an ordinary bed covered with a plastic sheet. He thought that they might keep up more of a pretence, even have a real massage couch. There was a bottle of Dettox spray and a cloth on the mantelpiece. So at least someone had done a bit of cleaning. It wouldn't have passed his nan's high standards, but it wasn't filthy.

'Massage with relief, forty quid,' Ponytail said from the doorway. 'Any extras sort it out with the girl.' And the door was slammed shut.

There was a slim Chinese woman standing looking at him. She was wearing a blue kimono-style robe, which hung open over a black bra and knickers.

'Can we talk, while the room warms up?' Sean said.

She said nothing but flicked a switch on an electric radiator and turned to him with a fixed smile.

'You like back rub first?'

Sean had been careful to move his wallet and keys to his jeans' pocket. He had no intention of removing his trousers and he didn't want to get ripped off. He had an image in his head of a guy, unable to find his jacket with all his valuables inside, being thrown out for refusing to pay. It might have been something he'd seen in a film because, to be honest, Sean had never actually spoken to any other bloke about visiting a massage parlour. There must be some guys at it, the statistics were there, but nobody he knew had ever mentioned it.

He lowered himself onto the bed, trying not to let his face touch the plastic sheet, and she slapped some oil on his skin, rubbing it in wide circles. It wasn't unpleasant, especially as the oil began to warm up. It was only when her thumbs started exploring the waistband of his jeans that he decided it was time to get on with what he'd come for. She stepped back as he rolled over and her hands went to his belt. He grabbed her wrists.

'No get nasty with me, mister, or I scream.'

'I'm not going to get nasty. I just want to talk, OK? I want to know about two girls who were

226

here. Arieta and Flora. From Kosovo. And a Chinese girl, she was here too, in the summer probably, maybe up to October?' She shook her head and pulled at his grip. 'Were there any other girls who left here, who you haven't seen again?'

'No. No, mister. You got to stop ask questions. Get out, get out!' Her voice rose to a shriek, then she dipped her head forward and bit his knuckle. 'Fuck!'

He thought she might have broken the skin. Now she was shouting in her own language, cursing him and pointing at the door. She picked up his T-shirt, jumper and jacket and thrust them at him.

'OK, calm down, I'm sorry...'

'What's going on?' The door was flung open and an older woman with blonde, almost white, bobbed hair was standing in the doorway.

'Crazy bitch. She got all wound up because I didn't want any extras.'

'How you expect girl make living here?' The girl was still shouting.

'I'm getting out of here,' Sean said. 'It's a fucking madhouse.'

But the older woman was blocking his way. It was dim in the room and the light behind her made it hard to see her features, but he remembered the set of her shoulders, and he remembered exactly where he'd seen her before.

'Forty pounds for the massage.'

Her voice was as hard as the hand she held out. He pulled out his wallet and thrust the notes at her. She stepped back and let him through.

On the street, a fine drizzle was beginning to fall.

He paused in the doorway of the How Hi, wedging his jacket between his knees to pull his T-shirt and jumper over his head. Miss Estelle. Of course, you bloody plonker. Divo Denton strikes again. That number, the one he'd written down and given to Sandy Schofield to check, was a personalised number plate. E something, definitely an L in there. He just hadn't seen it. Never could get them. Remember the number, yes, but read them as a whole word? No. Just didn't click for him.

As he was zipping his jacket up, he saw a black Range Rover pull up at the corner. He stepped back into the doorway and watched two men get out of the car. He recognised the first one straightaway. Almost as wide as he was tall, the passenger was Mr Forsyth, the agricultural contractor. The other one, getting out of the driver's side, was slimmer, with sandy red hair and a grey wool overcoat. A chill crept over Sean's skin. He'd seen that man at Philip Holroyd's funeral.

He watched them go into the All Star Massage Parlour before turning and walking quickly away, repeating the registration number under his breath until he was out of sight. On the high street he bought a newspaper and a biro and scribbled it down next to the crossword. He squinted at it, turned it on its side, but it didn't seem to make a word, just an ordinary plate.

He could have gone home then, or over to Doncaster Central to see if he could find Lizzie Morrison. But he was drawn back up to Carter Street. He was just in time to see the two men leaving. They hadn't been there long enough to have fully enjoyed the services on offer, so they

228

must have had some other business with Miss Estelle, or Stella Stubbs, as she was known to the DVLA. Forsyth got back into the passenger side, but the redhead opened the rear door and leant over the seat. When he stood up, he was supporting a small black woman, unsteady on her feet. With his arm around her shoulders, he walked her to the side door. She wiped her eyes, as if she'd just woken up, and let him help her inside. The redhead came back to the car and drove away. Sean stepped back into the shady doorway of the How Hi, holding his breath against the smell of stale piss as the car drove past him.

On the bus back to The Groves, he phoned Lizzie, but it went straight to voicemail. He didn't feel like talking to a machine so he sent her a text instead.

In his bedroom he stood and looked at the chart on the wall. The lines from the centre were beginning to link up around the outside like a spider's web. He added the All Star Massage Parlour and linked it to Arieta, Flora and Stella Stubbs. This meant that Lee, in red, was now connected, directly or indirectly, to everyone on the diagram. He picked up another pen, green for Mr Forsyth. It was then that he realised he'd left the newspaper on the bus. Shit. He closed his eyes to see the plate again. YD something, or was it YS? This was hopeless. He wrote 'redhead' next to Forsyth. It would have to do for now.

It was late when Lizzie phoned back and he could tell there was someone with her. Guy probably. He started to tell her about his visit to

Carter Street, but she cut him off.

'Can't it wait until the morning?'

'What time are you in?'

'Early. There's a big case conference. Top brass and Moon from the HTS is coming over.'

'I want to be there.'

'Sean, I'm not being funny but it's not, I mean, PCSOs aren't normally…'

'I know what you're saying, but I've got something important. Ask Rick to get me a seat at the case conference and I'll give you both everything I've got, first thing.'

She sighed. 'OK, meet me at half-seven up in my office. I've got a presentation to put together on all the crime scene evidence.'

'Fair enough. Save a couple of slides on your PowerPoint for me.'

Lizzie ignored him on the way out of the case conference, unless you counted her hissing, *Don't say a word about Carter Street or your nan's lodger, or both our careers will be up in flames.* She meant her career, of course. He had a job; she had a career. He was beginning to understand that there was a difference. He didn't mind the ingratitude, although it would have been nice to be thanked for providing her with the details of her natty little slideshow presentation. She hadn't even given him his chart back. She'd probably shredded it. No, what was really getting on his tits was the fact that somebody had spoken to the operations manager and he'd been detailed to full-time community beat, with no desk time at the station. Sandy Schofield was picking up all his admin tasks. He was completely out of the loop.

He was sounding off to Carly as they pounded along the crescent that divided the Groves from the bottom edge of the Chasebridge estate.

'What did you do to piss her off this time?' Carly asked.

'No idea, except be nice to her.'

'That would do it,' Carly's laugh rebounded off the concrete of the garages they were passing. 'You need cheering up. Fancy coming out later? Rick Houghton's got his divorce through and some of us are off into town.'

'Go on then.' Sean fancied getting off his face for a change. He'd been playing good cop and it had got him nowhere, except a patronising pat on the back from the Chief Super. Even that went for nothing when he saw them crowding round Lizzie, congratulating her for her excellent forensic work, telling her she was an essential part of the Philip Holroyd case. It was as if she were the most experienced detective at the station, not just some over-educated civilian from forensics. Which raised an interesting question, where was the most experienced detective at the station?

'What's going on with Burger?' he asked Carly.

'Gardening leave.'

'Is he into gardening?'

'Don't be a fool! It's what people say. I don't know, he messed up somewhere with the Chinese girl, the one you called Su-Mai.'

Sean wondered if there was more to it than that. He hadn't forgotten the moment in the car park when Burger had touched Stella Stubbs on the shoulder, or the moment he'd lied about

231

seeing a forensic report that hadn't yet been written. If he knew the caravan by the quarry was a brothel, maybe he knew Su-Mai was a working girl too. Sean thought back to the snippet of the phone conversation he'd heard in the lay-by and Burger threatening him to back off.

'Do me a favour, Carly, get Sandy to look up Stella Stubbs on the PNC.'

'Don't you think someone else is on to her?'

'Find out if she's ever been known by any other name.'

When his shift was over, he went home and cooked a couple of sausages and some oven chips for Maureen, and watched her poke them round the plate with her fork.

'Come on, Nan, you've got to eat something.'

'I just don't feel like it. I should have done more to help her; she's on her own. Even if she went back to her own country, she's got nobody. Just an alky for a father and cousins who would turn their back because she walked away from her marriage.'

'What else did she tell you?'

'How d'you mean?'

'Did she talk about the All Star Massage Parlour?'

'The brothel?' Maureen speared a chip. 'Yes and no. She told me a funny story about one of the other girls recognising the judge who'd put her away for benefit fraud the year before. And she said some days it was no worse than being married, some of the punters were all right and some weren't.'

'Did she say anything about the madam, Miss Estelle?'

'I asked her who was in charge.' She dipped another chip into a pool of ketchup. 'I told her I didn't know much about it, wondered how it all worked, well, she went right off on one, didn't she? Swearing in her own language. Funny how you can tell, even if you don't know the words. I kept off the subject after that.'

He sat down opposite her and picked up one of the sausages. 'You going to eat this?' She shook her head. 'You did what you could, Nan. You gave her somewhere safe to stay. It's not your fault.'

'Why did she take off then?'

He shrugged. He hadn't got a clue. Stupid to think he was part of it. He was eyes and ears on the ground, not expected to have anything between those ears, not expected to work anything out. Well, if that's how they wanted it, fair enough.

'I'm off out. Don't wait up.'

He found Rick and Carly among a big crowd in the pub. Most of the station was there, but no sign of Lizzie. At about nine, they went on for a curry. There were just four of them now, Sean, Rick, Carly and Steve. Rick waited until Steve had gone to the toilet, then he leant forward and said he'd seen the lab results on the heroin that was in the caravan.

'Not supposed to be talking shop tonight,' he said, 'and Steve wouldn't thank me for sharing, but it looks like it was from the same batch that killed your Chinese girl.'

'Not my Chinese girl. Not any more. Miss Morrison's case. PCSOs don't have cases, you know that.'

Carly played a mock violin and told him to cheer up, but he really didn't want to know. What was the point? His fourth pint of the night quenched the heat of the prawn jalfrezi and then he ordered a fifth.

Much later, in the heat and noise of Flares nightclub, it took him a moment to realise that Carly was trying to tell him something. Eventually she dragged him off the dance floor to a space near the toilets and shouted into his ear.

'The answer to the question is King. Stella Stubbs was formerly known as Stella King or Estelle King. She was also calling herself Estelle Kingsley for a while. She has a rap sheet as long as your arm. First picked up for soliciting at Grimsby Docks in 1982. Married to a Mr William Stubbs in 1991, divorced 1993. I was going to tell you earlier, but you've been in such a foul mood all night.'

Sean asked her to repeat the name and shouted back. 'So d'you think she's related to Burger? He touched her, in the car park, like this. How does that feel? Like an ex-husband?'

'Maybe it's just me, Sean, but that feels more brotherly.'

'Burger's her brother? Bloody hell! What happens now?'

'Fuck knows. Maybe it's a coincidence. Or maybe not!' Carly laughed, but the sound was lost in the music.

They were both drunk and way out of their

depth. Sean had been out of his depth for a long time, ever since those grubby kids met him on the glass-encrusted pavement of the Chasebridge estate. Shit, he thought, there's no going back.

Later, much later, he sat on the edge of the pavement and spewed up everything he'd eaten and drunk over the previous six hours. He wished he felt better, but he just felt worse. He started to cry. Rick crouched next to him and rubbed his shoulders

'Come on, mate, it's not worth crying over spilt beer.'

'Isn't it?' Sean slurred.

'I don't know. It depends if you're crying over the case or the girl.'

Sean rocked back and forth trying to stop the flow of tears. 'Fucking both. No, the case, yes, it's the fucking case, she's taken everything I've worked on and claimed it as hers, and the bastard, Guy-the-bastard, he's with her now. Well, he can have her. I'm not going to help her now. I still know stuff I haven't told her, she'll have to work it out for herself, she thinks she's so fucking clever.'

'Sean, mate, shut your gob, won't you?' Carly was there. He felt her grip on his arm. 'Save it for the morning, when you're sober.'

'D'you like me, Carly?'

'Course I like you, you're my mate.'

'But do you love me? Could you love me?'

'No, Sean. Don't take it personally. It's just that you're a bloke.'

# CHAPTER TWENTY-FOUR

In the weeks since the funeral, a kind of normality had settled over Karen's life. Normal but not normal. An altered state. She felt like she was waiting all the time. It was morning and she was watching her father perched, gnome-like on the breakfast stool, buttering his toast with precision, wasting nothing. Max had gone to Scotland for four days and Reg had arrived to keep her company and help with the children over the half-term holiday.

He wiped his fingers and pulled out his wallet. 'I've got that number tucked in here. Keith Clegg. I thought I might give him a bell.' He fingered the piece of beer mat, softened from weeks of being pressed against money and credit cards in his back pocket. 'I keep putting it off, funny that.'

'What would you say to him?' She tipped ground coffee into a cafetière as she waited for the kettle to boil.

'Just, you know, wondering if there's any news, a date for the inquest and how's Holly, that sort of thing. But then I thought I'd phone Stacey first, at least we know her. We don't really know Keith.'

'Did you? Phone Stacey?'

'Mmm...'

'Was she OK with you? She clearly doesn't want to speak to me.' The water steamed and bubbled as she poured it onto the grounds and plunged down to squeeze the flavour out.

'Don't you let it stand?' he said sharply.

'Shall I chuck it out and start again?'

'No, no, not on my account, I'm sure it'll be fine. I would have been perfectly happy with instant.'

She knew that wasn't true. She reached up for the cups and sat down on the opposite side of the breakfast bar.

'Stacey. You were telling me about your conversation with Stacey.'

'Ah, well, there's the thing,' he said. 'I did phone and I thought I'd got a wrong number. It was an older sounding woman. She said Stacey had moved out. Gave me another number, she's at something-or-other-farm. I just got an answer machine there, but I swear it was that bloke's voice, the one with the van.'

'Mackenzie?'

'I didn't feel like leaving a message.'

Karen was stunned. She swore and apologised to her father in the same breath.

'It's a lonely business being widowed.' He stirred his coffee, his eyes fixed on the brown whirlpool he was making. 'Don't be too quick to judge.'

She couldn't tell him that she was in no position to judge anyone else's morals. Just then Ben came crashing through the kitchen door and asked if Grandpa would take him to the park. Karen looked out of the window. The constant rain had finally abated and a watery sun was trying to break through.

'Would you, Dad? I think I need to go into the office for a while.'

Jaz was rummaging through file boxes in the boardroom. He looked pleased to see her.

'I can't find Mr and Mrs Moyo,' he said.

'Their file?'

'No, them. I've managed to postpone the appeal date until March, but they've disappeared. When they moved out of the house in Leeman Road, I thought someone from the church was putting them up. But they haven't been in contact.'

'Shall I try Reverend Wheatley?'

'Brilliant, thank you.' He took the stairs two at a time and disappeared into his tiny office under the roof.

Karen logged on and waited for her home page to appear. These computers were second- or third-hand from another charity and painfully slow to get started. She found the spreadsheet she'd made for the Moyos and rang the church. After speaking to a cleaner, who happened to pick up the phone, she finally got a number for the vicar. It wasn't good news. The Moyo family hadn't been to church for several weeks. He'd tried to find them somewhere to stay when they were evicted from their house, but it had fallen through. In his last conversation with him, Rudo had mentioned a job offer, which came with accommodation, but he'd been cagey about the details. Elizabeth had stopped attending school and it was really preying on the vicar's mind that Mrs Moyo's baby was due soon.

She thanked Reverend Wheatley, and made a neat set of bulleted notes, which she sent to Jaz's inbox. She stared at the screen for a while. It was like looking into a swimming pool and trying to

238

guess the temperature. She checked her contacts, picked up the phone and dialled a number.

'Can I speak to DCI Moon?'

'Give him my regards,' Jaz said, over her shoulder.

'Jesus, Jaz,' she covered the receiver, 'I wish you wouldn't sneak up on me. I didn't hear you come downstairs.' He'd taken off his shoes and a pair of purple socks stuck out from his suit trousers. The switchboard at the Human Trafficking Service was playing Nina Simone.

'Been doing yoga,' he said. 'Natalie's been teaching me. Trying to de-stress. You getting on better with Moon then?'

'How do you mean?'

'That night in the pub, he said you had a row and went home. He tried to follow you, to make sure you were OK or something.'

'Oh, that,' she shrugged, wishing Charlie would mention it, if he was going to tell lies on her behalf. 'I was worrying about my brother and he wasn't very sympathetic, that's all.'

At least that last bit had a ring of truth, even if it was ancient history. Jaz shuffled back upstairs as Charlie came on the line.

'I need to talk to you about Johnny Mackenzie,' Karen said.

'Oh? Hello. This is nice.'

'What do you know about him?' Karen said.

'Right. Mackenzie. In what context?'

'My brother was working for him and he was sniffing round my sister-in-law, now it seems she's moved in with him.'

'Ah.'

'What does that mean?'

'Well, let's just say he's of interest to HTS.' There was a pause. She could hear him breathing.

'Look Charlie, I can't bear the thought of that man being around Holly. He's dodgy.'

'Dodgy isn't a term that would stand up in court, but from the evidence that's coming together, I'd have to say that your instincts about Mr Mackenzie are probably bang on, but just for now, please, and I know this is hard, don't say a word to your sister-in-law.'

She promised and put the phone down. She opened up a document and punched some numbers into a spreadsheet, looked at them and deleted them again. She tried to force her concentration back onto her work, but her mind wouldn't stay on one thing. When the phone on her desk rang, she nearly jumped out of her chair.

'Let's meet up,' Charlie said.

'What?'

'Come on. I've been waiting for you to call and now you have, it just happens that I've got the afternoon off. I can be in York in an hour, if I make the next train.'

She met him at the station and they turned right, away from the city centre, cutting down a snicket. She let him hold her hand, dropping his when they emerged into a street of hotels. The chances of seeing someone she knew were too high.

He checked into an anonymous-looking chain hotel and she realised he'd booked it on his way there. Once inside the room, they began undressing each other, undressing themselves, heads stuck in jumpers, elbows poking through inside-out sleeves. She wondered if she needed a drink to see this through, but then he was laughing at himself, at her. They looked like a pair of scarecrows. The laughter carried them both onto the bed, where they lay looking at each other naked. They weren't laughing now, just listening to the sound of their breathing. He traced his fingers across her collarbone and smoothed his palm over her breast, while she ran her hands around his pelvis. He surrounded her lips with his and drew her tongue into his mouth. They kissed and touched and pulled back just to look, and then their hands and fingers found each other. When she could hardly bear it any longer, he eased himself over her, taking his weight on one arm, raising her back with the other, drawing her up to him as he pushed himself into her. She let go straight away, meeting his rhythm with her own. It was smooth and effortless, and as she buried her nose in his neck, she breathed in the smell of his skin.

When it was over, he wrapped himself around her back and they lay like spoons. In time, they must have fallen asleep because when she woke, she wondered why it was so light. She remembered then that it was mid-afternoon, that she was in a hotel bed and this was Charlie's arm curled heavily round her waist. It wasn't until she looked at her watch that she sat up with a jolt.

'Oh, my God, I have to make a phone call!' She scrambled to her feet, the bedsheet tangling around her legs. Her bag was by the door and she shivered, gathering her clothes haphazardly towards her. She was cold and naked and late again.

Charlie offered to make her a cup of coffee, but she had to go.

'My dad's with the kids. I wasn't going to be out this long. I'll have to say I got stuck at work.'

She made the call and dressed quickly, leaning against the doorframe, watching him making himself a drink in the nude. There was a copy of the *Guardian* newspaper on the floor where he'd dropped his coat. He must have been reading it on the train. The headline caught her eye. Beneath it was a picture of a crowd, waving red flags emblazoned with black eagles.

'Where's that?'

'Kosovo. My brother Hugh's been posted there with the Welsh Guards. Making sure they don't fry up the Serbs on their independence barbecues. Can't be worse than Basra.'

She'd been dimly aware of something on the radio in the past couple of days, but a missing child and an impending financial crisis had eclipsed it. She peered at the paper. In the photo, huge yellow letters spelt out the word NEW-BORN.

'Independence?'

'It was announced two days ago. They've had to wait a long time.'

In the photograph there was a crowd of faces, young and old, some halfway up lamp posts. There was an older woman in a headscarf and next to her a younger man was smiling, waving both arms in the air. He looked so like Phil. People, unremarkable people. There could be any number of faces in the world like his, or like the man on the other side of him, whose lined face smiled at the camera, or like the figure in the foreground, sitting astride his friend's shoulders.

'What are you thinking?' Charlie touched her cheek.

'About Phil. I think I would find it easier to believe that he's really dead if I'd seen him. I should have insisted.'

'It might not have looked like him, you know that, don't you?'

She did, and she knew that she'd rather remember him healthy, young and full of life, like the man waving at the camera in the photograph.

The journey home seemed interminable. Charlie wanted to come with her, stay with her as long as he dared, but she needed to be on her own. She had been shaken by the photo in the paper, even though she knew it was a common effect of grief, a kind of madness that makes us see the faces of the dead all around. The bus dawdled through the traffic, waiting for an eternity at the lights. The faces of strangers, flowing past on the pavement, blurred as she stared and crystallised when she blinked. Between two houses, she caught a glimpse of green: a playground with metal structures, red, blue and yellow, like a miniature circus. A roundabout was spinning and she could just see the edge of it. A child disappeared and reappeared, again and again, until the bus pulled away. Now you see him, now you don't.

At home, she rushed through her apology to her father. She needed a shower. She was heading for the stairs when the doorbell rang. Sophie opened it.

'Is your mum in ... oh, Karen, I'm so glad to see you!'

'Trish, hi! Come in.'

She tried to act normally, while they sat in the kitchen drinking tea. Karen was sure Trisha would be able to smell Charlie on her, but her neighbour was preoccupied with her own problems. She and Paul had taken a series of fertility tests and the results were strongly indicating that he was un-likely to conceive. Karen was only half-listening, but she could hear the desperation in Trisha's voice.

'I'll try anything,' she was saying.

'Unlikely though, Trish, that doesn't mean never, and the fact that he's got kids already.'

'That's something else. It turns out he and his first wife had fertility treatment too, he just never said. Seven years ago, I mean, the twins are nearly eight. His fish just don't swim, Karen. They were slow then, but it looks like they're going nowhere now.'

The clock in the hall struck six and Karen still hadn't had her shower. Max was due back anytime now. She found herself promising Trisha a girly lunch, when things were quieter at work, and managed to get her out of the door. She locked herself in the bathroom and was just about to step into the jet of hot water when she heard the phone ring. She willed Reg or Sophie to answer it. Tip-ping her head back into the water, she let it drum against her skull, tasting it in her mouth. Her mind raced, hammering a thousand different thoughts through her head. Then the hammering was outside her, a fist pounding on the door. 'Mum! Mum!' She heard Sophie's voice over the roar of the water in her ears. She stopped the shower, and stood dripping, starting to chill instantly.

'Grandpa says you've got to come. He says it's urgent!'

'I'm coming, I won't be a minute.'

Wrapped in Max's huge bath towel, water ran off her feet and into the carpet as she came downstairs.

'Funny time for a shower.' Reg sounded irritable.

'This isn't about my washing habits. What's happened? Is Ben all right?' She heard the snappiness in her voice and regretted it straight away.

'Stacey wasn't going to tell us, but I left a message for Keith Clegg, said I was here, he just phoned back. He thought we knew. It's the bloody inquest. It's tomorrow.'

## CHAPTER TWENTY-FIVE

'One more written warning and I'm out of a job.'

Carly Jayson was leaning against Maureen's kitchen worktop, cradling a mug of tea. Outside the window, the rain was coming down in spears.

'I'm not asking you to do anything you shouldn't,' Sean said. 'Just keep your ears open. Ask Rick what's going on.'

A pool of water had formed around Sean's feet.

They'd done a runner as soon as the rain got heavy, but they were still drenched. The jackets were fully waterproof, but their trousers were soaked.

'Well, all I know is that the whole of Doncaster Central is crawling with outsiders. There's an evil-looking pair from Serious and Organised, an internal investigation team picking over Burger's undeclared family connections and that bloke from Human Trafficking. They're like a bunch of flipping meerkats, popping up when you least expect them and demanding to see everyone's notebooks. Sandy's having a field day with the paperwork. Don't know how she sticks it.'

'I suppose Lizzie Morrison got the praise for finding out Stella was Burger's sister too.'

'Why should she?' Carly asked. 'I'm the one who told Rick Houghton to explore that murky little avenue. Don't look at me like that. I need all the Brownie points I can get at the moment.'

'How's she getting on?'

'Golden girl?'

'Don't.'

'Touchy! Seems to be keeping her nose clean. She's been sorting out the forensic statement for Philip Holroyd's inquest tomorrow.'

Sean looked up. 'Yeah? I've got to give evidence, about finding the caravan.'

'Hey, I might come along for a laugh, heckle you from the cheap seats.'

'I thought you were trying to keep a low profile.'

'It's a public court isn't it? And if I'm not on duty, I can go where I like.'

The door opened and the wind blew Maureen,

246

and another gust of rain, inside.

'Get us a cup of tea, love. I had to walk up from the number twenty bus stop. Hiya, Carly!' She dropped two large carrier bags of shopping and limped towards the stairs. 'I'm going to get something dry on, then I'm putting these shoes in the bin. Less use than my stockinged feet, they were.'

Carly started to empty the shopping, drying the packets and tins that had got wet and arranging them on the worktop.

'Lend us a hand, I don't know where any of this goes.'

But Sean was miles away, chewing over what he would say to Lizzie when he saw her. He was surprised she hadn't been in touch about tomorrow. He'd got his statement ready. He would need to check with the coroner whether he should mention the boy by name or not. What had they talked about at the quarry? Had he got it all written down? There was something that Declan was telling him just before they saw the body. Something he'd never followed up.

'Hang on a minute.' An arc of water sprayed off his coat as he grabbed it off the hook. 'I need to talk to someone.'

'You're not going back out in this. You're a bloody headcase–'

He didn't hear any more. The door slammed shut behind him and he was down the side of the house and away along the pavement. The back of his jacket was cold against his neck and water ran inside his shirt.

The estate was empty. Even the dogs had taken cover. The peak of his hat kept his eyes dry, but the rain ran down his nose and over his lips like tears. He found the flats where he'd watched the bull terrier tearing open the bin liner. The back door to the block wasn't locked and he went inside. He stood for a moment, trying to get accustomed to the darkness at the bottom of a piss-scented stairwell.

Everything was back to front in these maisonettes, bedrooms downstairs and living rooms up. The door, when he reached it, looked as if the last person to knock on it had done so with an axe.

'Yeah?' A woman in her twenties held it open two inches, making sure he couldn't see past her.

'Is Declan about?' He was about to add that the boy wasn't in any trouble, when she shut the door and shouted.

'Declan you little bastard, there's a copper at the door! If you've done 'owt, I'll batter you!' Then she opened the door again. 'Don't mind me, I wouldn't lay a finger on him.'

A wet brown nose pushed past her knees and Ruby came out, sniffing round his feet, wagging her tail.

'She likes you. Funny that.'

The boy followed the dog, ducking under his mother's sharp elbow to reach the landing. He was wearing a thin hoody and carrying the dog's rope.

'You wanna talk? We'll take the dog out. See yer later.'

Sean was lost for words. The boy seemed to have aged forty years and picked up an American accent in the process. God knows what he'd been watching.

'You sure?' Sean realised he wasn't going to be invited in, but even so, it was chucking it down out there. Declan was already halfway down the stairs.

They took the road that cut down through the centre of the estate. Water was flowing down the gutters in two rivers. There'd be flooding somewhere tonight.

'Where are we going?' Sean was surprised by Declan's pace. He didn't look well nourished enough to be walking so fast. Maybe it was the relief of getting out of the flat.

'Somewhere we can talk,' the boy said out of the side of his mouth. He was turning into a young Sean Connery now.

They crossed the road to the children's playground. The swings were twisted up around the top bar. Little buggers. He and Carly would have to get them down later, tick a box on *positive service to the community*. Tick bloody tick. He had an idea where they were headed and he was right. The dead end, where they'd chased Lee Stubbs. Declan went to the second garage and leant against it. A catch gave way and the up-and-over door creaked open to reveal an empty space. Empty except for a couple of upturned crates and some rubbish in a corner. Declan fished a lighter out of his pocket. He lit a candle in a bottle and stood it on the floor between the two crates. Sean watched the dog sniff around the edges of the garage.

'You can shut the door now.'

Sean did as he was told, trying to put aside all the nagging worries about how many different guidelines he was breaking. Declan sat and waved

249

at the other crate, every inch the little gangster in his hideout.

'What's this about then, copper?'

'Lights. Flickering lights. When we found ... you found the caravan in the quarry and we were up there, you said Brandon had been scared by a ghost. You never finished telling me, it wasn't a ghost was it?'

Declan shrugged. 'No. More likely a zombie. People change after they're dead.'

'I think you saw someone real, alive. Declan, this is important.'

'Me and Brandon went up to the woods to see if we could get anything to burn on the bonfire.'

'So this would have been what, the fourth? The day before Bonfire Night?'

'S'pose so, yeah.'

'Then what?'

'It was getting dark and Brandon was getting scared because he said we might fall into the quarry. I said it was OK because I know all the safe places. Then we went back on the path and there was this caravan. All weird flickering lights in the windows.'

Sean's hand went to his inner pocket for his notebook. Then he hesitated. The meerkats at Doncaster Central would pounce on anything that was written down. Maybe he should wait. A story about zombies wasn't going to do anything for his credibility back at the station.

'Go on.'

'When we got up to it, it was proper spooky. There was like a glow from inside the caravan. Brandon didn't want to go any closer but I made him. There was a little crack in the curtain. That's when we saw it.'

'It?'

'The zombie. Just sitting. Sort of like this.' He hunched his knees up and wrapped his arms round them, staring wide-eyed at the candle.

'What did this zombie look like?'

'Pale. They've got no blood, because they're dead. Well it was pale, like really white, and had mad, green eyes and red hair, sticking up all wild.' Sean shivered and Ruby began to whine at the door. 'Now d'you believe me?'

'I believe you saw someone, but it wasn't a zombie, was it?'

'Might have been.'

'Did you see anything else?'

The boy frowned and stared into the candle. He licked his finger and drew it back and forth through the flame.

'Declan?'

'What?' He didn't look up.

'Was there anything else?'

'You got any food, mister? I'm starving.'

Sean stood up and stretched his shoulders back. The dog circled him, hopeful that they might be on the move again.

'It's not far down to my nan's place and we could pick up a bag of chips on the way.'

'All right.'

It was lucky for Sean that Declan didn't have the suspicion of some kids, who'd accuse you of child abuse as soon as you spoke to them. The uniform helped, but it also bothered him. Declan trusted adults too easily. Half an hour later he asked his nan and Carly to stay in the room as chaperones, while the boy sat in front of the computer screen, stuffing chips into his mouth and staring at an image from the Star's webpage.

'What's it say?'

'It's about another girl who was found dead. The other woman in the picture was her flatmate.'

'And?'

'Declan, d'you think this is the woman you saw, the one you thought was a zombie?'

Maureen looked from the screen to Sean. She opened her mouth to say something but thought better of it.

'I think so. She's got the eyes.' He made a gun with his hand and shot at the screen. 'Pyaow! Zombie hunters!'

Carly walked back up to the estate with Sean and Declan. It was on her way home. Ruby had enjoyed a cold pie in Maureen's kitchen and trotted happily back by the boy's side. The rain was just a fine drizzle now. Declan had a spring in his step, karate-chopping phantom zombies and chattering on about how he was going to track them down. Once they'd seen him safely through the back door of the flats, Carly turned to Sean.

'Who was she?'

Sean shrugged.

'Maureen recognised her, and you seemed pretty sure the boy would ID her too.'

'It's hardly an ID. He thinks she's the living dead.'

'Don't fuck about Sean. This is a murder inquiry.'

# CHAPTER TWENTY-SIX

At Doncaster magistrates' court, the coroner had begun his introduction. An usher took their names and showed them in, then delivered a note to the coroner. Karen hadn't expected it to be so much like a trial, but an official was reminding everyone that this was a court of law and anyone who was asked to speak would be placed under oath. He explained that these were public proceedings and a member of the press was present. Karen saw a thin, pale girl with glasses and a shapeless grey suit sitting with a pad poised on her knee. Stacey was sitting between Keith Clegg, who had a protective hand on his daughter's arm, and Johnny Mackenzie.

A court official cleared his throat and began to read out the pathology report. Karen felt sick at hearing her brother's remains described so graphically. A forensic examination from the scene described partial decomposition, slowed by the cool and shaded nature of the quarry. Although the caravan had tipped into the water, the body had remained dry. It appeared that the deceased had fallen or possibly been struck, or both. The nasal bones were fractured and embedded in the brain. Blood samples from a gas heater and from the floor of the caravan matched the body. Residual facial features and personal effects were deemed sufficient for initial identification, confirmed by DNA samples from hair and skin tissue on an item of clothing supplied by the widow. A number of other fingerprints were found, belonging to numerous males and one female, they had yet to be matched with any others on the system. The man's voice was as level as a newsreader's.

Stacey was placed under oath and asked to take the stand. She was visibly upset and her voice quavered when asked to describe the last time she saw her husband alive. Reg clenched his pipe in his pocket.

'And did you speak to your husband during the day?' The coroner leant towards her, his voice soft and kind.

'No.'

'Would you normally expect him to call?'

'If he was going to be late.'

'What time did you expect him back?'

'By six, or a bit before. I was supposed to start my shift at the pub at six.'

'I know this is very distressing for you, Mrs Holroyd, but I have to ask you, did you realise that your husband was found in a location believed to be used for the purposes of prostitution?'

The coroner looked like an owl, Karen thought, his eyes widening under grey, bushy eyebrows.

'Yes, the police said it was.'

'He was reported missing by his sister, not by you.'

'Yes.'

'Why didn't you report him missing?' The eyes narrowed, but the softness was still there in his voice.

'I thought maybe he was having an affair. He's had affairs before, it turned out. I was told that he'd run off with another woman.'

'I see. While you are under oath, Mrs Holroyd, can I confirm that you identified your husband's body?'

'Yes.' She said, quietly but clearly. 'At the hospital.'

'And you supplied an item of clothing for a DNA match?'

'His jacket.'

The community support officer was called next. Karen was surprised to see Sean Denton again; he seemed to be all over this case. Denton was telling the coroner that he'd been led to the caravan by the same boy who'd found the unidentified body of a young Chinese woman on the steps of a snack bar van, on the Chasebridge bypass.

'The boy said, and I'm quoting: "My brother said it were another prozzie in there."'

The coroner cleared his throat and Keith Clegg patted Stacey's arm. Johnny Mackenzie stared straight ahead, while Denton read from his notebook in hesitant tones. He looked nervous, but the coroner was almost as kind to him as he had been to Stacey.

When Johnny Mackenzie was called, Karen noticed Stacey squeeze his hand as he stood up. He was asked about a text he'd sent to Mr Holroyd's mobile phone on the afternoon he went missing. Mackenzie said Philip had been very low, slightly crazy and he was just checking on him.

'What was your relationship with Mr Holroyd?'

'He was a mate, a good mate.'

255

Reg Holroyd coughed loudly, Karen wished he hadn't because at that moment Johnny looked in their direction, his scalp reddening under his thin hair. A court officer was walking down the aisle from the back of the room. The coroner beckoned him to the bench, where he handed over a note.

'Ladies and gentlemen,' the coroner said sternly. 'I'm going to call a recess for fifteen minutes.'

The court rose and Karen took Reg by the arm and hurried him out into the lobby.

'What the hell's going on?' Reg muttered. 'Why didn't he tell the truth? Mackenzie was his boss, not his mate. I need a bloody smoke.'

They kept going, out through the glass doors and into the fresh air. Reg wasn't the only smoker; a muscular-looking woman with short hair had just taken out a cigarette and offered Reg a light.

'You family?' she said.

'I'm the father, this is my daughter.'

The woman nodded and sized them up. Karen wanted to be alone with her father, but Reg was obviously feeling sociable.

'You got kids?' he said to the woman.

'A lad, he's eleven.'

'I can't get my head round it,' Reg continued. 'That's my boy they're talking about. I mean, I'm not saying Phil was a saint but I just don't recognise a thing they're saying. Phil, a serial adulterer? Phil with a prostitute? Where are those coppers? I want a word...'

'Wait.' Karen realised she had spoken at the same time as the other woman. They'd both reached a hand out to stop him.

Karen waited for the woman to say something, but she looked unsure now. Finally, she cleared her throat and suggested they go back in.

'Well, he'd better have something to say for himself.' Reg chewed on the stem of his pipe so hard it might crack.

She took Reg's arm and propelled him up the steps. 'Come on, Dad, let's see.'

Back in the courtroom, the coroner called Mr John Mackenzie back to the stand.

'May I remind you, Mr Mackenzie, that you are still under oath and that this is a court of law.' Johnny nodded and looked uncomfortable. The owl-like coroner had a new, steely edge to his voice. 'You say you were a friend of the deceased?'

'Yes.'

'Why did you not mention that you were also his employer?'

'He was helping me out a bit.'

'We're not the Inland Revenue, Mr Mackenzie. We are trying to ascertain what happened to Mr Holroyd on the day he died.'

'Yes. I asked him to deliver some stuff for me.' Johnny was barely audible. The journalist craned forward to catch what he said.

'Indeed. I have just been shown a missing person's report filed by the sister of the deceased, suggesting that Mr Holroyd was driving your van.' Johnny nodded, avoiding Karen's stare. 'What concerns me is that I am not satisfied that you have told us the whole truth. I would appeal to you Mr Mackenzie, as you are under oath, not to hide your business dealings in such a way as will jeopardise the outcome of this inquest.' More whispering, then the coroner, failing to hide his irritation, shuffled his papers and cleared his throat. 'I am afraid we are in no position to continue this inquest until we have reliable witness evidence. I am adjourning until further notice.'

Johnny wandered away from the stand as the court rose and people started to mill about. The ushers went to open the doors at the back of the room and two uniformed police officers left first. Karen and Reg followed them out into the lobby where the officers stopped and turned, standing like bouncers in front of the automatic glass doors to the outside world. She guided her father between them and, as they left the building, Karen heard a scuffle behind them and a familiar voice.

'John Mackenzie. Can I have a word?'

The doors swished shut and she and Reg were left to the sound of cars queuing in the traffic. She was sure it was Charlie Moon's voice, but when she turned to catch a glimpse of him, all she saw was the street and the sky reflected in the glass.

# CHAPTER TWENTY-SEVEN

Doncaster Central Police Station was getting crowded. The Community Support Team had lost their corner. They'd set up a temporary base in one of the interview rooms, but now the DCI from Human Trafficking had requisitioned that for a polite chat, as he called it, with the guy they'd pulled at the inquest. Sandy was buzzing. She'd been asked to write a press release to the effect that a John Peter Mackenzie of Common Gate Farm, Moorsby-on-Humber, had attended the police station voluntarily in relation to an on-going investigation into the employment of illegal immigrants. It was still under embargo awaiting further developments.

'Which means if they charge him, I'll have to delete it all and start again,' she told Sean. 'I've had that wimpy girl from the *Star* on the phone non-stop and I keep telling her she'll have to talk to the press office, but she won't listen.'

'I think there's more to it than that,' Sean paused, making sure he'd got her full attention. 'I'm not sure it's just about illegal immigrants. He was pulled at the caravan inquest.'

'So?' Sandy waited, twirling a ballpoint pen. 'Spill the beans! If there are any beans to spill. But be careful you don't let your imagination run away with you.'

Or the imagination of a ten-year-old boy. 'Never mind. Look, I'd like to chat but I need to find Lizzie Morrison. It's urgent.'

'Now, Sean, I know I'm old enough to be your mother and I don't see why you should take my advice, but—'

'PCSO Denton?' He looked round sharply to see a tall woman in a mac. Holroyd's sister. He was struggling for her married name.

'Karen Friedman,' she held out her hand, and coffee slopped onto Sandy's desk, as Sean put his cup down too quickly. 'I wanted to thank you for

259

attending my brother's funeral.'

'Right. We thought we should ... pay our respects.'

'And follow your nose.'

'Ma'am?' Sean tried to mop up the spilt coffee, before the brown trickle reached Sandy's keyboard.

'Actually I'm looking for DCI Moon,' Mrs Friedman said. 'Your friend Carly was kind enough to buzz me through.'

Sandy and Sean exchanged glances. Carly had clearly given up playing by the rules. He'd seen her in civvies, skulking around at the back of the inquest and now she was letting all and sundry wander around restricted areas. Not that anyone would notice yet another new face.

'Interview suite three,' Sean said, 'and there's an observation room next door. Come on, I'll show you. Just keep your head down.'

He was curious to hear what Johnny Mackenzie had to say. He peered through the one-way glass into suite three and flicked the switch that brought the two men's voices into the room. Moon had a map spread out on the table and was pointing at something, asking Johnny if this was where they arrived. Johnny shook his head.

'Wouldn't know, mate. They just answer job adverts, or they're friends of the ones we had last year.'

'Africans? Chinese? They've all got papers?'

'There's plenty of black people, and Chinese too, born and bred here. Someone's being a little bit racist if they think I'm employing illegals just because they're non-white.' He smiled at Charlie

Moon and his shoulders relaxed. Moon smiled back.

'Do you employ more men than women? Or is it about equal? And what about girls? Young girls?'

Mackenzie's smile vanished. 'Are you going to charge me with something? Because if you're not, then I've got a business to run.'

'Relax. You're being a great help.' Moon sat back, while the other man shifted in his chair, folding and unfolding his arms.

'Come on, push him a bit,' Sean whispered.

Mrs Friedman was about to say something, when the door to the observation room opened.

'Hello.' It was DI Rick Houghton. 'This is cosy.'

'Have you met Karen Friedman, Human Trafficking Service?' Sean said.

'Pleased to meet you,' Mrs Friedman said quickly.

'DI Houghton.' He shook her hand.

'PCSO Denton was kind enough to let me listen in, but I've heard enough, thank you.'

'No problem.' Rick turned to the window.

In the artificial silence of the soundproofed room, they heard Johnny Mackenzie giving the DCI some flannel about hardly knowing Forsyth. Sean opened the door for Mrs Friedman, and they stepped out into the hum and chatter of the first floor office suite.

Halfway down the corridor she burst out laughing. She sounded a bit crazy.

'Ma'am?'

'Please, don't keep saying that. You make me sound like the Queen. Why did you say I was

HTS? I'm not even a police officer.'

'That makes two of us.' He laughed too. It felt like the rulebook had been shredded. 'I'll just say I got mixed up, it won't be the first time.'

'What a strange old day.' She walked along the corridor slowly, looking at her feet, the laughter had subsided and her voice was sad. Sean sensed her unhappiness creep over him too.

'Thanks for covering for me,' she said.

'No problem.' The fluorescent lighting flickered above them as they headed for the stairs. He wanted to say more, but he held back.

Over a cup of canteen coffee, she asked him why they came to the funeral and if it was on official business.

'Not officially,' he said.

'Thought not.'

'It's complicated, but let's just say Lizzie Morrison, my colleague from Scene of Crime, was following her forensic nose.'

'What do you know about Mackenzie?'

Thin ice, thought Sean, very thin ice. 'This and that. None of it good.'

'You know, don't you, that my sister-in-law has moved in with him, with her five-year-old daughter?'

Sean shuddered.

'I need to know, was he involved in my brother's death?'

Sean shrugged. 'I really don't know.'

But I do know something, he thought, and I've kept it to myself. His heart was racing. Suddenly that old phrase, getting something off your chest, made sense. It was a real physical feeling. He was

262

trying to remember if Arieta had ever mentioned Mackenzie. He could ask Maureen. He felt a creeping chill up the back of his neck. The chill began to take the form of the question. What if Arieta was working with Mackenzie? Together they could have killed Philip Holroyd. Declan's zombie theory put her in the caravan the night before the murder. If Arieta was a suspect in the death of Philip Holroyd, the woman in front of him was the last person on earth he should share that with, however much he might want to tell someone. At that moment, to Sean's relief, he saw Charlie Moon weaving between the tables of the canteen, heading in their direction.

## CHAPTER TWENTY-EIGHT

Karen could have kissed Charlie, right there and then in the middle of the staff canteen. But she didn't. She smiled and hoped that Sean Denton was too young to read the body language between them.

'I'll have to go,' she gathered her coat. 'My dad's taken Holly out for a snack with her other grandad. I don't want to leave him too long. Did you get what you needed?'

'From our friend, Mackenzie? Yes and no.' Charlie turned to the young PCSO. 'You've been a great help, Denton. Keep in touch.'

'I will, sir.' He sounded like he meant it.

'Goodbye.' She liked this young man. There

was something about his face that she wanted to trust.

Charlie saw her out to the pavement. The cool air was a relief after the overheated police station.

'You OK?' He let his hand brush her arm.

'Bit dazed to be honest. I was beginning to think the inquest was worse than the funeral but then another part of my brain kicked in. Started playing detective, I suppose. Sorry.'

'And what did your brain come up with?'

'Mackenzie. Where was he when Phil went missing?'

'Fair question,' he moved a strand of hair off her face. 'Look, I want to catch Lizzie Morrison. There's something I need to follow up.'

She felt a surprising pang of jealousy. The young forensic officer was pretty, and young, and she'd worked with Charlie before. She pushed the thought away and headed for St Sepulchre Gate to rescue her father from McDonald's.

On the train, she bought her father a sandwich and a beer. She'd decided to go back with him to Hitchin and stay the night. He was shaky and she didn't want him to be on his own. Her own appetite had deserted her, so she got a half-bottle of red wine. They shared a table with two women in their seventies, travelling south from Newcastle to a Women's Institute conference. One was thin with straight hair, while her friend was round, red-cheeked and smiley, with a mass of white curls. Karen thought of Aunt Spiker and Aunt Sponge from *James and the Giant Peach*. She sat back as her father got drawn into a conversation about voting structures and jam recipes. When their neighbours went to the buffet, he asked her if she'd managed to see anyone useful at the police station.

'There was a very helpful officer there,' she said. Just an officer? The memory of Charlie's touch made the hairs on her arm stand on end. She gulped a mouthful of wine. 'It seems there's a link with human trafficking.'

'That's why they wanted to talk to Mr Mackenzie? I thought for a minute there, at the court–'

'I didn't find out much more.'

She cut him off just as the two women returned with tea and fruitcake. Before long, they'd moved on to a discussion about lawn management and Reg was offering them gardening tips. She recognised the brittle cheer in his tone. She remembered how whenever things got too grim with her mother's illness, Reg would always change the subject, be ready with a joke or an anecdote. Now he was entertaining these two ladies with the tale of the time he'd drawn a hammer and sickle on the lawn with weedkiller.

'I remember! Mum made you re-sow it, she was mortified.'

'Not the done thing in Hitchin.'

'But fascinating. You must tell me your method,' Aunt Sponge leant forward, as much as her size would allow. 'The possibilities are endless if one wanted to make a protest.'

Karen stared out through her own reflection at the occasional dots of orange light in swathes of nothing. She hardly heard the conversation going on beside her. Her father was asking the women about the village where they lived. He knew the name of the place and they began talking about its history.

'*Miners moving from Cornwall to North Yorkshire and onwards to County Durham.*' Her father's voice lingered somewhere just beyond her consciousness. '*Seventeenth-century migrant labour.*' She thought about Johnny Mackenzie and his comment to Charlie about the Africans and Chinese. How had he got Phil involved in all of that? The more she tried to understand, the more she realised she had no idea what her brother's life had been all about.

When it was time for them to change trains at Peterborough, she got their cases down from the rack.

'What a day, Dad, what a bloody day.'

'Wasn't it? That old Confucian curse, my dear, may you live in interesting times. I'd settle for some boring ones myself.'

He shook hands with Aunt Spiker and Aunt Sponge, who looked more than willing to provide him with all the boring times he could handle. If they'd been of another generation, they would have exchanged numbers, or email addresses. But as it was, they didn't even know each other's names.

Karen passed a sleepless night in the bedroom she'd occupied all her childhood. She couldn't get comfortable in the single bed, brushing up against the cold wall, or waking with her arm hanging over the side. In the morning she made her father's breakfast and took it to him on a tray. He scolded her for fussing over him, but she

266

could see how tired he looked.

'Takes it out of you, all this,' he waved his toast to demonstrate the strange new world of grief they were now inhabiting.

Later, when he was dressed, they went to the shops and she made sure his cupboards were stocked.

'Anyone would think there was a war on,' he said. 'I shall be well prepared in my bunker with all these baked beans.'

Eventually he persuaded her that he was fine, well rested, and that she should get home to Max and the children. She sat on the local train, numb with tiredness, but once she'd changed onto the main line, she finally let herself drift into a deep sleep, waking with a stiff neck and dribble on her cheek as the train slowed its way into York.

By ten o'clock that night, Karen was on her own doorstep, rummaging in her handbag for her front door key. As she went inside, it sounded like Max had company. Trisha's yelping laugh from the front room reminded her of something Ben had learnt at school about hyenas. He said the ancient Egyptians believed they lived in the caves of the dead and fed on corpses. She pushed the door open, hoping that Trisha and Paul weren't going to stay long. She was exhausted.

The hall light was off and the glow from the living room picked out a path across the tiled floor. There was a jumble of shoes under the radiator and she kicked off her boots to join the pile. The low rumble of Max's voice was punctuated by Trisha's yelp. Bless her for finding his

267

jokes funny, most of them were a hundred years old, but Karen wished she'd keep the volume down. As she pushed the door open she was hoping there was some wine left. She saw two empty glasses on the floor a second before she took in the fact that they were both naked. Trisha was sitting in Max's lap and he was still wearing his socks. There was no sign of Paul. For some reason Trisha screamed.

Karen said quietly, 'Please, don't wake my children.'

She went to shut the door, not sure which side of it she should be on. It seemed like slow motion, but she managed to put one foot in front of the other and leave the room. The door clicked shut. Silence. She stood in the hall. She thought she might faint; dots of light danced around the edge of her vision. She realised she was holding her breath.

No point being jealous. What right did she have anyway? She ran her hand along the wall, as if she needed to feel her way to the kitchen. She turned on the tap for a glass of water. She wasn't jealous. It was something else. Nausea maybe. But that might be because of the lack of food in her belly. She opened the fridge and took out some pastrami, which she ate straight from the packet. Then she cut some bread and put it in the toaster. She was just spreading Marmite on it when there was a knock on the kitchen door. Max stood in the doorway, waiting for her to say something. He was fully dressed and had a small suitcase in his hand. He was wearing a dark suit and a clean shirt and tie. Wherever he chose to spend the night, he'd be able to go straight to work in the morning. Typical Max. She scraped the Marmite towards the crusts so it was an even pale brown all over the slice.

'I would appreciate it if you didn't say anything to Paul at this stage. Trisha is in a very delicate emotional state.'

The Marmite-covered knife hovered in the air. She didn't seem to be controlling it. She heard a strange voice say, 'Is she?' It was hers, but it didn't sound right. Like a medium channelling a voice from the other side.

Yesterday she'd been sitting in an inquest, hearing about the state of her brother's body, the condition of his skin, the decomposition of his vital organs. And now Max had the temerity to tell her that Trisha was in a delicate emotional state. The knife fell out of her hand and clattered onto the lino.

'Just go, Max.'

'I ... look, Karen, I'm...'

'A fool.'

She wanted to ask him if he'd used a condom but she decided it could wait. Perhaps she should ask her neighbour first. Trisha might not have been quite so open with Max about her desperation to have a baby.

She heard the front door close and came out to check the living room. Trisha had gone. Home to Paul presumably. Would she sneak into the shower without waking him? No. He was probably away somewhere, making money out of someone else's cracked-up marriage. Jesus. It didn't matter, she knew the answer anyway, even if Max hadn't realised what the deal was. What was it Trisha had said? *I'll try anything.*

They'd left their empty champagne bottle and two dirty glasses on the carpet. They were Dartington crystal, a wedding present from Max's parents. If she'd been wearing shoes, she would have stamped them to pieces, but instead she picked them up and carried them through to the kitchen where she hurled them into the sink. One stem snapped and the other sprung a crack like a demented smile. She held the side of the sink and began to cry.

When the doorbell rang, it was well past midnight. She had no tears and no anger left. Max must have forgotten his keys and she decided she wouldn't turn him away. He could sleep on the couch if he had to. She turned the Yale and opened the door.

The woman standing on the doorstep looked tired. She had pale-olive skin and deep circles under her green eyes. Her hair was pushed back and it looked like it hadn't been washed for a week. She looked at Karen for a moment before she spoke.

'You are Ffilip's sister?' She blew the f sound in Phil's name as if she was blowing out the candles on a cake.

'Phil's sister? Yes.'

'Thank to God!'

Karen had no time to step out of the way. The woman threw her arms around her and kissed her on both cheeks.

# CHAPTER TWENTY-NINE

The picture frame hung above Sean's bed. When he turned out the light, the reflection of his room vanished and the dim glow of the streetlight disclosed the white goose on the lacework. Maureen had explained that it was traditional in Kosovo to do lacework. They'd ordered special needles and the fine cotton yarn on the Internet and she and Arieta had plotted his Christmas surprise all through December.

He must have closed his eyes. When he opened them he was reaching for its neck, surprised to find it warm and feathery in his hands. He knew, from inside the dream, that he was asleep and he tried to wake up, but he wasn't in his bed any more. He was in Stanley Mayhew's yard. It was full of white geese, running out of the barn. Behind them waddled an impossibly fat Mr Forsyth, now swelled to Michelin Man proportions. Forsyth was telling Sean that he had to strangle the geese when they reached him.

The dream altered, the colours changed. He was wearing a green waistcoat and red bloomers like some idiot in a pantomime. He didn't want anyone to see him like this. It was *'Jack and the Beanstalk'* and he was saying, *It's all right, I know what to do.* He had a goose under his arm and was coming down the beanstalk when the fat man appeared with a kitchen knife and started to hack away at the plant. Only this time the fat man was Barry 'Burger' King. Sean's feet were tangled in the leaves and he lost his hold, the goose slipping out of his hands, and when he looked down, he saw it had turned into a rabbit. He dropped it and it fell, spinning round and round, and then he was falling too.

He woke up for real then. Put the light on and sat upright against the pillows. The space on the wall where his flipchart had been was marked with four blue smudges on the wallpaper. The goose was in its frame. The dream receded but he was left with the feeling that there was something he should have done.

## CHAPTER THIRTY

When Karen woke up, Ben was kneeling on the bed, leaning over her.

'Mummy, there's a lady on the sofa.'

As her head cleared, she remembered Max going and the girl arriving. Last night, she'd wondered if the two things were connected but now she realised that they couldn't be. Interesting times, as her father would have said. The girl had mainly cried. She was in a bad way, very hungry and thirsty. Karen tried to persuade her to have a shower but she crumpled up on the sofa and didn't look like she would even make it up the stairs. When she answered Karen's questions, she made no sense and kept drifting into her own language.

'Mummy?' Ben said. 'The lady on the sofa is asleep. Can I put the telly on or will it wake her up?'

She sat up. The clock said seven-thirty. 'Don't you have to get ready for school?'

'It's the holidays. Half-term. Remember? Daddy and Trisha took us to Flamingo Land yesterday. Where did you go?'

She rubbed her face. 'Grandpa's house.'

Downstairs it was very quiet. She looked at the shape under the blanket on the sofa, rising and falling, just a tiny movement. This frail girl seemed to need very little oxygen to keep her alive. Arnold was nesting in the curve behind her knees. Karen closed the door and let her sleep on.

One floor up, Sophie was curled up in an identical position, cocooned in her pink duvet. Karen sat on the end of her bed and watched her waking, turning slowly, eyes half open, peering against the light.

'Hello, Mum. You're back.'

'Yes.'

Sophie wiped some sleep dust from the corner of her eye. 'Did Grandpa come with you?'

Karen shook her head. She didn't know how much she should tell Sophie about the inquest or about Max and Trisha. She would have to begin by telling her about the woman downstairs.

'There's someone staying over, on the sofa. She's a friend of Uncle Phil's and she's not very well, so we need to be quiet.'

'Did she come when Trisha was here? She was really noisy, I couldn't get to sleep.'

That bloody woman.

'Mum? Are you OK? You look like you're going to cry.'

'Just tired, really, really tired.'

Somehow she dragged herself back upstairs and got dressed. Sophie was listening to her MP3 player when she passed her door on the way back down. She would let her eat breakfast later; there was no rush. In the kitchen she put bowls and cereal, milk and orange juice on the table. She fed the cat and turned the kettle on. It was all so automatic and yet it felt like she was doing these things for the first time. It came to her then: Max had let her go. He didn't even know it, but he had freed her. This was the first day of her post-Max life. She wanted to tell someone. Charlie. She wanted to phone him, better still, see him. She stood still. There were voices coming from the living room. Ben and the girl. Damn, he'd woken her.

He had a jigsaw puzzle out across the floor. The girl was sitting, the blanket wrapped round her shoulders, pointing at one of the pieces.

'Is corner piece, no? You should start with corner, it becomes easier I think.'

'It's going to be a steam engine, like Thomas.'

'Tomass?'

'The Tank Engine, you must know who that is.' Ben stared at her as if she'd just stepped out of a spaceship.

'Hi,' Karen said. 'Did you sleep OK?'

'Yes. Very OK. I need it very badly.'

Karen handed her a cup of tea and left them to the jigsaw while she went to empty the dishwasher. Her mobile was ringing where she'd left it on the kitchen worktop, spinning as it vibrated on the marble.

'Charlie! You must be psychic. I was just about to ring you.'

'There's been a development. South Yorkshire Police are about to release it to the press.' It was his work voice, DCI Moon on the case, she almost laughed. 'They're looking for someone in connection with your brother's murder. A young woman, Arieta Osmani, she comes from Kosovo and was working as a prostitute in Doncaster. I wanted to tell you before you saw it on the national news.'

'National news?'

'She's not in the area, as far as we know. She could be anywhere.'

When he rang off, Karen turned the radio on in the kitchen. Weather. That meant she'd missed the news. She went upstairs and switched on the computer. Sophie came in.

'What you doing Mum?'

'Nothing.' Her hands didn't move on the keys. 'Just going to check emails.'

'Can I go on MSN?'

'Later.'

She unfroze when she heard Sophie go downstairs. It was there on the BBC website. Just posted. God, they were quick. Arieta Osmani, wanted in connection with the death of Philip Holroyd, and a photo, credited to *The Star*. She'd seen it before, she realised, when she'd looked up the heroin deaths, two young women squeezed into a photo booth. The girl downstairs was much thinner now and her hair had grown, with several inches of black roots showing before the red. She could hear Ben laughing and the girl laughing too. Then Sophie was running back up the stairs.

'Mum! Uncle Phil's friend is so funny. She's doing magic tricks. She can make a puzzle piece disappear then pull it out of Ben's ear.' She stopped behind Karen's shoulder. 'Oh ... my ... God.'

It was too late.

'It'll be all right, Sophie. Go and check the back door is locked and put the key in your pocket, then put a film on for Ben. Something long. Try to act normal. I'm going to call the police.'

Sophie nodded and backed out of the room. Charlie's phone rang to voicemail. She cut the call and rang again. This time he picked up.

'Sorry, I didn't get to it. I'm in a meeting...'

'She's here.'

'What?'

'Arieta Osmani. She's downstairs doing a jigsaw puzzle with my son. She turned up last night. She had my address, Charlie.' She was speaking quietly but making sure he heard every word.

'Is your husband there?'

She almost laughed. 'No. No, he's gone away.'

'Is there anywhere you can send the children?'

Not Trisha. She racked her brains. 'Sophie's got a friend. They can go there.'

'Wait, I'm passing a note to a detective here. He'll get the ball rolling. There'll be someone with you from North Yorkshire Police in a few minutes. It may be better to keep the children there for now. Don't do anything to arouse her suspicion.'

'I need to go downstairs. She's with them, with my children.' She heard her voice crack and he was trying to calm her. She kept the phone to her ear as she came downstairs. Then raised her voice, injecting a false note of normality. 'Bye then, thanks for calling.'

Sophie had put *The Jungle Book* on for Ben. She searched her mother's face as she came into the room. 'Do you want me to make another cup of tea, Mum? So you can watch the movie.'

She could have hugged her. 'Thank you, darling, that would be lovely.'

She realised she sounded like Mary Poppins, trying to keep everything normal. She stole a glance at Arieta Osmani, curled up again on her side, her energy dissipated, staring at the television. If the doorbell rang now, Ben might go to answer it and be confronted by police, possibly armed, but if she went, he would be alone with the girl. Come on, Sophie. It seemed to take ages but finally she heard a sound from the kitchen: the bolts being pulled open on the back door, unfamiliar voices.

'Ben, can you run upstairs and get me a tissue, my nose is running and I haven't got one.' She might have known it wouldn't work. He didn't even hear, he was so engrossed in the movie, his shoulders rocking to a song he'd heard a hundred times. The girl sat up.

'There is people outside.'

Sure enough there were several dark shapes at the front window.

'I'm sorry, Arieta.'

'How you know my name? Did Philip tell you?'

'What are you talking about? Phil's dead, you know that, and those people outside are the police.'

The door to the living room opened and a young policewoman stood there. Someone in the hall was opening the front door. Ben looked round, confused by the interruption.

'Ben, go with this nice police lady into the kitchen, you're not in trouble, she just needs you to show her where the biscuit tin is.'

It must have been the effect of the uniform, because this time Ben did exactly what he was told. Within seconds the front room was full of uniforms. Karen thought for an awful moment that they were going to take her, not Arieta, but the girl got shakily to her feet in time for an officer to read out the charges. On the television screen the snake, Kaa, was wrapping its body around Mowgli.

'I come. It's OK. I don't want to make trouble here,' she hesitated, her face so close that Karen could smell milky tea on her breath. 'It's not possible I kill Philip. You know, it is not actually possible.'

After they'd taken Arieta Osmani away, a policeman stayed behind in the kitchen to take a statement. Ben was upset that nobody had paused *The Jungle Book*. Sophie led him into the front room to rewind it and Karen caught a look from her which made her shiver; it was like looking into her own eyes, staring back at her, demanding an explanation. It would have to wait.

Paul appeared at the back door asking for Trisha. He seemed mildly puzzled at the presence of the police officer but didn't comment. When Karen said she hadn't seen Max or Trisha since ten-thirty the night before, he just nodded, as if he understood that his new wife was about to become his next ex-wife. Maybe he'd known for a long time. He excused himself and left.

After the police officer had gone, Karen sat down on the sofa and stared at the TV. The monkeys were doing their dance again. Something dug into her hip. She put her hand down the side of the cushion, and pulled out a small handbag. She remembered seeing it last night, across the girl's thin shoulders as she stood on the doorstep. She picked it up and took it upstairs.

## CHAPTER THIRTY-ONE

Sean stood on the steps on Doncaster Central Police Station and breathed in the clean air. Rain was drying on the pavements and the buildings looked like they'd been washed. It was three days since Declan had identified Arieta as the zombie in the caravan. This morning, the weight had finally lifted from Sean's chest as Rick listened to what he had to say, never for a moment showing any frustration that he hadn't spoken up earlier. He knew it pointed to Arieta being. Philip Holroyd's killer, and that one day soon he was going to have to sit Maureen down and tell her, but he'd done what he had to do.

He turned towards the bus station. Off duty and out of uniform, he had nothing planned for the whole afternoon. His fishing rod was in the attic. He hadn't done any fishing for a while. There was a lake a short bus ride out of town where he could get a one-day licence. He still had a few hours before it got dark. He didn't notice the blue car moving next to him until he heard the whine of its electric window.

'Fancy a lift, Denton? I'm going your way.'

It was Burger. Sean hesitated, but Burger was smiling at him. It looked like he'd lost a bit of weight. Maybe he really had been gardening. Sean got in. Neither of them spoke as they nosed through the traffic and headed towards the edge of town, towards the Chasebridge estate.

'You been back into work then?' Sean finally said.

'You haven't heard? I've taken early retirement. Working for myself now.'

Sean wondered how the top brass had edged him out so quietly. There'd been no announcement. They slowed down for the roundabout where Pets At Home nudged up against Morrisons. Burger told him to open the glove compartment. Wedged on top of the car manual was a small plastic bag.

'Get it out.' Burger said.

It was a Boots bag, the size they give you when you've just bought one or two items, like a deodorant or a toothbrush, but this bag was folded over in a money shape, a wad-of-notes shape. Sean waited for another instruction, torn between wanting and not wanting to see how much was inside.

'It's a down payment from my client. If we're successful, there'll be more.'

'We?' It was warm inside the car and Sean

became aware of the smell of sour milk rising up from the carpet.

'We could be a team.' Burger rested his hand on the gear stick and Sean thought, for one horrible moment, that the fat hand was going to reach over and pat his knee. 'Especially as this job's right up your street.'

They were level with the entrance to Pets At Home, and Sean tried to think of an excuse to get out. He could look up some old workmates, or hang around the guinea-pig pen, until Burger had forgotten about him.

'You have the advantage over me, Denton,' Burger was accelerating and changed into third gear. Sean had missed his opportunity. 'You have the information which my client is looking for. My client pays me and I subcontract to you. I buy, if you like, a little of your intellectual property.'

'You've lost me, sir.'

'Yes, I know.' Burger sighed theatrically. 'Let me put it more simply; one hundred pounds to you if you can help me find a girl; a particular girl.'

They were on the ring road now and Burger was slowing for the turning into the Chasebridge estate.

'I can't help you,' Sean shoved the bag back into the glove compartment. 'And, if it's all the same to you, sir, I'd rather walk from here.'

'What a pity. Don't worry, I'll deliver you right to your front door, all in good time, but I've got to see a man about a dog on the way.'

They turned up the dead-end towards the garages. Lee Stubbs was standing outside the one where Sean had his meeting with Declan.

281

'I think you know my nephew,' Burger said.

They were going quite slowly. Sean calculated that he could jump out and run, but as his hand reached for the door, Burger flicked the central locking on.

'Bit jumpy, Denton? Now in my former profession I would say that was a sure sign of having something to hide.'

The car stopped a few feet away from Lee Stubbs, who made no sign of having seen them. He got something out of his pocket. Light flashed off metal as he released the blade. Sean used to have a flick knife like that, when he was about fourteen and thought it was cool. This one looked very sharp.

Burger switched the engine off and Sean stared out at Stubbs, who started casually picking at the dirt under his nails with the tip of the knife.

'If you don't want to accept my offer, I'm sure we can find another way. Why don't we have a little chat, Denton, about some family business? My family. Not yours. You haven't really got one, have you? Not a proper one, just an old granny down on the Groves and an alky dad who you never visit.'

Sean didn't move. He tried not to twitch an eye muscle. Nothing that would antagonise Burger. He tried to see him as he once had, doing his job, tucking into his second breakfast in the staff canteen, wheezing with his allergies in the old man's farmhouse. But it didn't add up. He was the same, but different, thinner, meaner. He was back to being the Barry King who'd twisted Sean's ear in the lay-by.

'We could visit your granny. She's a bit over the hill but Lee's not fussy. He's a sick fucker as it goes.' Lee continued to pick at his nails. 'I blame his mother; he saw too much too young. She gave him his first taste of the ladies when he was only twelve. He's driven a few used cars in his time, if you know what I mean.'

Sean felt the heat rising up to his face. He clenched his fists. But Burger carried on, in a steady tone, like they had all the time in the world. He wanted to make it clear that he was angry with Sean, on several counts. First, he was very upset for his sister, whose business premises had been raided.

'She's always paid her taxes, Denton, not to mention National Insurance. All her ladies are genuine self-employed, but no, that's not good enough for some people.'

He also wanted Sean to understand that he was upset about the Internal Affairs Investigation Team, the meerkats who'd been all over Doncaster Central, poking their noses much deeper into his private business than was necessary.

'All a fuss about nothing, Denton, nothing they could prove, not until you and that stuck-up little tart came plodding in with your big fat feet.'

Sean kept his mouth tight shut and watched Lee Stubbs approach the car. As Burger clicked off the central locking, Stubbs opened the door. He leant towards Sean, stinking of sweat and stale smoke. His fingernails were chewed and brown round the edges.

'I've told you,' Sean tried to keep the quiver in his voice under control, 'I can't help you.'

Stubbs laughed his high-pitched doper's laugh and did a weird dance. He was clearly off his head.

'Can't or won't?' Burger made it sound like it was everyday police work, as if there wasn't a nutcase skipping up and down with a flick knife in his hand. 'The thing is, are you going to tell us where the girl is, or are we going to have to ask your gran?'

'Which girl?' he dared to say.

'The one you had tucked away in your love nest.'

Sean shook his head. Stubbs stopped dancing and lunged towards him. Burger clicked the catch to unfasten Sean's seatbelt and gave Sean a hard shove. Stubbs grabbed the collar of Sean's jacket and dragged him out of the car.

'In that case,' Burger said. 'You can wait here, while we have a chat with her on our own.'

Stubbs had Sean's arm twisted up his back. Sean could have thrown him off but out of the corner of his eye, he saw the knife dipping and arching with Stubbs's erratic movements. Barry King was opening a garage door. Sean recognised it straight away. The crates were still there, but the candle and bottle had gone. In the middle of the floor was a blue plastic chair with a roll of duct tape on the seat. He wanted to shout out, but his throat was tight and when he tried to say *wait*, Lee Stubbs spun him round and punched him across the mouth. His lips went numb and he tasted blood on his tongue. Stubbs kicked the back of Sean's legs and folded him down onto the chair.

'The thing is, if you don't tell us what we want to know,' Burger smiled, his slack cheeks pushing up until his eyes almost disappeared, 'I'm sure your dear sweet granny will.'

Stubbs was winding the duct tape around Sean's ankles, then round his wrists. He split the tape off the roll with the knife and Sean felt its chill against his skin. Sean tried to keep track of the blade, as the other man's hands moved over and across his body, pinning his upper arms to his sides.

'It's such a relief not to have to play by the rules, Denton,' Burger said.

'Night, night, Plastic Percy.' Stubbs ripped one last length of tape off the roll and stuck it over Sean's eyes. The garage door slammed shut and he heard the click of a bolt.

## CHAPTER THIRTY-TWO

Karen was beginning to feel at home on this train line and Ben and Sophie were visibly enjoying the novelty. Ben took the window seat and spread his comics out across the table. A thin-faced man sitting opposite him looked dismayed at being joined by a family. After ten minutes he turned to Karen.

'Will you please tell him to stop kicking me?'

Ben was sucking a pencil and staring out of the window, swinging his legs under the table. She didn't care any more.

'No,' she said, 'I can't. He's got a medical condition, he doesn't understand a word I say.'

Sophie rolled her eyes and hid her face behind a magazine. The tea trolley came past and Karen bought the children crisps, cola and chocolate, much to their amazement. The man stared hard at the passing fields. She hoped they'd be sick in his direction.

'Will Daddy remember to feed Arnold while we're away?' Sophie said.

Good point. Perhaps she should tell Max they'd gone, if only for the cat's sake. She got her phone out to text him and noticed a message from Charlie. She replied with her arrival time in Doncaster.

'Grandpa! Mummy, there's Grandpa!'

Outside the window Reg was waving. As he got on, Karen was ready to get off.

'Barely had time for a sleep and a bath and then she drags me out on another adventure.'

'How did you get here, Grandpa?' said Ben.

'Got the train up from Hitchin this morning and now I'm heading south again. They'll think I'm some poor tramp trying to keep warm, going up and down the same line!' He gave Karen a peck on the cheek. 'Run along or the doors will close. Are you kids ready for a Grandpa mystery tour?'

'It's not a mystery,' Ben said. 'We're going all the way to London to see Buckingham Palace, then we're going to stay at your house.'

'That's right, and I've got twenty-two cans of special-offer baked beans waiting for you.' Reg sat down next to Ben and the man opposite stiffened at the realisation that his ordeal would last another two hours.

Karen waved back at them from the platform. She felt a lightness in every bone, every muscle, as if she was buoyed up by helium. The brick walls of the station were redder, cleaner than she remembered. People were smiling and she smiled back. They couldn't know what breeze was carrying her along. But it was the breath of a miracle.

When the police had gone, Karen had waited quietly in the upstairs study, weighing the girl's bag in her hands like an unopened gift. Its strap was frayed and the vinyl was peeling away from the cardboard that held it together. The clasp gave way with a muffled click. It wasn't too late to phone the officer who'd interviewed her in the kitchen. He had written his mobile number down and Karen had pinned it to the noticeboard. It wouldn't have been difficult to say: *there's something else, she left her bag. Do you need it?* Or she could just look inside. There was a dirty tissue and a battered lipstick tube, a small purse containing two ten pence pieces and some coppers. And then, wedged deep into the seam of the bag, Karen felt a small piece of card. She pulled it out and saw that it was actually a larger card, folded up into a tight square not much bigger than a postage stamp. It unfolded easily, as if it had been opened out and refolded many times, and despite the criss-cross graph of creases, it was clear that it was a picture postcard of a large yellow building with a sweeping staircase and a balustrade. The building looked European, but in the background there was a tall concrete minaret. Karen turned the card over. *Pristina, Kosovo.* A stab of recognition stopped her breath. The handwriting was Phil's.

# CHAPTER THIRTY-THREE

At first Sean shouted, then he gave up. From a gap under the tape, he could see the light under the garage door turn greyer and darker. The air grew colder. Somehow, finally, he slept. When he woke, his bones ached with cold and his feet and fingers were numb. The tape round his ankles was so tight he was afraid it had stopped his circulation. He had no idea how long they'd left him but he knew it was overnight. The smell of his own piss surprised him but then he remembered finally letting go at some point and peeing on the floor. He drifted off again and when he woke, he remembered his nan. Jesus, what had they done to her?

A line of sunlight was visible under the door of the garage. He wanted to shout again, but who would hear him? He listened. There was something there, something moving. It might have been a leaf or a bit of plastic, blowing up against the door, blocking out the light intermittently. Or an animal; Sean thought he could hear a snuffling sound. He whistled, as quietly as he could manage, and the thing stopped moving. He whistled again louder this time and this time he could hear the thing whining.

'Ruby?' No need to shout. Thank God dogs have sharp hearing. She barked. He was sure it was her. 'Ruby! Good girl. Is he with you? Is Declan there?'

She barked again and must have stood on her hind legs; he could hear her claws scratching against the metal. Someone tried the handle, and then he heard a voice.

'Who's put a padlock on here?' It was a woman. He thought it could be the boy's mother and he tried to remember her voice, it sounded familiar, but perhaps older than Declan's mum.

'Hey!' He risked shouting now. 'Can you get me out of here?'

'Someone in there?' She knocked against the door.

'Yes, can you open it?'

'No, I can't. Someone's put a new lock on. Cheeky buggers. It's ours, is this garage.'

'Call the police. Please.'

There was silence for a few seconds. 'Bloody hell. I'm out of credit. Hang on, there's someone coming.'

Sean wriggled as hard as he could. There was some give in the tape but it was cutting into his wrists. He wanted to shout out that having no credit didn't matter; she could still get the emergency services if she dialled 999, but it was too late. The sound of a car engine filled the space outside the garage. There were voices but he couldn't hear what was being said. Then the door was opening. The first thing he saw was three different pairs of shoes and the dog's four paws. A pair of Nike trainers moved first. The big leather shoes and the pink plastic clogs stayed where they were.

'Bloody hell, Barry!' It was the woman again. 'Get him out of my garage. I told you what you wanted to know, now I want nothing more to do with it.'

'Don't you worry, Carole, he's coming with us. We're going to take him to see your friend Johnny Mac.'

Carole. The one with the spicy crisps and knock-off T-shirts. The one who Maureen thought was her friend. Shit. The door was wide open now, and Stubbs was on him. He willed the dog to defend him, to bite Stubbs's hand as he pressed the blade of the flick knife against Sean's neck. He could feel her sniffing his feet. Stupid animal. This wasn't a game.

'Get him in the car,' he heard Burger say.

Stubbs shoved him forwards but the tape binding his ankles made him stumble, pins and needles stabbing up through his legs. From the bottom of the tape across his eyes, he could see the light was brighter for a moment and they were outside. He caught a glimpse of blue paint on metal before he was pushed down onto a gritty carpet. The sour milk smell was overpowering and he guessed he was in the rear footwell of Burger's car. Someone was following him in, then the door slammed and he felt a weight on his back. Two feet had him firmly pressed to the floor.

Sean couldn't tell how far they'd come, but it was the better part of a Michael Jackson album. There was something under his hip, which crumpled as his weight shifted. He couldn't tell if it was a newspaper or a discarded food wrapper. There were straight stretches when it felt like they were doing a reasonable speed, and then they were on slower, winding roads where the motion threw him against the metal undercarriage of the driver's seat. He could feel the heels of Stubbs's trainers digging into the side of his legs, as the evil sod tapped his feet, singing along in a weed-cracked voice to *Wanna Be Starting Somethin'*.

'Club remix!' Stubbs shouted above the music. 'Fucking brilliant!'

Then the feet got carried away, dancing over his curled-up body. A foot landed with a sharp crack on Sean's elbow. The pain seared up his arm and he whimpered. Burger turned the music up louder. Lee was laughing and singing. Sean caught a whiff of something that smelt like newly cut hay. The feet paused and there was lighter fuel in the air. Then the music stopped.

'What the fuck?' Stubbs whined.

'I've told you, you little bastard, don't smoke that crap in my car.'

'Uncle Barry? It don't matter now. You ain't still a copper.'

'Gives me asthma. Just have a fag like a normal person, can't you?'

'Fuck.'

Another kick to Sean's side. The road surface got worse. Bumping over stones and potholes, it felt like a rough track. And then they stopped.

'What's the plan, Uncle Barry?'

'Shut it. Pigs have big ears.'

'We could put him in a pigpen. Eh, Uncle Barry, how do you stop a pig squealing?'

'Dunno.'

'Slit its throat.' Click. The flick knife. 'We could just leave him here. Middle of the yard. Job done.'

The engine cut out. It was windy outside. Sean

could feel the car shifting slightly. He moved his head and realised that the corner of the tape had caught on the carpet. Slowly, slowly, he turned his head. The tape began to peel off his face like a sticking plaster, tugging at his skin.

'Lee, you're a twat. Now stay here, and don't move.' Burger opened the driver's door. 'I'm going to see if I can find that ginger bastard. Let him ask the questions.'

'Don't know why you take orders off him,' Stubbs whined, 'after the way he's treated Mam, robbing girls off her and that.'

'Shut it,' Burger growled and slammed the door shut.

The smell of skunk again and the rustle of a cigarette paper. Stubbs just couldn't help himself. Sean waited until he heard the lighter. The metal lid rattled back and the flint caught. It had to be a two-hand job. This was his chance. He clenched his stomach muscles and pulled himself up and round. The tape flapped off one eye. It was caught in his eyebrow on the other side, but he could see enough. Stubbs stared over the fat joint in his mouth. As the flame caught and smoke billowed between them, Sean brought his head down on Stubbs's nose. He felt a sting on his cheek as the burning end fell to the floor. Then he remembered the knife. It was on the seat next to Stubbs, whose hands were free while Sean's were still taped at the wrists. He rolled sideways and sat on it. Stubbs's hands came up to his throat and gripped tight, squeezing his windpipe. He could feel the knife blade; it must have slit through his trousers and cold metal

292

touched the back of his thigh. He prayed it would stay flat against him – if it punctured the skin it could hit an artery – but it was almost impossible, he was struggling for air, trying to twist out of Stubbs's grasp. His eyes were stinging and the car was filling with smoke. The newspaper Sean had been lying on was now alight and a crisp packet began to singe and crumple. The hands fell from his neck and the door flew open. Before it could slam shut again, Sean threw himself at the gap and slid out onto the wet, muddy concrete. Stubbs aimed a kick at him, then turned and ran. Sean tried to stand but he had no feeling in his taped-up legs. He held his breath and rolled over and over, as fast as he could manage, away from the burning car.

A little girl with a halo of white blonde hair was looking down at him, her eyes wide in astonishment. Sean had come to a stop against a wall. Something hard dug into his shoulder blade. When he twisted his head he could see that the girl was sitting on a concrete step in front of a green door. The sharp thing in his back was the corner of the step. He moved a little and heard the tape tear. With a few wriggling twists, he loosened it enough to free his arms and push himself up to a sitting position. The car was about fifty feet away, clouds of smoke billowing inside and flames sneaking out through the sunroof. He could hear raised voices coming from around the side of the building. He pulled his wrists down over the corner of the step and felt the tape beginning to tear and split. With his hands free, he started on the tape round his ankles.

'What are you doing?' she said.

'Playing a game.'

'What game?'

'Hide and seek. Where's a good place to hide?'

She looked at him and sucked her finger. 'Umm, let me think.'

The voices were getting louder.

'What's through that door?' He tried to keep his voice level; he didn't want to scare her. 'Why don't we hide in there?'

'Is that car on fire?' She sounded quite matter of fact; as if burning cars were an everyday feature of life. Perhaps she was like Declan and watched too much TV.

'We'd better go inside, hadn't we? In case we get hurt.'

He was up the steps and turning the door handle when he clearly heard Burger's voice shouting an obscenity and Stubbs's whine in response. To his relief the little girl stepped cautiously through the door. He slipped in behind her, slammed it shut and pushed a bolt across the top. His pulse thundered in his ears.

'It's all right. It's all right,' he babbled, more to himself than to the child. There was a bolted door between him and Stubbs, between him and Burger. He was safe for now; he hadn't died.

'Mister?'

He turned round. They were in some sort of barn or cowshed. One side was taken up with farm vehicles. He identified a rusting John Deere tractor and something that might have been a plough. There was a newer tractor too, a great big thing with a glass cab and wheels as high as Sean was tall. Behind it, covered with a blue plastic tarpaulin, was a rectangular box-shaped trailer and beyond that, a dusty green car. The glass windows, high up under the roof, cast a hazy light over a series of stalls. Low walls, topped off with metal railings, divided each space into a fifteen-foot square. But there weren't any cows. In each section, there was a mattress and a sleeping bag. Some had a blanket or a neat pile of clothes; others were surrounded by cardboard boxes or brightly covered plastic bags. The girl was holding his hand very tightly.

'Mister,' she whispered. 'Uncle Johnny says I'm not allowed in here on my own.'

'Well, you're not on your own. I'm here. My name's Sean and it's OK, I'm a policeman. What's your name?'

'Holly Holroyd and I've got a fierce dog called Marvin and a rabbit called Frank, but when Mummy and Uncle Johnny get married I'm going to be called something else but I can't remember what it is.'

Sean had a pretty good idea that it was Mackenzie.

'I've seen you before, haven't I?' Sean said gently. 'At a place with lots of stone angels?'

'Heaven. Where my Daddy is.'

She was moving away from him now, along a track where once the slurry from the cows must have collected. It was like a little concrete lane between the stalls. She stopped and when he caught up with her, he found her staring at a bundle on a mattress. The bundle had a face. Two eyes opened and a black woman with neatly braided hair was looking up at them. Sean crouched down to get a closer look.

'Hello,' the little girl said. 'Who are you?'

'Please,' the woman said to Sean, her voice thick with tiredness, 'don't tell Mr Mackenzie I am here. The baby makes me sick so I cannot go to work.'

Her voice sounded African, some place like that. She struggled to sit up and as her sleeping bag dropped, Sean could see she was heavily pregnant.

'What's going on?' Sean said. 'You should be indoors.'

Holly was exploring the few possessions around the woman's mattress. She picked up a magazine and sat down, cross-legged, turning the pages. Sean crouched on the cold floor and tried to unwrap the tape that was still sticking his left arm to his torso. He winced from the pain in his elbow, where Stubbs had stamped on him in the car.

'Let me look. In my own country I was a nurse.'

The woman's fingers moved swiftly, tearing the tape in small movements that caused much less pain than his own jerky attempts. Then she rolled up his sleeve and whistled at the state of his elbow. It was swollen and tinged with a blue-black bruise.

'Man, someone hurt you. Have you been fighting?'

'Bit of a one-sided fight.'

'What does that say?' Holly said, pointing at a picture in the magazine of some C-list celebrity in a tiara. 'Is she a princess?'

'I don't know. The magazine belongs to my daughter.' There was a catch in the woman's voice. She looked from Holly back to his elbow and blinked hard. 'Right now, what are we going to do with this mess? Bind it, I think, then you need to see a doctor for real, young man.'

She pulled his sleeve down and used the discarded tape to fashion a bandage, which held his arm stiff, the elbow slightly bent. He almost laughed, he had an Action Man with an arm like that when he was little. He remembered being upset that he couldn't afford the one with the proper moving joints.

From somewhere outside the barn, the shouting reached a peak. A massive bang punched the air and sucked out all the sound. When Sean could hear again, glass was raining down around them. He threw himself across the girl and the woman, ignoring the shrieking pain in his arm.

He was sitting with his back to the woman, while she picked glass out of his hair and told him her story in a soft voice, which rose and fell in a rhythm designed to smooth the fear out of the three of them, but especially the child. Her name was Florence Moyo and she lived here with her husband, who was out with the others at a bacon factory. They wouldn't be back until late and she was worried about the glass, which had spread over their beds and possessions.

'You really are going to have to see a doctor now. Some little bits I can't get out without hurting you more. But mainly you are a lucky boy.' He didn't feel lucky. 'Tell me, what is going on out there exactly? It sounded like a bomb.'

'It was just a car.' He turned to look at the little

girl, who was hugging the magazine and sitting as much in the woman's lap as she could manage, considering the size of her bump. There was no point in scaring her any more. 'Some naughty men set fire to it, and the petrol tank must have exploded.'

The woman seemed to understand his tone and stroked Holly's hair. 'Yes, yes of course. I forgot. In my country children of Holly's age are used to loud explosions.'

'Is that why you're here?' Sean asked.

'My husband had some enemies in the police.'

He knew what that felt like, the ex-police anyway.

'Do you think we should call them, the police I mean?' she continued.

'You've got a phone?' He couldn't believe it, all the time he'd been in here, and he could have called for back up.

'You understand, I am reluctant to draw attention.' She spoke more urgently now, lowering her voice as if they could be overheard. 'My husband and I've lost our claim to be here. But my daughter, she's found a job. The people here, they have an agency for nurses, I saw their advertisement. I wanted her to stay if we are sent back, so I gave her my papers. My nursing qualifications. Was that wrong, to make people think she is a nurse?'

He didn't know, hardly cared now. All he wanted was that phone. 'I need to call someone.'

She hesitated, then handed it to him.

'It's all right,' he said, hoping it would be. He punched in the direct number for the station and got through to the desk sergeant. He gave her

Maureen's address. She said there was a flap on, but they'd do what they could, then she hesitated.

'Did you say Barry King?' she asked. 'Are you sure?'

'Yes, and his nephew, Lee Stubbs. I think they might have hurt her, they threatened to, but they're not there now,' he looked at Florence. 'They're here.'

The desk sergeant was asking if he needed assistance.

'I don't know where I am, to be honest, but I'm OK. Just send someone up to my nan's, please.'

'When I ring off, leave the phone switched on, Sean,' the desk sergeant said, 'And I'll see if we can put a trace on it.'

'You didn't say anything about this place? The explosion?' Florence said, when he handed the phone back to her.

'Not yet. Not until we have to.' He hoped it wouldn't take them long. The car would probably burn itself out before it did anyone any harm, but he didn't fancy his chances against Stubbs. From the brief glimpse he'd had of the farm itself, it seemed to be entirely surrounded by country-side. He might be able to hide, but the night would be cold if there was no shelter nearby.

'Thank you,' Florence said, and stroked Holly's hair until the little girl relaxed and began to trace her finger over the picture of the actress.

The air smelt of burning tyres and the wind carried voices from the yard. Sean wondered if there was another way out of the barn. If they could let the little girl run safely back to the house, they could disappear into the fields. Or he

299

could disappear. He didn't think Florence would be able to move fast enough, but he didn't want to think about her spending another night in here, with no glass in the windows.

He stood up slowly. The pain in his arm and the long hours without food made him dizzy. He blinked and waited until his vision cleared. Then he stepped into the slurry channel and began to explore the barn again. Apart from the small door he had come through, which opened in the shorter wall, there was also a large double door on the longer side of the barn. He pushed it gently but nothing moved. It seemed to be locked from the outside. As far as he could work out, the barn was at such an angle that the large door opened directly on to the yard. The smaller door was around the corner, but he would still have to run fast to get out of view of anyone who was near the burning car. He looked at the vehicles. The old tractor was useless. He peeled the corner of the tarp away from the rectangular box, hoping it might be a van of some kind. Peeling cream paint gave way to a metal shuttered hatch. The last few letters of a sign were visible. MENTS. He lifted the tarpaulin up higher; it was Su-Mai's catering trailer. He tried to focus. Burger and Stubbs had brought him to meet Mackenzie, so this was his farm, his barn. He looked at the car, tucked behind the trailer. The registration plates were missing.

Sean thought about that day in the lay-by, the girl folded in on herself, the wind catching her hair. Just a straightforward smack OD. Why would anyone want to hide the trailer? Probably because they didn't want it left behind as evidence. If Mac-

300

kenzie had hidden the trailer here, then he could have been Su-Mai's pimp. The fuzziness in Sean's head was beginning to clear but he was struggling to see why Mackenzie wanted to know where Arieta was, although of course, he was probably her pimp too. A caravan on the edge of a quarry was the new opportunity she'd told Maureen about. But then Mackenzie had taken a young girl to Stella Stubbs. Was he working with her? Or was he coaxing girls away from her and setting up his own franchise? In the middle of all this was Lee Stubbs, dealing fatal amounts of heroin.

'Young man?' Florence Moyo called across to him. 'Can you smell it? Burning?'

'Yes, it's the tyres.'

'No. A new smell.'

She was trying to stand up. The little girl held on around her legs. She was right. It was different smell, something acrid that caught in your throat.

'That's petrol!' Sean spun round to work out where it was coming from.

'Look!' Florence pointed at the double barn door. The tongues of tiny flames were licking underneath.

A massive surge of adrenaline cleared Sean's vision and numbed the pain. He had to live. He understood what had happened, what had been happening all along. He couldn't die now and he couldn't let Holly or the pregnant woman die either.

'It's going to be all right. I'm going to get you out of here.' He turned back to the looming shape of the new tractor, its wheels like the shoulders of an elephant.

301

# CHAPTER THIRTY-FOUR

The afternoon light was starting to fade as Charlie turned off the road onto the farm drive. Ahead of them there was a glow in the sky. Soon they could see a cluster of barns and a small farmhouse lit by a fire in the centre of a yard. There was a loud bang, followed by a plume of black smoke.

'Petrol tank. Someone torching a car.'

Charlie made it sound almost normal, but this wasn't joyrider country. Something was going on. Karen had been hoping to talk to Stacey on her own, while Charlie dealt with Mackenzie, but there were figures running across the yard. Charlie turned the headlights off and carried on driving. He stopped the car on a grass verge, just outside the entrance. The gate was hooked open.

'CCTV,' Charlie said. 'The camera's angled on the gate itself, with any luck it hasn't picked us up.'

'If they're even looking. Sounds like they've got other things to worry about.'

They could hear male voices shouting. Charlie took her hand and led her close to the hedge and around the gatepost. From there they had a better view of the remains of a burning vehicle and three men, all shouting at each other, none of them looking their way. They went closer. A large, red-faced man turned and stared, open-mouthed, at Charlie, who had produced his warrant card, and was using it to fan the black smoke away from his face.

'Who the fuck...?' The fat one started, and Karen recognised him. The big copper from Doncaster Central, what had Sean called him? Burger, that was it. One of the figures backed away into the shadows; it was unmistakably Johnny Mackenzie and she was pretty sure it was Charlie he was trying to avoid. The other guy was younger, skinny and jittery. He was dancing on the spot, looking from Burger to the car and back to Charlie, as if he was trying to work out whether to run or fight.

'King, isn't it? My name's DCI Moon. Is everything all right?'

'Pleased to meet you.' Although it didn't sound like he meant it. 'All under control here, just an unlucky accident.'

'Where did Mackenzie go?' Charlie peered through the smoke. There was a movement over by a large wood and brick-built barn. Someone was moving along the side of the building. Whoever it was, was carrying a heavy object in their hands, bending at intervals as if they were pouring something on the ground.

'Looks like a petrol can,' Charlie said. 'Jesus Christ, he's going to set light to the barn!'

The young guy let out a sound like a banshee wail. Karen couldn't tell if it was pain or pleasure. She expected King to react but he just stood there, watching, as Mackenzie stood back from the barn and threw something at the liquid. It puffed up immediately into a flame, which licked along the ground, retracing his route until it reached a high double door at the front and tore up the wood.

Charlie ran towards Mackenzie, who dodged him and disappeared through a gap between the farm buildings.

King made no move. He just stood and watched. She pulled out her phone and he turned towards her, hand outstretched.

'I'll take that.'

'What? Why?'

He didn't answer.

'Give 'im your bloody phone! Shall I make 'er Uncle Barry?' The skinny boy jostled her elbow and she instinctively fended him off.

Still the police officer didn't react. Why did the boy call him uncle? She couldn't see Charlie any more and the flames were taking hold around the wooden sides of the barn. She judged that the distance between where she was standing and the farmhouse was about fifty metres. She could outrun King if she had to, but she wasn't sure about the skinny one. He made a grab for her arm and she dodged him, nearly slipping in the mud. She turned and made a dash for it.

There was a light on in the farmhouse kitchen and through the window she could see Stacey sitting at a table, an empty bottle of wine next to her. Karen burst through the door and slammed it behind her.

'Call the fire brigade, Stacey, the barn's on fire!' A television was on in one corner, the volume turned high. Stacey stirred from a deep sleep, oblivious to the car on fire or the shouting in the yard. The door was opening, Karen leant her back against it but she couldn't hold it.

'Holly.' Stacey got up, rubbing her eyes. 'Where's Holly?'

'She went to check on her rabbit.'

As Karen hit 999 on her phone, Stacey pushed her aside. She opened the door and the skinny boy fell in. Karen ran deeper into the house, looking for a door, any door with a lock on it. Where the hell was the toilet?

'Emergency services. What service do you require?'

'Police, fire.' She was in the dark hallway, a staircase on her left. She took the stairs two at a time. Somewhere ahead of her a dog was barking.

'What is your location?'

She tried a door on the landing, Holly's room. No use. She tried the next. There were footsteps on the stairs and a door banged. She heard the policeman calling from the kitchen: 'Lee! Leave her to me!'

'Hello?' the operator kept saying. 'What is your location?'

Here was the dog, Marvin, jumping up, trying to lick her face. It looked like she was in the master bedroom. She prayed they had an ensuite bathroom.

'A farm, Moorsby-on-Humber.' What was the address? 'Exchange something...'

'I'm sorry, can you repeat that?'

A door in the bedroom led to a bathroom. She and the dog were inside. She closed the door and pushed the flimsy bolt into place and put all her weight against it.

'Labour. Exchange Labour.' She was breathing heavily. 'It's a business address, near Moorsby-on-

305

Humber, a farm. Tell them to go to The Volunteer Arms, take the smaller road at the crossroads, then after half a mile, turn left, keep going, I don't know, after another quarter of a mile maybe, there's the farm drive. Go to the top of that.' A thump against the door. 'And get a message to who ever is in charge at Doncaster Central, that one of their officers, a detective called King, is here, but there's something wrong.'

'You're saying there's already an officer on the scene?'

'Yes, two, but one's behaving weirdly, really weirdly. Please, hurry up!'

Another thud and Marvin let off a round of frantic barks. Then someone coughing and a voice that sounded half strangled.

'Jesus,' King spluttered. 'Fucking dog hairs, get me out of here!'

He was gasping for air. The boy mumbled, too low for her to hear, and then their voices seemed to be moving away. She strained to hear beyond the house, praying for the sound of distant sirens.

It was quiet in the bedroom. Karen drew the bolt across and eased the door open a crack. There was nobody there. She crept to the window. Outside, the car was almost burnt out; just two small fires remained, under the front and rear axles. The tyres had collapsed unevenly and it sat at a drunken angle. Flames were licking up the sides of the barn. Stacey stood in the middle of the yard, her mouth open in a scream, but Karen couldn't hear her because the window was rattling in its frame. When she opened it, she realised that some sort of engine was causing a powerful, rumbling vibration. From much further away the wail of sirens was just audible, fading in and out on the wind, but the rumbling noise was coming from the barn. With a loud crash, the double doors bent outwards, splintered in the centre and fell open. A tractor as high as a lorry drove through the flames and into the yard. In its cab she could see a man, a woman and a child.

Marvin got her legs up onto the windowsill and shoved her nose out of the window. She sniffed the bitter air and barked at the huge tractor. Just then, another vehicle moved away from behind a low shed at the back of the yard. It was a black Range Rover and its only way out was between the tractor and the burning car. Just as it looked as if the car was going to make it, the tractor lurched forwards and clipped the rear of the driver's side, sending the Range Rover spinning on the muddy concrete. The front end smashed into the back of the burning car. Immediately the driver's door flew open and Mackenzie ran out. Stacey caught him. She had him by the shoulders and was shaking him, pointing up at Holly in the tractor cab. The Range Rover now had flames pouring out of the bonnet and a yellow glow behind its tinted windows.

Mackenzie started running, not towards the house but into the prefab office. Stacey followed him. Karen knew she had to stop them. She ran out of the bedroom and down the stairs, the dog nearly tripping her up in its excitement. Where was Charlie? And where the hell were Burger and the skinny guy? The kitchen was clear. As she reached the yard, there was Holly, hand in hand with a heavily pregnant African woman, walking

307

towards the kitchen door. Karen stopped. It was Florence Moyo. Behind her limped PCSO Sean Denton, torn bits of tape flapping off his clothes. She wasn't sure what to do now, but Sean had a look in his eyes that made the decision for her.

'Stop Mackenzie!' she shouted. 'He's going to destroy the office.'

He turned and ran, while she led the other two, and Marvin, back inside and locked the kitchen door firmly behind them. Florence sat down heavily and rested her head in her hands.

'Mrs Moyo, what are you doing here?'

She began to cry, silently. Tears running down her face and onto the wooden table. Eventually she started to speak.

'My husband found a job with this man, Mackenzie. There was work for me and my daughter too. I was cleaning, and she was going to be caring for old people. We lied about her age and her qualifications, I'm so sorry, but we had to get money. Was that wrong?'

Karen shook her head. 'Where is she? Where's Elizabeth?'

'I don't know. Mackenzie takes my daughter, he says it is to a care home. My husband says at first the other men, the men he works with, just give him looks. Then they are smirking and laughing, making disgusting jokes. One man, a Polish one, he is kind, takes my husband to one side and tells him, there is no care home.'

Her head sank back into her hands and she began to cry again. Holly crept up to her and stroked her arm.

# CHAPTER THIRTY-FIVE

Sean didn't think he'd ever seen so many blue lights. If only they wouldn't all flash out of sequence, it was making his head hurt. There were three fire engines working on the barn and a single firefighter with a hose extended towards the two cars, nudged together like smouldering wreckage in a war zone. The ambulance was standing by and two paramedics were with the pregnant woman in the farmhouse. Lizzie said he should get them to check he didn't have any more glass in his skin. She was picking over his head like his nan used to check for nits, but more gently. As her fingertips stroked through his hair, he didn't want her to stop. He almost let himself believe that her tenderness meant something, but then he remembered that combing for evidence was her job. He was sitting on a little stone platform with steps up to it. Lizzie said it was an old mounting block from the days when ladies rode side-saddle. She seemed to know a lot about it. Lizzie Morrison riding ponies as a teenager was an image he was going to have trouble wiping from his mind.

'Tip your head a bit this way, so it's in the light.'

Someone had found the switch to override the movement sensor on Mackenzie's security system and this side of the yard was lit up like a football pitch. He watched Rick Houghton stroll across from where he'd been talking to DCI Moon.

Behind them Sean could make out Mackenzie's miserable features in the rear seat of one of the police Volvos.

'All right, Lizzie,' Rick was saying, 'If you've finished playing Florence Nightingale, as soon as the fire brigade say it's safe, get yourself into the barn. It's a crime scene for at least two live cases.'

'Three,' Sean said. 'I think it might be three.'

Back up had arrived just as Sean was rugby-tackling Mackenzie to the floor of his office. He'd caught him unawares, apparently trying to find his lighter. Nobody had known what to say when they saw ex-DCI Barry King and Lee Stubbs being frogmarched across the burning yard, with Charlie Moon carrying a double-barrelled shot-gun behind them. Moon said he got it off Mackenzie. Sean wished he could have seen that.

'We've had a call, about your nan. She's all right by the way. Just a bit shaken,' Rick said, as he tapped a cigarette out of the packet and into his palm, then glanced over at the firefighters and put it away again.

'What happened?' Sean asked.

'Stubbs tied her up and threatened to set light to the house. They were asking about the girl, Arieta. I think they were planning to use your nan as a hostage, to get you to talk. Burger must have thought better of it and let her go, but not before he'd cut her landline, taken her phone and house keys and locked her in her own house. Carly's with her now. She's had the locksmith round and she's now trying to persuade her to let the doctor check her over, but she says she's fine.'

Sean was relieved Carly was there. He knew his

nan would never ask, but he was sure it would make her feel safer tonight to have someone in the house. He'd call her as soon as things calmed down here. Rick looked him over, as if he was testing to see how he was bearing up too.

'All right, son?'

'Right as bloody rain, mate.'

Rick seemed satisfied with that and went over to speak to the firefighters.

'All done,' Lizzie said.

Sean stood up. His legs felt like jelly but he wasn't going to let on. He took a deep breath and concentrated on getting down the steps of the mounting block.

'I imagine Arieta's miles away by now,' he said.

'As it happens, she's at North Yorkshire Police HQ in York. Rick's been there all night, questioning her,' Lizzie said.

'Right.' He nodded numbly. He couldn't really take it in.

'And Sean,' Lizzie lifted his chin gently, to make him look her in the eye. 'When we get back to work, when you're fit again, I've got a form I want you to fill in.'

'What are you on about?'

'An application form to train for the force as proper police. I'll write you a reference. So will Rick.'

'I can't,' Sean said.

'Yes, you can. You'll be amazing.'

'No, Lizzie, I'm totally fucking dyslexic.'

'Oh, right.'

'What?'

'I'm sorry. I should have realised. The spelling

311

on your flipchart was atrocious.' She was smiling. She better not bloody laugh at him now. 'That explains why you got taken off admin duties.'

'I thought that was down to you.'

She shook her head, offended, and was about to reply when he saw something coming up the lane beyond her. 'What the hell's that?'

It only had one working headlight, so at first he thought it was a motorbike, but as it got closer, he could see it was a minibus. It had just made it through the gate when it stopped abruptly and the driver tried to put it into reverse, crunching the gears. The sharp-eyed officer at the entrance swung the gate shut. The minibus stalled and it was trapped on the edge of the yard. Sean recognised the logo from the charity that used to do the transport for the special school. He hoped Mackenzie had found it second-hand and not actually nicked it from disabled children, but he wouldn't have put it past him.

Within seconds, Rick was at the driver's door, helping a man down with a firm grip to the upper arm, while Moon and another officer opened the side door and helped the passengers out. None of them made any attempt to run. They climbed down wearily and lined up, staring in horror at the barn, as Rick asked to see ID and the uniformed officer radioed for police transport to come and pick them up. Twenty people had been squeezed into the twelve-seater Variety Club Sunshine Bus. Mostly white, two Chinese and one tall African man. Sean watched as Charlie Moon approached him.

'Mr Moyo?' Moon said.

312

The man pulled his gaze from the burning barn and Sean could see the fear in his eyes. 'My wife? Please, is she all right?'

'Yes, sir, she's fine,' said Moon. 'Denton? Take this gentleman inside.'

As Sean led the man towards the farmhouse, Mr Moyo caught sight of Mackenzie, waiting in the squad car.

'Where are they taking him? They should ask him, where is my daughter? She was only fifteen.'

'Was she small for her age?' said Sean, gently.

'Yes.'

Like a child. There were men who would pay much more for a child. He hoped they weren't too late.

## CHAPTER THIRTY-SIX

Karen phoned Jaz at home and told him that she'd found the Moyos in time for their appeal hearing and he might have some new clients waiting for him at Doncaster Central. Jaz asked more questions than she could answer, but she told him he'd have to wait, she'd call him again when she could. Charlie assured her someone was getting on to social services to find out what had happened to the young girl they'd picked up in the raid at the All Star Massage Parlour. Karen could see him in Mackenzie's office now, picking over sheets of paper in latex gloves.

She wandered across the yard. Two of the police

cars had left, carrying Burger, Stubbs and Mackenzie. The fires were out, but the smell of burnt rubber and paint lingered in the air. A tang of petrol caught in the back of her throat, mixed with the scent of steam and charcoal coming from the barn. She saw Sean standing alone, looking up at the stars, as if he'd never seen so many.

'Hello, Mrs Friedman.'

'You're a bit of a hero,' Karen said.

'I don't feel like one.'

'Why on earth not? You caught Johnny Mackenzie red-handed; he was about to destroy all the evidence in his office. Employee records, money, God knows what else on his hard drive. It's fantastic for the Human Trafficking Service. He was the missing link.'

'I put my own grandmother in danger. I could have told Burger that the police were looking for Arieta, and then they wouldn't have bothered my nan.'

'Why didn't you?'

'They didn't give me much of a chance and, I don't know, I thought I could find something out.'

'And did you?'

'I think so. Mackenzie's been branching out, setting up girls in caravans. Maybe he's got more, parked all over South Yorkshire. Burger realised when we found the first victim; he recognised her from Stella's massage parlour. He must have known that Mackenzie had poached the girl off his sister. I don't know if he realised what Lee Stubbs was up to though.'

'The young guy? He looked completely out of it.'

'He's always been like that, not sure if it's what

he takes or just how he is.' Sean Denton rubbed his arm. 'Stubbs was picking his victims carefully. They'd all worked for his mother, except one. Stubbs didn't want anyone to leave his mother, so he spiked them with pure heroin. He got to Flora, but not before he'd tried to get to Arieta. Trouble was, Arieta wasn't a user. I think your brother stumbled on something he shouldn't and Mackenzie pushed him over the edge of the quarry.'

'It's an interesting theory.' Karen tucked a strand of hair behind her ear and pulled her coat closer around her.

The barn was lit with the eerie coldness of arc lights. Sean said the forensic team was working on a trailer and a car. He looked startled.

'Shit, I've done it again. I keep telling you stuff I probably shouldn't.'

'Don't worry,' she reached to touch his arm, but he winced. 'Sorry.'

She watched him limp across to the doorway of the barn, where he stood watching the action inside, his fingers resting on the incident tape. They all knew things they probably shouldn't tell, and things they should. The pieces of the jigsaw were beginning to fall into place. She shivered inside her coat, wishing Charlie could give her a hug to warm her up, but she'd have to wait. The secret burning inside her would have to wait too. Everyone around her was so busy. She looked back at the farmhouse and wondered if there was something she could do for Holly. She'd left Stacey holding her, rocking back and forth. The thought of doing something practical gave her a quick burst of energy and she headed for the kitchen.

The paramedics had decided to move Florence to hospital. She was dehydrated and they wanted to get a monitor on the baby.

'You've saved my wife,' Mr Moyo shook Denton by the hand. 'We will call the baby Sean, if it's a boy.' He was still waving as the ambulance doors were closed behind him.

'I need a note-taker, Sean.' Rick stood next to him as they both watched the red tail lights getting smaller, heading towards the main road. 'Stacey Holroyd's got a few things she wants to get off her mind.'

'Yeah?' Sean said. 'If you don't mind rubbish spelling, I'm your man.'

It was hot in the farmhouse kitchen. Someone had made toast and it gave a new edge to the smell of burning that Sean was beginning to get used to. The little girl was sitting in her mother's lap, a buttery slice clutched in her fist.

Mrs Friedman handed him a plate.

'Here,' she said. 'You were looking envious.' Her voice sounded different, as if the anxiety had gone out of it.

He took the plate and sat down at the end of the long wooden table. Rick pulled up a chair opposite Stacey.

'When you're ready, Denton.' He slid a pen in Sean's direction.

Sean caught the pen and tried to chew the toast faster, but his mouth was dry. Mrs Friedman took a blue-and-white mug off a hook on the dresser and filled it with water.

'Let the poor boy catch his breath.' Her voice

was kind.

'Karen?' Stacey Holroyd spoke for the first time. She sounded like she'd been crying and her face was blotched with red. 'Can you put Holly to bed for me? Go with your Aunty Karen, Holly, there's a good girl.'

The child looked up and held out her arms to be carried. Mrs Friedman gathered her up and the toast fell, to be caught by the waiting dog.

'Night, night, sweetheart!' Stacey looked like she was going to cry again but once the door was closed, she cleared her throat and clasped her hands together on the table. 'Are you going to arrest me?'

'Why don't you tell us what happened?' Rick said. 'PCSO Denton is going to take some notes. We may need you to come into a police station at some point, but you're not under arrest. We're just trying to understand what's been going on.'

She kept her eyes on her clenched hands and began to speak.

'Phil was a lovely feller. Too good for me. But you know what? Nice doesn't pay the bills.'

Sean wasn't sure if he was supposed to start writing.

'Do you know where your husband is?' Rick said.

She looked up at Rick, a frown tightening between her plucked eyebrows. Sean looked at him too, trying to read his expression. It seemed an extraordinary question.

'No,' she said, 'I don't.'

Sean picked up the pen and started to write.

'I didn't know what to believe,' Stacey spoke

quietly, her eyes dropping to the table again, 'when they said they'd found a body, a man, they said, who matched Phil's description and they said they'd found his phone, I remember thinking, oh my God. I mean I was shocked but, something else, I think I was angry.'

'Go on,' Rick almost whispered it.

'If he'd left me for some rich woman, like Johnny said, I could have understood. I wasn't going to forgive him, but there would have been a reason. But to end up in some grotty caravan, a ... a ... what would you call it? A whorehouse? Whorevan, that other copper said. To end up like that.' She paused, picking the skin off the side of her thumbnail. 'Look, I'm sorry. I'm still trying to get my head round all this. What I mean is, if he'd gone off with another woman, I was going to be all right. Johnny was treating me like a lady. We had things that we could never have afforded before. Good riddance, I thought. But when I heard the copper saying all that stuff on the phone, like he was enjoying rubbing it in, that's it, I was so angry.'

Sean could imagine Burger's lack of charm in breaking the news.

'Anyway,' Stacey continued, more quickly now, as though she might change her mind if she hesitated too long, 'we went to the morgue and there was this room with the body under a sheet and they pulled it back and for a second I saw Phil.'

Rick held his hand up to stop her. Sean was relieved to have time to catch up. His hand was beginning to ache.

'And Mr Mackenzie went with you?'

'Yes.'

'And did he think it was Philip Holroyd?'

'We both did, I think. And then as I looked at it, the face changed. It was swollen and messed up and a weird sort of colour but it wasn't that. The hair was wrong, shorter than Phil's and it had grey hairs in it. His ears were too big. I looked at Johnny, I remember, and he said, "Yes, that's him" and the woman turned to me and I said, yes. And that was it.'

Sean was writing so fast he was afraid the biro was going to tear through the page.

'Did you discuss it afterwards?' Rick leant forward as if willing her to meet his eye.

'I was in a kind of trance. I remember later someone saying they'd want a DNA match and did we have anything of Phil's? Johnny said he'd bring something, a jacket Phil had left up the farm; it would have his hair and skin he said. My phone kept ringing. It was Karen but I couldn't speak to her. I kept putting it back in my pocket until eventually Johnny took it and switched it off.'

'Did you see the jacket?'

Stacey shook her head.

'Did Phil own a grey suit jacket?'

'No. Phil's never owned a suit in his life.' She sighed and no one spoke. The tap dripped into the sink. As Sean wrote Stacey's words on the pad, he heard someone moving about upstairs.

'Did you have any idea who the man in the mortuary was?'

She shook her head again. 'I never asked. Johnny moved us in here, and I've been on tablets ever since. Nothing's real.' She waved her hand at the television screen on the wall and towards the

319

dresser stacked with expensive looking china. 'I've got all this. Everything I wanted. But all the time I've just been waiting for a knock on the door.'

'Mrs Holroyd,' Rick's chair creaked as he shifted in his seat, 'was your husband's life insured?'

'Yes.' Her voice was almost inaudible. 'My dad got him to start paying into a scheme when Holly was born.'

She sank her face into her hands and started to sob. Rick pushed his chair back and stood up. He looked around and picked up a roll of kitchen towel, which he plonked down in front of her. He patted her shoulder, just once, as if he wasn't sure it would help.

'You're doing very well,' he said.

She reached for the kitchen towel and tore off a sheet, dabbing at her face. Sean had got as far as *when Holly was born* when Rick began to speak again.

'Did you know that John Mackenzie was operating brothels in several temporary vehicles?'

'Several?' she looked up. 'No, I didn't. Several?'

Rick ran his finger down the bristles on his cheek. He said nothing.

'Wait.' Stacey seemed to catch her breath, to calm her own sobs. 'There's a trailer in the barn. I knew there was something wrong. It's the one they were looking for, isn't it? Where that Chinese girl died?'

Sean wrote furiously while Rick waited for Stacey to say more.

'Holly's rabbit is a bit of a Houdini; he gets out all the time and he heads for the barn. You know there are people sleeping there? I think he's after

320

their food. I wouldn't have gone in there other-wise. I always keep out of the business side of things. Anyway, I went to look for the rabbit. I'd never been in that barn before, so I had a look about and there was this trailer. I was just curious, so I looked under the cover to see what it was.' She paused to blow her nose on another piece of kitchen towel. 'It was like a chippy van. I was thinking it might be good to get it going again in the summer, out the back of the pub. Jackie might like it for barbies and that. Anyway, when I asked Johnny about it, he went mental. It's the only time he's laid a hand on me, but it put the fear of God in me. I had to cancel my mum coming round for a week because I couldn't let anyone see what he'd done to my face.'

Sean guessed Lizzie was in there now, dusting the tarp for prints, exploring Su-Mai's trailer. If Stacey was telling the truth, her prints would be on the tarp, his too. He hoped Johnny had left some of his own, enough to nail him as Su-Mai's pimp.

'Do you remember seeing any other vehicles in the barn?' Rick asked.

'I think there was a car and a couple of tractors. That big tractor was there.' She looked up at Sean. It was the first time she'd acknowledged his presence. She hadn't said a word about him saving her daughter's life. He told himself she was probably too embarrassed.

'Did you ask Johnny about the car?' Rick walked slowly back around the table to his seat and sat down heavily. Sean thought he looked knackered. He wondered what Arieta had told him during their all-night chat.

'You must be joking,' Stacey said. 'Not after he flipped his lid about the trailer. Anyway, I thought it was just some junk.'

'Did you ever see him drive it?'

'No, he always drives the Range Rover. He wouldn't be seen dead in a green car, he thinks green's unlucky.'

Someone knocked on the door from the hallway.

'Come in!' Rick called.

It was Karen Friedman.

'I'm sorry to interrupt, but would it be OK for Stacey to come up and give Holly a goodnight kiss? She won't settle.'

'Aye, go on, we're more or less done here.' Rick stood up again and offered Stacey a hand. She let him help her up from the chair. 'You've been a real help and now I think you should get some sleep. There'll be an officer here all night and then maybe we could ask you to come in tomorrow and put this on tape. Would you do that?'

Stacey nodded. 'I don't owe Johnny Mackenzie a bloody thing any more. He could have killed my daughter in that fire. I'll tell you whatever you need to know.'

'Thank you.'

Sean put the pen down after she'd gone and waited for Rick to speak. Mrs Friedman was putting on her coat. She muttered something about getting out of their way and went outside into the yard.

'So,' Sean said when she was out of earshot, 'if the body wasn't Philip Holroyd, who was it and who killed who?'

'Whom.'

'What?'

'Who killed whom,' Rick said with a grin. 'It's more grammatical.'

'Whatever.' Sean wanted to know how Arieta was. His nan was sure to ask. But he wasn't sure about the protocol. He tried to sound casual. 'Did you get much from Arieta Osmani?'

Rick's smile faltered slightly. 'Has Lizzie been sharing?'

'Not exactly. I suppose it's none of my business. Sorry.'

'Look, you're a lucky bastard, Sean. You've done some good stuff on this case, but you've also broken a few rules. I suppose on balance you and the Force are about even.'

'So?' He knew he was pushing his luck, but Rick was a mate, or so it seemed when they'd been out clubbing. When someone's wiped the sick off your face it kind of bonds you. Or maybe it was the other way round. Maybe he was bonded to Rick in grateful servitude. Thinking about it made his brain fuzzy again. God, he was tired. 'Fuck it, Rick. Is she OK? I understand if it's off limits, but my nan's going to ask and right now, I've put her through hell, so...'

'All right! Keep your hair on!' Rick sighed. 'In answer to your original question about who killed whom; well, according to your little Kosovan friend, the victim was the driver of a green car very like the one that's in that barn, but she doesn't know his name and until we find the plates, neither do we.'

'So Mackenzie killed him!' Sean hit the table

323

with his fist and sent the dog running out from underneath. It stood at the door, looking back, one ear raised warily. 'I knew it.'

'Slow down. Mackenzie just tidied up the mess. His little business plan was going horribly wrong, so he was on damage limitation.'

'Then who, or is it whom?'

'You're too impatient. You wanted to know how the girl is.'

'Yes?'

'Thin, not very fragrant but remarkably well, considering she's just confessed to manslaughter. Now, why don't you nip out and see what Lizzie's got for us? She's been sniffing round that barn for at least half an hour. If you'll excuse me, I need a piss.'

As Rick disappeared further into the house, followed by the dog. Sean sat still at the table, tracing a pattern in the wood with his finger. The grain was like a contour map, getting steeper and steeper. He kept feeling as if he was almost there, but the hill just kept getting higher. There was a murmur of voices upstairs, a creak of a floorboard but no more answers. He signed and dated his notes, put the notebook in his pocket. But he didn't get up. He was thinking about Arieta. When they'd travelled on the bus into town, she'd pressed her face up against the window. *Nobody must run, nobody should leave.*

When Rick came back he was still sitting there.

'Taneesha McManus,' Sean said. 'We've been assuming she was an accident. But I bet she wasn't. I think she was planning to leave Stubbs. We need to talk to her friends.'

Rick laughed. 'OK, boss, I'll get on to it first thing in the morning.'

'Sorry, way beyond my pay grade, I know.'

'Don't worry. Let's get finished here first. Stubbs has got so much shit coming his way, he won't know what's hit him.'

Karen walked towards the drive. The air was cleaner away from the farmyard and she breathed it in slowly. Leaning on the gate, she stared across dark fields, lined with the looming outlines of hedges. Here and there the black skeleton of a tree jutted up, fingers pointing at the moon. She imagined it must be pretty in the summer and suddenly it occurred to her that by next summer all their lives would be completely different. Perhaps this whole farm would belong to someone else and Holly wouldn't have all this space to play in. Karen would have a holiday with Sophie and Ben, but without Max. Maybe he would have the children and she would be free to do something on her own. The cold metal of the gate worked through her coat to her elbows. It felt like there would be a frost tonight, maybe even snow. Perhaps she would go on a walking holiday to the Pyrenees or one of those charity hikes to Machu Picchu; anywhere warm would do.

She heard the office door open and footsteps behind her on the concrete.

'Are you all right out here?' Charlie put his arm round her waist. 'I won't be long. Just a few loose ends I need to check with Rick Houghton.'

Karen turned to face him, searching his eyes for information.

'Karen?' he said, and she wondered if she'd spoken her thoughts out loud. 'There's something you should know. The body in the caravan wasn't Philip. Arieta Osmani made a statement. She confessed to manslaughter. The man was a client.'

She held her breath. On the way here in the car, and through all the chaos around them since, she'd tried to think how she was going to tell him. Now he was making it easy for her.

'I know,' she said. 'I know it wasn't Philip. I've spoken to him.'

Charlie didn't say anything.

'Arieta left her handbag in my house yesterday morning.' Karen measured her words, laying each one out carefully for him in the order she'd planned. 'There was a phone number. I checked on the Internet and the code was Pristina, Kosovo. I dialled the number and the man who answered spoke no English. He put someone on the line to translate. It was my brother.'

'Why didn't you tell me?'

She couldn't make out if he was angry or disappointed in her, or both.

'I wanted to confront Stacey, but not on my own. That's why I asked you to come with me. I wanted to know why she'd identified the wrong man.'

'She lied. People do. Mackenzie had quite a hold on her.'

Karen turned away from him. There was more she needed to say. 'Phil took Mackenzie's van and some stock he was supposed to deliver. But he didn't push the caravan into the quarry. They just panicked and left it where it was.'

'They?'

'I don't know what she told you. But Phil says it was his fault, not hers.'

Charlie didn't move a muscle. She wondered if this was what it was like being interrogated. It felt like hypnosis. If he didn't say anything, she knew she would have to fill the silence. She ground her boot into the gritty concrete.

'He's coming back, Charlie, he'll be here by tomorrow. He wanted me to tell you. He thought the man in the caravan was attacking Arieta. She was tied up and this guy was about to hurt her.' She was surprised at how calm her voice sounded to her own ears. The joy at knowing Phil was alive had altered every other feeling. She had no fear about what would happen next. They'd agreed, she and Phil, that the truth mattered now: nothing else. 'The man turned on him. I suppose it will all come out in court, but there's no reason why you shouldn't hear it from me. Phil thumped him, and then – it sounds almost farcical when you think about it – the other guy went for him, but tripped over his own trousers. They were still round his ankles. He fell and hit his nose, full force, on the gas heater. Then he didn't get up. That was it.'

'And they ran away and left him?'

'He was dead, Charlie. Phil wouldn't have just left someone, I know he wouldn't.'

'That's not the point.'

'He told me that he tried to use his phone, but Arieta was scared. She stamped on it to break it. They didn't move the caravan though.'

'No. I know. The track fragments were from a Range Rover. I think Mackenzie must have

327

reversed it to the edge and then let gravity do the rest. I hope those tyres haven't melted too much to get a match.'

The door to the farmhouse kitchen slammed and PCSO Denton came into view, heading for the barn.

'I've promised I'll help Sean Denton trace the Chinese girl's family,' Karen said, watching him standing at the barrier of incident tape, speaking to someone inside. 'He wants to make sure her ashes get sent back home for burial.'

Charlie didn't reply. He put his arm around her shoulder and pulled her towards him. He kissed her on the head and let her go.

'I'm a police officer, Karen, you need to tell me everything you know.'

She turned away from the barn and faced him. Phil's voice on the phone was still fresh in her mind.

'OK,' she said. 'He left from the ferry terminal in Hull. He waited until the last minute for the girl. She said she had to check on a friend, but she never came.'

Karen could imagine Phil, sitting in the van, queuing to get on the boat, edging forward minute by minute, getting closer to the point where he couldn't go back. He did what Arieta told him to do if she didn't make it. Keep going. Carry on. Go south. He followed her instructions to the letter. Found her country. Her city. Her apartment. Found her father, an alcoholic when she left, now a reformed, remarried man, devoutly attending the mosque and preparing for his country's independence. Karen pictured the man and the woman in the newspaper, solid middle-aged people, either side of her brother. He said he'd sold the van to the girl's cousin, who carried his building tools in it. Tools to build the new Kosovo. He went into the city with Mr and Mrs Osmani, where young men danced on the roofs of cars and automatic gunfire filled the air.

'Do you remember the photo in the paper, Charlie? The giant yellow letters in the square on the night of the declaration that spelt out *Newborn?* It really was Phil. He got to Kosovo. He was there for the celebrations.'

He told her on the phone that they had danced all night and gone home to the small apartment. They waited for Arieta to come, but she didn't and he knew he couldn't stay forever.

'He said when he heard my voice, it was a relief. He knew it was over.'

Charlie sighed. 'Why didn't he call you before, or call your dad, just to let you know he was safe?'

'He thought we were better off thinking he was dead than thinking he was a killer. He got close to taking his own life, but he couldn't do it. He's going to hand himself in as soon as he lands.' She reached up and put her hands on Charlie's shoulders. Their faces were close enough to kiss, but he wasn't meeting her eyes. 'I'm sorry, Charlie. I should have phoned you last night, when I knew. Does this change things between us?'

'I don't know. It depends.'

There was a streak of dirt on his cheek. She wanted to wipe it off but she hesitated.

'Are you going home to your husband?' he said.

'That's over.'

'I'm sorry.'

'Don't be,' she said. 'It was over a long time ago.'

She broke away first and thought he was about to say something else, when she noticed some movement in the doorway of the barn. The young woman from the forensic team was carrying something, wrapped in thin plastic. Charlie seemed to snap back into police mode as he strode across to see what she'd got. The other detective, Rick Houghton, was coming from the farmhouse. They all seemed to forget Karen and although she hung back, she was close enough to see that the bundle of plastic contained a yellow-and-black car number plate. Houghton got into one of the police cars and a few moments later jumped out again.

'Got it!' he shouted. 'Registered to a printing company in Somerset. Must be a sales rep. Doesn't ring any bells with me, so I don't reckon it went national as a missing person. Either he was way off his route or no one cared enough to go looking.'

Or maybe, Karen thought, they'd been looking all this time, but just in the wrong place.

## SUMMER

Marvin was pulling Ben along the river path while Holly ran after him, calling to him that it was her turn to hold the lead. Sophie walked behind them, listening to her music. York was full of families enjoying the heatwave. Karen felt Charlie's hand in hers and thought how like a perfect family they must look. If only that woman on the bicycle knew, or that man, throwing bread to the ducks. The children ran up on to the Millennium Bridge and Charlie sneaked a kiss on Karen's ear.

'Where does the river go?' Ben called to her. She let go of Charlie's hand.

'To the sea.'

'But before that?'

'Well,' she was on the bridge now, helping him up onto the bench, which ran the length of the curved arch. 'It goes down to Goole and it joins another river called the Humber, which becomes a big, wide estuary and then it goes past Hull and out into the open sea.'

'Hull,' said Holly, leaning her forehead against the metal meshwork. 'It starts with a haitch. Like Holly. That's where we went to see my Daddy.'

Karen waited to see if she said any more. The social worker said it was good to get her to talk about it, not to pretend. The front of HMP Hull didn't offer much scope for pretending. The hard Victorian stone screamed jail as soon as they got out of the taxi.

'It was supposed to be heaven,' Holly said, more to Ben than anyone else, 'but someone was silly and got it wrong. It was Hull.'

Ben nodded sagely, watching a pleasure boat nosing its way under the bridge. 'They must have got mixed up with their haitches.'

They walked back through the park so the children could go to the playground. Sophie found a school friend and they swung together on the swings, laughing. Karen and Charlie sat on the grass with Marvin and watched Ben and Holly climbing up a rope structure shaped like a spider's web.

'She's a tough little thing, isn't she?' Charlie said, looking at Holly.

'Gets that from her mum.'

'I was going to say she takes after her beautiful aunt.' He plucked a piece of grass and tickled her wrist.

'You're so cheesy!' She pulled her hand away but he caught it and held on.

'Can I stay tonight?' he said.

She thought about the state of the house. She'd given up on housework. The bookcases were full of gaps where Max had taken his books away. Over the fireplace a ghost frame of dirt marked the place where he'd removed a picture she'd never liked. On the mantelpiece there were two visiting orders with a Home Office crest, one for Stacey, one for Phil, and a postcard of Taunton Castle from the real victim's elderly mother, thanking her for her sympathy. She and Max had argued over the photograph of their baby, Cara, but in the end, he left it for her. She thought it might look nice in a new frame. Maybe she'd paint the wall and hang something else up there, a landscape would be good, with plenty of wide open space.

'Soon, Detective Moon, you can stay over soon. When I'm ready.'

The children were running back towards them now and Marvin was straining to greet them, as if they'd been gone for months or years.

'Come on, everyone,' Karen said. 'It's time we got back. Holly's rabbit will be getting hungry.'

# ACKNOWLEDGEMENTS

Many thanks to the PCSOs and forensic professionals who have advised me during my research. I assure you that any flexibility in procedural accuracy is down to my own artistic licence.

Thank you to everyone who has given me encouragement along the way, especially Carole Bromley and Lesley Glaister, without whose teaching this book would not have happened. Many thanks to my original editor, Will Mackie, whose collaboration and kind advice was invaluable; and to Claire Malcolm, Olivia Chapman and Andrea Murphy for seeing the potential in new northern crime fiction. Many thanks to Laura Longrigg and Fiona Barrows for looking after me so brilliantly and thank you to Susie Dunlop, Lydia Riddle and Sandy Draper for taking *To Catch a Rabbit* onto the next stage.

Thank you to David Nicholson, Allison Loftfield and Kate Vernon-Rees for being my first readers and gently pointing out my spelling mistakes. A huge thank you to my family for all your support and particularly to my mother, Jill Cadbury, for encouraging my love of reading from a very early age and to my late father, Charles, for always being the voice of reason.

Particular thanks to the residents and colleagues at HMP Askham Grange, who have been travelling this journey with me.

The publishers hope that this book has given you enjoyable reading. Large Print Books are especially designed to be as easy to see and hold as possible. If you wish a complete list of our books please ask at your local library or write directly to:

**Magna Large Print Books**
Magna House, Long Preston,
Skipton, North Yorkshire.
BD23 4ND

This Large Print Book for the partially sighted, who cannot read normal print, is published under the auspices of

**THE ULVERSCROFT FOUNDATION**